# Naughty 4:

## *Naughty by Nature*

D0555634

# Naughty 4:

## *Naughty by Nature*

*Brenda Hampton*

www.urbanbooks.net

Urban Books, LLC
97 N18th Street
Wyandanch, NY 11798

Naughty 4: Naughty by Nature Copyright © 2011
Brenda Hampton

ISBN 13: 978-1-60162-389-8
ISBN 10: 1-60162-389-5

First Mass Market Paperback Printing September 2013
First Trade Paperback Printing August 2011
Printed in the United States of America

10 9 8 7 6 5 4 3 2 1

*This is a work of fiction. Any references or similarities
to actual events, real people, living or dead, or to real
locales are intended to give the novel a sense of reality.
Any similarity in other names, characters, places, and
incidents is entirely coincidental.*

Distributed by Kensington Publishing Corp.
Submit Wholesale Orders to:
Kensington Publishing Corp.
C/O Penguin Group (USA) Inc.
Attention: Order Processing
405 Murray Hill Parkway
East Rutherford, NJ 07073-2316
Phone: 1-800-526-0275
Fax: 1-800-227-9604

# Naughty by Nature:

### He Makes It Good
### To the Very Last Drop

# Scorpio

## 1

It was almost two years later and there I was lying in bed thinking about Jaylin. Bitter was a word that surely described me, and revenge was recently added to my list when I discovered no other man could take his place.

Finding a replacement for the man I once loved was like finding a million dollars in a sack right in front of my house. Since Jaylin ended our relationship, I'd dated several men, but no man could compare. It wasn't that I was looking for somebody *exactly* like him, but was it that impossible for a brotha to have a decent job, a nine-plus inch stick, and work it for more than ten minutes? It couldn't be. If bad sex and employment weren't the issues, then playing games was another. I was tired of the lies, and if one more man told me how much he loved me, and two weeks later I just happen to run into another one of his "love ones", I was going to scream! I couldn't help but wonder where in the hell were all the good men?

When I heard Spencer mumble something in his sleep, I rolled my eyes over to the back of his head. He mumbled something again, and when I heard him moan, "Yvette" and quickly paint a grin on his face, it was time for me to go. I tried not to wake him, so I carefully eased out of bed. I looked for my panties on the floor and tip-toed over to them. Spencer's snores got louder and louder. I stood in my panties while shaking my head with disgust. I had high hopes for the bro-tha. He delivered the mail at Jay's, the place I own that's designed to make women look beautiful. The first time Spencer came in, I figured he was going to be something special. With a six foot frame, 210 pounds of solid Hershey's Chocolate, light brown eyes, and my mail in his hands—who would have thought that in the bedroom he couldn't deliver.

I'd been seeing him for almost a month and was anxious for this day to come. We'd had plenty of dinners, a few late night walks, and he even had the decency to send roses the other day. That's what kind of made me feel as if it was time to show him what I was working with. I was prepared to do just that—until he broke out a half of a pencil between his legs. Damn! I was disappointed. I tried to work with it, but I couldn't. He caught me shaking my head in disbelief, but I couldn't help myself. All that muscle and it wasn't even in the right place.

I spotted my black mini dress that I wore over to his house last night by the door. Just as I was about to make my way to it, Spencer's head popped up and he rubbed his fingertips over his closed eyes.

"You're leaving already?" he mumbled.

I stopped in my tracks. "Yeah. I gotta open up the shop early today so that Bernie can get in by the time her nine o'clock appointment arrives."

He looked at my half naked body and smiled. "It's only six o'clock. Why don't you lay with me for awhile longer? Your body felt warm and—"

It was kind of early, so I tried to be nice and eased my way back in bed with him. He wrapped his arm around my neck and I laid my head on his muscular bicep. His fingers ran through the waves in my long black hair, and seeing that his mini monster was rising, I turned my head to address him.

"Spencer, thanks for a good time. I'm only staying for another hour or so and I can't see you tonight as promised."

He continued to stroke my hair. "Can you make love to me again before you go? Last night was spectacular. Give me a little something extra to keep on my mind until we meet again."

I hated to reject him, so I touched his manhood and stroked it. It was hard as cement, but it did nothing for me. I wasn't even sure if I wanted to go there with him again, so I told him that I needed to go to the bathroom.

"Now?" he griped.

"Yes, now."

He sighed and I got out of bed.

While looking in the mirror, I saw the woman I had worked so hard to be. I'd finally gotten my business degree, had my own business, was a good mother to Mackenzie, could have just about any man I wanted, and my body was one that many women craved for. Then, why? Why was it so hard for me to find Mr. Right? Yes, Jaylin had scarred me, but I still desired to have what we shared with somebody else. Or, did I? I thought. At times, it was hell living with him, but we always seemed to make it through. No matter what though, my days with Jaylin were some of the best days of my life.

I flushed the toilet that I hadn't used and washed my hands. I opened the bathroom door, finding myself face-to-face with Spencer. He backed me into the door and stood tall in front of me.

"What took you so long?"

"I was handling my business," I said with a fake smile.

"Your business was out here waiting for you," he said. He lowered his head and cupped my left breast in his hand. After he swayed the tip of his finger around my hard nipple, he covered it with his mouth. His tongue turned in circles and my breast took on a shiny look from the saliva that drizzled from his lips. I'll admit, by the time he worked my other breast, and massaged both in his hands, I squirmed like a slithering snake against the door. My breasts were quickly abandoned and Spencer lowered himself. He held my hips with his hands, lifting my leg and gently placing it on his broad shoulder. He was directly in front of my coochie and before exploring me with his tongue, he looked up at me.

"You got some good ass stuff. It's potent, baby. I want you to be my woman, all right?"

I couldn't even respond. I knew if I did, it would be out of pure lust. How dare him have me pinned up against the door with his breath breathing on my clit that was waiting to be licked, and ask such a question.

I kept quiet and Spencer dove right into it. He licked around my swollen clit and traced the furrows of my walls with the tip of his curled tongue. As he felt my juices coming down, he went in deeper. I stood on the tip of my toes, encouraging him to have at it. The feeling was much better than his sex was, and as his licks got more intense, I pulled the ends of his neat corn-rowed braids. I was almost *there,* and when my body jerked, it was all over with for me.

Spencer licked around his lips and stood up. He took my hand and walked me into his bedroom. Knowing exactly what he wanted, I lay back on the bed and opened my legs. He placed a condom on his mini-monster, and within seconds, it had found its way inside of me. I closed my eyes and hoped that it would be over with soon. As he pumped hard, it felt as if a needle was pricking my insides. I quickly dried up and Spencer noticed that I just wasn't feeling him. He stopped the motion.

"What's up with you?" he asked.

"I . . . I'm fine," I said, and then rolled on top of him. I knew that he couldn't handle what I was about to put on him; and surely enough, after three good strokes on top, the party was over.

"Damn, baby," he moaned and tightly pulled me forward. "Why'd you have to do that?"

"Do what?" I whispered. He held my face in his hands and moved my hair away from my light brown eyes.

"Why'd you have to put it down like that? You badder than a mutha, and I'm gon' keep you around for a very long time."

*Not if I could help it*, I thought. I reminded Spencer that I had to get to the shop, and certainly after getting what he wanted, he didn't mind my attempt to depart. I hurried to put on my clothes and damn near broke my neck as I tried to make my exit.

Spencer stood naked and opened the door for me. "I'll see you around noon when I deliver your mail. Don't be telling your girlfriends at the shop how good I was to you," he bragged.

I rubbed the side of his face. "Never," I smiled. "How good you were stays between us. Besides, I wouldn't want no one to come over here and experience anything like what I just experienced."

He smiled again—as if I was giving him some props. Only if Spencer knew, he'd go down in my little black book as a serious LAZY FUCK!

I gave Spencer a peck on his lips, and took off in my convertible Thunderbird. I let the top down, so that allowed the cool breeze to blow vigorously throughout my ride. My hair was already a mess so I didn't mind that it had blown all over my head. But as soon as I got to a stop-light, I combed my fingers through my hair and reached in my purse for my lip gloss. I slid the gloss over my lips while looking in my rearview mirror. Then I turned on the radio and listened to "Missing You," by Tamia. I hadn't heard that song in a long time, and like many songs that I listened to, they made me think about Jaylin.

As much as I hated to admit it, my life had never been the same since my last encounter with him. I should have never asked him to meet me for dinner and make love to me at the Four Seasons Hotel that night. Had I known he wasn't able to forgive me for sleeping with his cousin, Stephon, I would've chalked up my losses and went on my merry way.

The light turned green so I sped up to make it to Jay's. Of course, I named my business after Jaylin, and the name was perfect. All of the money he and Nanny B had given Mackenzie and I, sure in the hell paid off. Not only did I have Jay's, but I also had some property that I rented on the Southside of St. Louis. That, along with investing some of the money, made me one well-off sista. I didn't need no man to take care of me as I had before, but I sure as hell missed the one who had made all of this possible.

I pulled in front of Jay's on Carondelet Boulevard in Clayton. I had one of the nicest places on the block, and for the neighborhood to be considered upscale, I felt blessed.

The phone was ringing inside, but by the time I got to it, it had stopped. I looked around at the stylists' work stations and they were all pretty much tidy and clean. I checked the back rooms where my girls, Lacey and Deidra worked and they were tidy, too. They gave the best massages in St. Louis, so our customer base was huge. Lastly, I made sure China Doll, Yasing's work station was in order. She was responsible for giving pedicures and could make anybody's feet feel and look like a million dollars.

Once I saw that everything was clear, I went into my spacious office in the back. It was furnished with a soft yellow leather sofa and chairs. White and silver were my choices for accessories and the contemporary style made my office look as if it belonged in a *Better Homes & Gardens* magazine.

I sat at my glass top desk, thinking hard about my evening with Spencer. My thoughts prompted me to open my desk drawer. I pulled out a cracked picture of Jaylin and held it in front of me. I felt anger inside as I'd felt it many times before when I glared at his picture. I hadn't heard from him at all, and frankly didn't know if he was dead or alive. I did know, however, that he no longer lived in Chesterfield. And, the only reason I'd known that was because I'd been by his house several times since our breakup and an elderly white couple came to the door.

Honestly, I was afraid to find out his status, but the more I thought about it, a part of me wanted to know. I knew Stephon still had his barbershop in the Central West End, but I didn't know if he'd be willing to share anything with me about Jaylin. I wasn't sure if Jaylin had forgiven Stephon for having sex with me and I doubted that they had reconciled their differences.

While in thought, my eyes were closed, until I heard a knock at my door. It was Bernie.

"Good morning," I said, placing the picture back into the drawer.

"Good morning to you, too. Or is it?" Bernie sat in front of my desk and crossed her legs. "So, tell me, how was last night?"

Tired for nothing, I covered my face with my hands and yawned, "It was awful. Girl, that fool Spencer need to be put in jail for performing like he did."

Bernie laughed. "Are you kidding me? You mean to tell me that good looking man who be coming in here to deliver the mail ain't no good in bed?"

"That's exactly what I'm saying. He fooled us all!"

We both laughed.

I looked at Bernie and prepared myself to ask for advice. Since she was forty-five years old, and the oldest woman who worked for me, I kind of trusted her advice. I had shared *my past* with her before, but not much with anyone else.

"Bernie," I said. "How do you know if you're still in love with somebody?"

"I assume you're talking about Jaylin, right?"

"Who else?"

Bernie's forehead wrinkled, as she placed her index finger on the side of her temple and glared at me. "Do you still think about him?"

"A lot."

"In your thoughts, does he creep into your bed in the middle of the night when you're alone?"

"Yes. Even when I'm not alone."

"Are your thoughts good or bad?"

"Both."

Bernie let out a deep sigh. She turned her head and pointed her well manicured fingernail toward the door. "If he walked through that door right now, what would you do?"

I gazed at the doorway and Jaylin appeared in my vision, only to soon disappear.

"I'd kill him! I'd wrap my hands around his neck and choke the shit out of him. Then I'd—"

"You'd rip off his damn clothes and fuck him to death. Ain't no need to pretend with me, Scorpio. There's no need to ask me nothing when you already know how you feel."

I stood up and so did Bernie. "Can we go workout now? I don't want to talk about Jaylin anymore," I said. My thoughts of him were making me crazy.

Bernie smiled and gave me a hug. We headed to the gym on the lower level and changed into our workout clothes. Afterwards, we waited for our instructor, Calvin, who I'd had a previous relationship with, but cut it short. Since I'd played him off by not returning his phone calls, he was upset with me and did his best to ignore me

"All right, ladies," he yelled. "Get your fist up and let's get ready for boot camp."

Bernie and I were always ready. She had an immaculate figure like mine, but my heart shaped butt couldn't be duplicated. I can't say that she was as attractive as me, but she knew how to get a man's attention. Not only that, she was a smart woman. She was classy, sweet as pie, and looked out for me and the other stylists in the shop as if we were her daughters. She grilled me a lot about sleeping around with different men. Said that even though Mackenzie was eight years old, I was teaching her some bad habits. I reminded her that everything I did was done on the downlow and it was done outside of my home. Mackenzie hadn't met any man I'd been with, and as far as I was concerned, she never would. Jaylin had become only a memory to her, and after the first year of him being away, she never really asked about him anymore. I couldn't believe my own child was stronger than me, but something inside of me yearned to know his whereabouts. There was still that unknown about him and I needed closure. Once I found out what I needed to know, maybe I'd get it.

Bernie and I finished our workout. I headed for the showers and she headed for the locker room. Her short layered hair laid flat on her head and both of our abs dripped with sweat.

"I'm outtie," she yelled into the shower stalls. "I'm gonna shower at home and come back in a few. Will you be here to let my nine o'clock appointment in?"

"Yes," I yelled back. "I'm sure some of the others are already here, so go ahead. I'll see you in a bit."

I heard the door slam and continued on with my shower. I closed my eyes, and routinely, thoughts about the many showers I'd taken with

Mr. You Know Who swam in my head. I had come to the conclusion that my time was either now or never. Now, I had to know what was up with Jaylin. Davenports, Shane and Felicia's Architectural Firm, was located in Clayton as well. I had a good feeling that if anybody knew what was up with Jaylin, Shane would. I prepared myself to place a phone call to Davenports by the end of the day.

# Shane

## 2

The last few years had been all about business. Everything had been going cool with Davenports, but when things got good for a brotha, there were some things I had to leave behind. My boy, Stephon, was one of them. Even though he was Jaylin's cousin, and they'd fallen out over Scorpio and Stephon's obsession with drugs, I still tried to be there for him. For whatever reason, he couldn't seem to get himself together. And when he started demanding money from me to support his habit, I had to cut that fool loose. Last I heard, he was in rehabilitation. I hoped it all worked out for him because there was basically nothing else I could do.

Felicia, as always, had been bugging the shit out of me. Sometimes I felt as if this partnership was a big mistake. Then, there were times we'd land a big account and all we could do was celebrate.

Since she had the most knowledge in the business, I agreed to name Davenports after her, and we both decided that she would be the president, but me the CEO. I guess it wasn't such a bad idea since she landed the majority of our accounts. She'd worked her charm on many men, and they were never able to resist. I, on the other hand, did resist her. After sleeping around with Jaylin, she proved to me what a slut she could be, and all of my feelings for her had vanished. Our partnership was cool just the way it was, and I respected her for keeping it as platonic as it could possibly be.

Because she was "the boss lady" she straight up had her nose up her ass. There were times I had to put her in her place and remind her that even though I hadn't brought in as many accounts as she had, I was the one who kept us in tune with one of the biggest investors we had. And that was my man Jaylin. He'd believed in our dream from day one and supported the idea simply because of me. When shit got rough, he encouraged me to keep my head up and sent more funds so that Felicia and I could make ends meet. Things didn't really start to jump off for us until he hooked us up with one of his investors. They were looking for some designers and Felicia and I worked together to give them exactly what they wanted. Since then, more accounts rolled in. Every once in awhile, Jaylin hooks me up with new clients and I'm grateful. He's not only a friend with millions, but also a friend with connections and power. Power that can make major deals happen for us overnight.

As I sat at my designer's table working on a project for the Mayor's Group, a new account from Jaylin, I could hear Felicia on the phone in her office running her mouth. She was loud and obnoxious and I couldn't believe some of the things I'd heard her say to people. Basically, she down talked everybody. And with all the money that we'd been making, she felt as if she was on top of the world.

I listened to her ask the caller to hold, and soon after, she yelled my name.

"What?" I yelled back. I looked at her behind the glass windows to her office. She held her hand over the phone and gritted her teeth.

"Would you come in here, please?"

I placed my drawing pad on the table and stood in her doorway. She placed the caller on speakerphone and plopped down in her seat.

"Mrs. Carlson, are you still there?" she asked.

"Yes, Felicia, I'm still here," she announced.

"I have Shane in my office now. What time would you like for him to meet your daughter for dinner?"

My eyes widened. "Dinner?"

"Hello, Shane," Mrs. Carlson said. "Felicia told me that you wouldn't mind taking Cassidy to dinner. She recently got divorced and I need someone who can help lift her spirits. Felicia and I thought—"

I eased my hands into the pockets of my Levi's 501 and shook my head. "Well, I'm sorry, but Felicia and you thought wrong. I don't know if she shared this with you or not, but I'm already in a relationship—"

Felicia cut me off. "Mrs. Carlson, he'll pick her up around seven. Call me back with her address and I'll be sure to pass it on."

"Shane, are you sure? I don't want to—"

"He's sure," Felicia said, beating me to the punch.

My eyes shot her down quickly, "Mrs. Carlson, I apologize, but there's no way that I can take your daughter to dinner. As I was saying, I'm in a committed relationship with someone and I don't think that would be a good idea."

"But . . . but Felicia said it would be okay."

"I know what Felicia said, but I said I can't do it."

Felicia was furious, as she placed her finger above the conference button. "Mrs. Carlson, we'll call you back, okay?"

"Okay, but—"

"Give me ten minutes, and we'll call you back."

"All right. And, thank you."

"You're welcome," Felicia said, and then punched her finger hard on the conference button. She stood up and folded her arms in front of her.

"How dare you reject an offer from one of our major clients like that!"

I walked further into her office and stood face-to-face with her. "And, how dare you treat this business like it's some kind of escort service. I don't need you making no damn dinner arrangements for me."

She sucked in her jaws and rolled her big round eyes. "It's just dinner, Shane. You act as if I asked you to go somewhere and screw the bitch! I saw an opportunity to help out one of our clients and you have some nerve rejecting my offer. It ain't like your relationship with Sam is all that tight anyway. The last thing you told me is that y'all were on the verge of breaking up. So, what's up with that?"

"Whether we're breaking up or not, I determine who the fuck I date. Not you." I turned and left Felicia standing there to argue with herself. She was so mad at me, and as soon as I exited, she slammed the door behind me.

I continued on with my sketching and I saw her running her mouth on the phone again. I assumed she'd called to make other arrangements for Mrs. Carlson's daughter because I sure as hell wasn't the one. I'd met her daughter before and she was one ugly chick. Really, I didn't care if she was fine or not, I just wasn't going to put myself out there for nobody unless I wanted to.

After Felicia ended her call, she opened her door and calmly walked out with her Chanel purse clutched underneath her arm. She wore a peach linen business suit that hugged every curve in her awesomely shaped body. Her braids were neatly wrapped into a bun, and for her to be such a bitch, she was still a very attractive woman. Attractive or not, I'd become accustomed to ignoring her.

"I'm going to lunch. Would you like for me to bring you something back?"

"Nope," I said, still not looking up. She hated to be ignored, and today, I didn't mind getting underneath her skin.

"Are you sure? I'm going to one of your favorite places."

"I don't have no favorite place."

"I thought you liked J. Bucks?"

"I love J. Bucks."

"Then, what would you like for me to bring you back?"

I put my drawing pencil down and looked up at her, "I said nothing. Now, go have your lunch and I'll see you when you get back."

"What's your problem? If it's about Mrs. Carlson, don't worry about it. I took care of it, okay?"

"I'm sure you did."

"Look, Shane, I was just trying to help you out, too. You are too darn fine to be cooped up in this place all the time. That's probably why things ain't working out between you and Sam. I'm sure that poor woman is dying for some quality time."

"Felicia, you know nothing about my relationship with Sam. If I didn't put so much time and effort into this business, Davenports wouldn't be as successful as it is today. If the woman in my life doesn't understand how important this is to me, then she doesn't deserve to be my woman. It's as simple as that."

Felicia moved her single braid that dangled in her face away from her eye. "All I'm saying is, you're young, you're gorgeous, and the last time you've had a good woman in your life is when you were with me. Unfortunately, I'm not available—"

"Please, don't flatter yourself. As a matter of fact, you were the worst woman I ever dated. You cheated on me and you fucked my friend. Sorry, but getting rid of you was one of the best things I ever did."

She smiled. "Well, you cheated on me, too."

"Are you crazy?" I yelled. "I never, ever cheated on you! I should have, but I didn't."

"Well, I thought you did. Besides, that was a long time ago. I apologized, and I can't help it if Jaylin put something on me that you hadn't."

"Yeah, that's what they all say," I grinned. "Now, get your butt out of here so you can get back and do some work."

Felicia bent down and gave me a kiss on the cheek. "I'm sorry for yelling at you earlier. I get wrapped up in being the boss sometimes. I appreciate everything you do and I know Davenports wouldn't be nothing without your partnership."

"I'm glad you recognize that. On another note, you never told me if you'll be able to attend Friday's meeting with the Mayor's Group."

"Jaylin's coming in town that day, right?"

"Yeah, he'll be here. Just to kind of introduce everybody and then he's heading back out."

"Then, yes, I'll be here. Even though he don't give me the time of day, it's always good to see him."

"He's a changed man, Felicia. You gotta learn to respect that."

"I don't give a hoot what anybody says, once a ho, always a ho. He might have y'all fooled, but

I can see right through him. I bet any amount of money he's had his share of women in Florida. Nokea probably down there pulling her damn hair out like she was when they lived in St. Louis."

"And, that's your opinion. I know for a fact when I see a man that's in love, and whether you want to believe it or not, he's in love."

Felicia tooted her lips out of jealousy. She rolled her eyes and switched her way to the door. Before she walked out, she turned toward me. "Just in case you haven't noticed, being in love ain't never stopped no man, that I know of, from cheating."

I ignored Felicia because we could debate our differences forever. I knew she wished, as every other previous female in Jaylin's life had wished, that his marriage to Nokea would fail. From what he told me, their marriage was strong and I truly believed him.

By 2:00 p.m., Felicia still hadn't made it back yet. My trash can was piled high with sketches I'd completed for the Mayor's Group and I decided they wouldn't work. My brain couldn't even come up with any more ideas, so I leaned back in my chair and closed my eyes. I placed my hands behind my head and hoped my creative mind would kick in soon. As I was in deep thought, I heard the door squeak open. It was Sam. She had a wide grin planted on her face and headed my way. I stood up to meet her halfway and held out my arms to greet her.

"Hey, baby, what brings you by?"

"I was in the neighborhood," she said. We wrapped our arms around each other and she planted her lips on mine. "Mmmm," she moaned, and then wiped her lipstick off my lips. "Were you busy?"

"Sort of." I slid my arms from around her tiny waistline and walked her over to my cluttered designer's desk that sat in the middle of our 4,000 square-foot office. I picked up one of the sketches I'd been working on and showed it to Sam. "I can't think of what else I want to incorporate into this design. Actually, my mind knows, but I can't sketch it out on paper."

She took the paper from my hands and looked at it. "Baby, this is awesome. I mean, it looks fine to me. I don't see what else you could be aiming for."

"Trust me, I can do better."

I sighed from frustration with the design and walked over to the tall glass windows that overlooked the entire city of Clayton. Davenports was on the twenty-first floor and showed an awesome view of St. Louis.

Sam came up from behind and put her arms around my thirty-four-inch waist. Standing just as tall as me, she dropped her chin on my shoulder and whispered in my ear.

"It's gonna be okay. Just relax, clear your mind and I'm positive you'll come up with something. You always do, so I don't know what you're so worried about."

I nodded. "I know. But, from what Jaylin said, these are some impressive people that are coming in on Friday. I just want to show them my best."

"And, you will," Sam assured. "There's no doubt that my man will win them over. You always do."

I stood quietly as Sam continued to hug my waist. She raised my loose fitting black V-neck shirt and swayed her hands across my rock solid abs. Trying to excite me, her hands touched my muscular chest and tickled my nipples. I knew what was on her mind when she lowered one of her hands down to my belt buckle. She then placed her warm lips on my earlobe.

"You look amazingly good in your wide legged Levi's, baby. I hope you don't mind if I have a sudden desire to remove them."

I gave off a soft snicker and continued to look out of the window. My dick was already growing, so I reached for my belt buckle, even though Sam had no problem undoing it herself. She lowered her hand down inside my pants and massaged my sacks. My pipe had grown past my navel, and since we hadn't had sex for a little over three weeks, I turned to face her. I held her thin face in my hands and moved her long dark brown hair away from her cheeks. I brought her sweet lips to mine and our tongues took a slow dance.

The phone rang, but I ignored it. We broke our kiss and I reached for Sam's silk blouse to unbutton it. It wasn't the first time we'd made love in my office and we released our sexual appetite for each other anywhere we could get it done.

Sam removed her hand from down inside my pants and worked on removing her skirt. I dropped her blouse to the floor and created a small pile that was right behind her. She stood in her pink Very Sexy bra and matching boy shorts I'd just purchased for her at Victoria's Secret. She hadn't much breasts or ass to fill the ensemble, but her tall model shaped legs and her bronze toned skin still made her look magnificent.

My Levi's were barely hanging onto my ass and I was anxious to dive into her. I crept my hand between Sam's legs and massaged her hot spot. I could feel her wetness and rubbed my index finger between the creases of her shaved lips.

Getting overly excited, she let out soft moans and placed her hands on my shoulders. She looked into my eyes and spoke with passion.

"Let's get married," she suggested.

My enthusiasm vanished. "What?" I said, as my rubbing between her legs came to a screeching halt. Now wasn't the appropriate time to discuss marriage.

She seductively rubbed her fingers on my twisties and traced the minimal baby hair on my forehead.

"You heard me. I said, let's get married."

I dropped my hands to my sides and tilted my head slightly to the side. "Let's not go there right now, all right? Why do you wait until our intimate moments to question me about marriage?"

"Because you never want to talk about it. If all you want to do is fuck, then just go ahead and fuck me. At least I know where things stand between us."

I wrapped my arms around her waist. "Making love to you is not the only thing on my agenda. I would love for us to get married someday, but now ain't the time to discuss it."

"Then when, Shane? We've been together for almost two years. I refuse to spend years with a man and nothing comes of it."

The phone rang again and saved me.

"Hold that thought," I said making my way over to it. "Davenports," I answered.

"Shane Alexander, please."

"Speaking."

"Hello, Shane. This is Scorpio."

An instant smile grew on my face and I was shocked to hear her voice. I quickly took a seat in my chair. "Scorpio Valentino?"

"Yes."

"Hey, Lady. What's up?"

"A whole lot," she laughed. "But the reason for my call is, I need to speak to you about something."

"Uh, sure. When . . . where would you like to meet?"

"I'd like to meet soon. I know Davenports is in Clayton and Jay's isn't too far from it."

"Jay's? What's Jay's?"

"I'll tell you about it when I see you. Can I come over within the hour?"

I glanced at Sam, still standing partially naked by the window. Then, I thought about Felicia coming back. Since they'd had major issues with each other in the past, Felicia seeing Scorpio here would be a big mistake.

"Say, why don't I meet you for dinner this evening? I'm kind of in the middle of something right now and I can't get away."

"Okay. That's fine. What about six? Can you meet me at Cardwell's around six?"

"I'll be there."

"Thanks, Shane. I'll see you then."

Scorpio hung up and I held the phone in my hand for a few seconds. I hadn't heard from her in quite some time. Since her and Jaylin's breakup, she'd kind of disappeared.

Sam cleared her throat. "Who was that?"

"Aw, that was Jaylin's ex-girlfriend. She said she wants to talk to me about something and asked if I would meet her for dinner. She wanted to come here, but we're in the middle of something, right?" I walked back over to Sam.

"Yeah, we *were*, but now, I'm feeling a li'l dry down below. Especially, since my man tends to avoid me."

Seeing that nothing was about to go down with us, I picked up my shirt from the floor and slid it over my head. I reached for her clothes and held them in my hand to give to her.

"Here," I said. "Why don't we continue this conversation tonight? I got too much on my mind right now, baby, and I don't need the additional pressure."

Sam took her clothes from my hand and slid back into them. Before leaving, she gave me a tiny peck on the lips and told me she'd see me later. I was relieved that she had left and quickly got back to work.

Later that day, I'd come up with some ideas I thought the Mayor's Group would like. Felicia hadn't made it back yet and when I called her, she said that she'd gotten tied up. I figured she'd been literally tied up when I heard a brotha laughing in the background. I informed her of my suspicions, but she laughed and told me if she didn't make it back by 5:00 p.m., then she wasn't coming back until tomorrow.

At a quarter to six, I tidied up and made my way to Cardwell's to meet Scorpio. I was more than surprised to hear from her and wondered what she wanted to talk about. I was sure it had something to do with Jaylin, but I wasn't sure to what extent it would be.

I pulled in front of Cardwell's and one of the valets came out to park my Lexus. I was under-dressed for dining at such an exquisite place, but casual attire was something I simply loved. I didn't wear suits that often and the last time I'd had one on was many, many years ago.

I grabbed my black jacket from the backseat of my car, and handed my keys to the valet. As soon as I entered Cardwell's, my cell phone vibrated and I reached for it clipped to my jeans.

"Shane Alexander," I answered.

"Where are you?" Felicia asked.

"I'm about to have dinner." I looked at the maître d' and held up two fingers. "Can you seat me for two? Someone else will be joining me." I followed behind him.

"Tell Sam I said hello. I wanted to tell you that I'm looking at your sketch for the Mayor's account."

"And," I said, taking a seat at the small candlelit table the maître d' had taken me to.

"And, it looks good. I think you did a phenomenal job."

"Thanks. But, if you don't mind, I need you to add your touch to it, too."

"Oh, I plan to. After I get finished, we are going to knock the Mayor's Group off their feet."

I smiled and felt a tap on my shoulder. When I looked up, I could have fallen out of my chair. Scorpio stood beside me wearing a canary yellow mini dress that had a haltered top. Just a sliver of her meaty breasts crept out on the sides and she accessorized her neckline with a silver and diamond necklace that fell between her breasts. Since the last time I'd seen her, her hair was full of long thick curls that draped down her shoulders. Now, her hair had been straightened and hung at least four to five inches from her shoulders. Bangs covered her forehead, and she was by far, the sexiest woman I had seen in a long, long time.

She immediately noticed how mesmerized I was, and smiled before taking a seat in the chair in front of me. I got a glimpse of her nicely shaped ass that so many men craved to hold in their hands. My dick thumped in my pants, so I placed my hand over it to calm it down.

"Let me call you back," I said to Felicia. "I'm getting ready to order dinner."

"Okay. Don't forget to tell Sam I said hello and I'll see you in the morning."

I laid my phone on the table and quickly stood up.

"Sorry about the call, but you know you'd better stand up and give me a hug."

Scorpio stood and put her arms around me. She rubbed my back and pressed her breasts against my chest.

"It's good to see you, Shane. Thanks for coming."

Even though I didn't want to, I finally let go. Her sweet smelling perfume and soft body had me unable to get myself together. I took a hard swallow and cleared my throat before sitting back down.

"Hey, what can I say, Scorpio. You . . . you look magnificent."

She blushed and winked at me. "Thanks, Shane. I do my best to look good and I'm pleased to hear when people appreciate my efforts. You look awesome, too—even better than I remember."

We both smiled and there was no doubt that our previous encounter together was playing out in our minds.

"So," I said. "What brings you out of hiding? I thought I'd never see you again. Honestly, I thought you'd left St. Louis."

"No, I didn't leave St. Louis. After Jaylin and I broke up, I almost did, but I decided against it."

The waiter approached the table and displayed the special of the day, then asked if we wanted something to drink. As he spoke, my eyes were glued to Scorpio. She was so stunning; I knew Jaylin had to be missing her like hell.

"I'll have a dry martini," Scorpio said to the waiter.

The waiter looked at me, "And, you sir."

"Rémy, no ice."

The waiter said he'd be back shortly with our drinks. Scorpio noticed my stares and questioned me. "Shane, you really don't have to put on a front like I'm the most gorgeous woman you've ever seen. I'm sure you've had plenty."

I smiled at her comment and licked my lips. "Are you telling me, Miss Scorpio Valentino, that you're unaware of how attractive you are? Woman, as you stood there, do you know that every head in this place was turned. And, still is. I am honored to even be sitting here with you."

She turned her head and noticed some people, women included, gawking at her. "Those women are looking at you, and possibly, Mr. Shane Ricardo Alexander, some of the men are, too."

"Ricardo? How in the hell did you know my middle name?"

"Jaylin told me. We were talking about you one day and he told me your middle name."

"I hate that name. My mother knew she was tripping when she gave me that for a middle name."

"Well, I kind of think it's cute. Now, don't get me wrong, Shane fits you to a capital *T*, but Ricardo is kind of a suave name."

I shamefully dropped my head. "Please. Suave or not, I ain't feeling it. And you, pretty lady, better not ever call me that again."

She laughed and agreed not to. The waiter came back with our drinks and took our orders. Scorpio ordered a Caesar salad and I ordered a steak.

"No wonder your body is intact like it is. Hell, you don't eat nothing," I said.

"Oh, I eat plenty. I just know how to work it off."

That statement went in another direction for me, so I left it alone and changed the subject.

"I . . . I would assume you called me to discuss Jaylin. There couldn't possibly be no other—"

"Yeah, you're right," she said, and then clinched her hands together on the table. I could tell that my mentioning his name made her nervous. "Lately, my mind has been preoccupied by the thoughts of him. I know it's been a long time, and I have been able to move on. However, a . . . a part of me wants to know what he's been up to. I thought you might know, since the two of you are so close."

I hesitated to talk to Scorpio about Jaylin, but I only thought it was fair that she knew the truth. After all she'd been through with him, if I was able to put her mind at ease, then that was the least I could do.

"Jaylin is doing well, Scorpio. He lives in Florida and things are going well for him."

"Florida, huh? Has he been in Florida since our breakup, or did he recently move there?"

"He's been there for," I looked away to think. "almost two years."

"Then, it was right after we broke up."

I shrugged my shoulders. "I guess."

Scorpio swallowed and looked down at her lap. "You're not going to hurt my feelings, Shane.

If I didn't want to know the truth, then I wouldn't be here."

"What do you want me to say, Scorpio? That . . . he's married to Nokea, they have another child, and they're living out their dreams together as a happy couple."

She looked up and gasped. "Is that true?"

"I . . . I wouldn't lie to you," I said. "I know it's not what you wanted to hear, but it's the truth."

Seeming a bit shaken, Scorpio took a sip from her drink. She placed the glass on the table and cleared her throat. "I knew he always loved her."

"Yeah, but he loved you, too. As a matter of fact, he loved you just as much."

"I guess I really blew it when I had sex with Stephon, huh?"

"Honestly, I can't say it really mattered either way. If I can voice my opinion about the situation, I think Jaylin would have married Nokea someday either way you look at it."

Her voice rose. "And, I disagree. I think my betrayal is what drove him to Nokea. We would have stayed together forever . . ."

I kept quiet because I wasn't in the mood to debate the issue. Instead, I picked up my drink, admired Scorpio's sexy lips and listened to her vent.

"So," Scorpio said. "When is the last time you've seen him?"

"I visit him from time to time. He and Nokea have a beachfront home and I go there to get away some times. The last time I visited was about three months ago. He had a surprise birthday party for Nokea and invited me to come."

"I see," Scorpio said. Even though she said my words wouldn't hurt, hurt was written all over her face. When her eyes watered, she excused herself from the table and headed for the restroom.

By the time Scorpio had gotten back, our dinner had been served. I had already cut into my steak and was on my second piece. I placed my fork next to my plate and stood up to pull her chair back. I couldn't tell if she'd been crying, but if she had been, she covered it up pretty well.

I went back to my seat and dabbed my mouth with the napkin. Scorpio looked at her salad and twirled her fork in her hand.

"Shane, does Jaylin ever come back to St. Louis?"

"Yeah, sometimes. He'll be in St. Louis on Friday to introduce Felicia and I to some possible new clients."

"On this Friday?"

"Yes."

"If you don't mind me asking . . . what's the plan for that day?"

"Plan? What do you mean by plan?"

"I mean, what time will he be here? Where is he staying and for how long? I guess the big question is . . . is Nokea going to be with him?"

I wasn't sure how Jaylin would feel about me telling Scorpio about "his plans" so I hesitated. I guessed it wouldn't do no harm, so I went ahead and told her. "His plane arrives at 9:00 a.m., our meeting starts at 2:00 p.m. Most likely we'll have dinner that evening, and by morning he should be heading back home. That's if—"

"If what?"

"If I can persuade him to stay Saturday night for a li'l get together I'm having for my cousin Trey. He's turning twenty-one and I invited a couple of his friends to Davenports for drinks and a li'l entertainment."

Scorpio slightly tooted her lips. "Yeah, right. Your cousin is turning twenty-one and all y'all having are drinks and a little entertainment? Shane, please. I know better."

I smiled because she'd definitely seen through my bullshit. "Okay. There might be a little more entertainment, but not much. I have a woman and she would kill me if she found out about anything raunchy going down."

"What's the stripper's name?"

"There ain't gon' be no—"

"Shane, don't lie. If I know you like I think I do, you're the one who's making all of the arrangements."

I laughed and reached into my back pocket. I pulled out my wallet and searched for the stripper's business card. "Her name is Lady Ice. Now, what's it to you?"

"Curious. I just wanted to know."

Scorpio picked at her salad and hadn't taken one bite. I could tell something was still on her mind.

"On Friday," she said. "Do you mind if I stop by Davenports to see Jaylin?"

"Scorpio, feel free to do whatever you like, but I don't think that's a good idea. I don't know how Jaylin is going to react and Nokea and I have become very good friends. I don't want to be responsible for—"

"Look, all I want to do is see him. Nothing more and nothing less. All I need is five minutes of his time. I promise you that I will not interfere with him and Nokea's marriage."

"I know you wouldn't. But, please don't come dressed as you are today. I don't know of any man who can keep their hands off you, being dressed like that."

"You seem to be doing a pretty good job of it."

I displayed my dimples and gave her a wink. "If, pretty lady, I was not in a committed relationship with a somewhat decent woman, and if you were not previously engaged to my boy, this shit would be on. I'm telling you now, and I do not lie, we would be leaving here right now and indulging into some hot and heavy sex."

Scorpio pulled her head back and smirked. She seemed stunned by my words, but sat quietly. I wasn't sure if she was thinking about my previous licks between her legs or not, but being speechless implied that something was on her mind.

"Let's wrap this up so I can get out of here," she said. "Your offer sounds tempting, and I'm glad that you have a *somewhat decent* woman at home. If I learned one thing from my mistakes with Jaylin, that is to never get involved with a man who is with someone else—if I can help it. In this case, I'm not sure if I can."

I wanted a piece of Scorpio so bad, but because of her past relationship with Jaylin, I changed the subject. After we finished yakking about old times, she headed her way and I headed mine. She told me she'd see me on Friday, and whether Jaylin liked it or not, his marriage to Nokea was about to be tested. I had faith in my boy, but as fine as Scorpio was, I wasn't sure if he'd survive seeing her again.

# Scorpio

# 3

Having dinner with Shane was very enlightening. More than anything, it was my final wake-up call. Jaylin and Nokea had tied the knot and the hopes I had of us someday getting back together had finally washed down the drain. A part of me really wished that maybe our time would come again, but then there was something inside of me that knew it was over for good. I guess I really didn't need Shane to validate anything for me, when I knew deep down Jaylin had moved on.

If I really knew that, then why was I still so willing to see him on Friday? Getting my feelings hurt again wasn't on my agenda, but I wanted to see him and wish him well. In addition to that, I wanted him to know Mackenzie and I were doing fine. There was no way he hadn't thought about us from time to time. I didn't care how happy he was, I was positive that we occasionally crossed his mind.

On Thursday, Jay's was jam-packed. Brian McKnight was coming to town, and everybody was dying to see him. Every last stylists' chair was full, about ten people were waiting, and Yasing couldn't handle all the pedicures she had lined up. I could have helped, but my job was to run the business not handle the business. I wanted to make sure everything flowed smoothly, and if things got out of order, I had to step in. We were way behind schedule, so I ordered one of my masseuses from the back to help out. She didn't mind because she was a jack-of-all-trades.

Things started to slow down, so I grabbed a *Black Hair* magazine and took a seat on the leather sofa near Bernie's station. She was working on one of her customer's hair and had it laid out.

"Girl, you know you can do some hair," I said.

"Can't she," Bernie's customer replied, as she looked in the mirror with approval.

"That ain't all she can do," said Jamaica, another stylist. "From what I heard, she's damn good at giving a blow job, too."

Everybody laughed except for Bernie. She cut her eyes at Jamaica and pointed her comb in her direction.

Her voice dragged as she spoke. "You bony, ugly, nappyhead rooster. The next time you talk about your mama giving blow jobs in here, I'm gonna call and tell her. From what I hear, though, you are the queen of all queens when it comes to that. Darious just happened to mention that the other day, and even though he said you bit him, he truly understood you couldn't help it because of your big beaver teeth."

"Y'all need to stop," I said, laughing hard. Everybody else continued to laugh, but they were use to Bernie and Jamaica going at it—all in good fun.

Just before Jamaica started in on Bernie again, the bell on the door chimed and in came Spencer. The place got quiet and everybody shifted their eyes to me. I'd eased the magazine up over my face so he wouldn't see me. That didn't work and I could see him coming my way.

"Hi," he said, standing in front of me.

I lowered the magazine and put on a fake smile. "Hey, baby. I haven't seen you in a few days. Have you been sick or something?" I asked.

"Naw, I took a few days off. Why haven't you been returning any of my phone calls?"

I stood up so we could go to my office and talk. The last thing I needed was for the women in here to know *all* of my business. Spencer followed behind me, and after I closed the door, we took a seat on the sofa.

He took my hand and placed it in his. "So, why haven't you called me?"

"I've been busy, Spencer. You can see for yourself how busy Jay's is."

"Yeah, but it ain't stopped you from calling me before."

"Well, it's getting close to the weekend. I was going to call you, but there's been one thing after another." I stood up and walked over to my desk, pretending to be occupied with a piece of paper on it. I didn't want to hurt Spencer's feelings anymore than I'd already done.

He stood up and placed his bag full of mail up on his shoulder. "I get the feeling that you don't want to be bothered. If so, just tell me. I'm not the kind of man who hangs on to a woman who doesn't want me."

"It's not that Spencer, but . . . but you and I just . . . we didn't click."

"Didn't click?" he shouted. "We clicked like a mother-fucker the other night. Unless I was dreaming or something, that night was off the chain."

"With who? Me or Yvette?"

He gave me a blank stare. "What are you talking about?"

"I'm talking about you calling her name in your sleep. If I was that good to you, then why are you dreaming about somebody else?"

"I don't even know no damn Yvette." He snapped. "If this is your way of calling this off, then fine. But don't go making up no lame ass excuse about me calling another woman's name in my sleep."

I broke him down easy. "Look, let's just chalk up this one as a loss. If you just make sure to deliver my mail, honestly, I'm cool with that."

He walked over to the door. "No problem. Women come and go in my circle, baby, and it definitely ain't no loss here."

I shrugged my shoulders and followed behind Spencer on his way out. By the time we reached the work area, the women got silent again. Some held their pinky fingers in the air and I hadn't a clue what was up, neither did Spencer. He passed the mail to Bernie and closed the door on his way out. After he left, everybody burst into laughter.

"What is so funny?" I asked, as they still had their pinky fingers in the air.

"It's a sista thing. This means short-dick-nigga alert," Jamaica said. "Every time we see one, it's a warning for the other sistas to stay the hell away."

I looked at Bernie because I knew she had spilt the beans about me and Spencer. I couldn't help but laugh myself.

Thursday night didn't come to a close until almost 2:00 a.m. And even though I wasn't "hands on" I was still exhausted from all the fires that had to be put out.

As usual, Jamaica's boyfriend came in clowning, another one of my stylist's customers was upset about her hair, Yasing wasn't moving fast enough for some customers, and when two women got into it over some money being owed—all hell broke loose.

There was only one stylist left, so I headed back to my office and kicked off my shoes. I unbuttoned my tight jeans and undid a few buttons on my silk blouse so my breasts could breathe. Before soaking my feet, I reached for the phone to call Mackenzie. My sister, Leslie, and her kids had been living with me for three months. My condo sometimes didn't feel like home and I hated to go there. She was never a good housekeeper and all the yelling and screaming at her kids drove me crazy. When she asked if she could live with me, I really didn't want her to. Then, I'd thought about all the times I'd run to her when Jaylin and me had our problems. There was no way for me to tell her no. Since I had a tenant soon moving out of one of my apartments on the Southside, I told Leslie she could move there rent free. It seemed as if time wasn't moving fast enough, but I had to bear with it.

I called home and Leslie said that everyone was asleep. She sounded down for the count too, so I told her I'd be home soon and ended the call.

Finally, the last customer was out, so I locked the door and changed into my white and black swimming suit. I put my hair in a ponytail and turned on the water jets to the Jacuzzi in one of my rooms. I dimmed the lights and sunk deep down into the water. I tightly closed my eyes and leaned my head back on the contoured headrest. With it already being Friday, seeing Jaylin was heavy on my mind. I didn't know what I was going to say, how I would say it, or why I wanted to say anything. I recited my words over and over but they never seemed to come out right. I'd even skimmed over some notes I'd taken earlier, but I realized that they hadn't made much sense. My stomach was tied in a knot, but I knew once I saw him that I'd soon be able to breathe.

*"I love you," he said, standing over me.*

*"I love you, too," I responded back. "But, why'd you stay gone for so long."*

*"Because I needed time to get myself together, baby." He touched the side of my face, as he sat on the edge of the Jacuzzi. "Now that I've thought about things, I'm ready for us to do this. I want you to be my wife."*

\*\*\*

Before I could respond, the sound of my cell phone ringing awakened me. I'd fallen asleep in the Jacuzzi and quickly reached for my phone.

"Hello," I snapped.

"Can we talk about how you played me?"

It was Spencer.

"Spencer, I didn't play you. Like I said, I didn't think we clicked. That's all."

"After I sucked your pussy the way I did, and now, you don't think we clicked? That shit doesn't sound right to me."

"Well, I didn't ask you to suck my pussy. You took that upon yourself. Besides, don't be mad, I returned the favor, didn't I?"

He was silent, and then calmed his tone. "Just give me another chance. Let me take you out tomorrow night."

"I don't think that's a good idea."

"And why not?"

"Because I don't want you getting the wrong idea about us. Besides, I'm seeing somebody else right now." I lied.

The phone went dead, and I had a feeling that Spencer was going to be a problem for me. What was it that he didn't understand? I said no, and as a matter of fact, I'd been saying no to a relationship with every man who'd come my way since my breakup with Jaylin. I guess I was kind of making them pay for what had gone down between us. Maybe I wasn't feeling anybody else because my heart wouldn't allow me to. Hell, I didn't know, but it did make sense.

I glanced at the clock on the wall and it showed 6:45 a.m. Being in the Jacuzzi felt so relaxing and I couldn't help but fall asleep. And then, to dream about Jaylin really made me feel good. I hadn't dreamed about him in awhile, but since he was heavy on my mind, I couldn't help myself.

I was so anxious to see him that I hurried home to find something to wear. The sun was up and the streets were nearly empty. I drove nearly thirty miles to my condominium in Lake St. Louis and was furious when I pulled into the driveway. The kids had all kinds of toys and stuff in the yard. Before Leslie had moved in, my place had remained pretty tidy and clean. Mackenzie would have her toys in the yard from time to time, but nothing like this.

I opened the door and headed upstairs to my room. Leslie and her kids slept in the basement, so I was quiet enough not to wake anyone. Mackenzie had her own room, but always wanting to be close to me, she was laid across my bed with her dog, Barbie, lying beside her. Jaylin had gotten her Barbie as a Christmas present, and she was very attached to her.

I figured I'd go to Davenports around 11:00 a.m. That would give Jaylin time to get settled and it left a little time before his 2:00 p.m. meeting. I had a few hours to take a nap, but before I did, I went into my closet, filled to capacity with clothes and shoes, and searched for something to wear. If I hadn't worn my canary yellow dress that had Shane drooling, I probably would have opted for that. Instead, I pulled out three more seductive little numbers then decided against those as well. Realizing that I looked good in just about anything I wore, I decided on a simple pair of Apple Bottom jeans and a red fitted shirt that left my back bare. Two strings tied it together in the back, and since my bra could be seen, I was forced to go without one. My shoes weren't a problem, so I reached for my red strapped shoes that had a three-inch heel.

Once I decided what to wear, I changed into my pajamas and climbed into bed with Mackenzie. She woke up just long enough to wrap her arms around my neck and had fallen right back to sleep.

The kids downstairs arguing and Barbie's barking was what awakened me. I pounded my fist into the pillow and screamed. Sleep in this place was a thing of the past and I was damn mad about it. Mackenzie was already out of bed, so I yanked the covers back and screamed again. Nobody heard me; as the noise downstairs was enough to drown me out. Instead of going downstairs to kick some butt, I hopped out of bed, noticing it was already a few minutes after 9:00 a.m. I showered, changed into my outfit for the day and looked at my gorgeous body in the mirror. *Eat your heart out, Beyoncé,* I thought. *You my girl, but I can work it just as good as you do.*

I headed downstairs and the kids were still in the kitchen making much noise. Leslie was cooking pancakes and had totally tuned them out.

"Please," I yelled, while reaching for the orange juice. "Can a sista ever get some sleep around here?"

They laughed and the noise came to a halt. I gave Mackenzie a kiss on her forehead. "Hi, baby. Did you sleep well last night?"

"Yes, Mommy. I tried to wait for you, but you took too long."

"Well, don't stay up trying to wait for me. Sometimes, I get real busy and I don't want you losing your beauty sleep, okay?"

She smiled.

Leslie looked me up and down before saying anything. "You look cute," she said in her ghetto, but sassy voice. "Maybe I need to go to Jay's today since all the men are going to be following you."

"Girl, please. Ain't nobody gon' be following me nowhere. Especially, if I put on my don't-fuck-with-me mug."

We both laughed.

The kids were out of school for the summer, so Leslie said she'd take them to the zoo today. The good thing about having her around was Mackenzie got a chance to spend time with her cousins rather than being cooped up with me at Jay's.

"I'll see y'all later," I said on my way out. "If anybody needs me, you know where I'll be."

I gave Mackenzie another kiss and I was finally on my way to see what I'd been missing.

# Shane

## 4

Jay and I sat on two stools by my designer's table and cracked up at the pictures he'd shown me from Nokea's surprise birthday party. I'd gotten messed up and had passed out on the beach.

"I can't believe you took a picture of me under those conditions," I smiled and continued to look through the pictures.

"Hey, don't blame me, my brotha. Nokea was the one with the camera. I suggest you take your beef up with her."

We laughed and when I'd gotten to a picture of Jaylene, his baby girl, he was all over it.

"Ain't she beautiful, man," he said, standing up like a proud father.

"More than beautiful. I can't understand how a Negro as ugly as you pulled off something like this."

Jaylin snatched the pictures from my hands. He rubbed his goatee with the tips of his fingers. "Fuck you, fool. Both of my babies got me written all over them. LJ and Jaylene are a spitting image of this handsome brotha that stands before you today."

As we were talking, Felicia came in. She wore a soft white suit with a skirt that had a major split in the back. The suit tightly hugged her hips and showed off her hour glass figure. Her braids were in a bun and I could tell she went out of her way to impress Jaylin.

"Hello, boys," she said, wiggling her fingers in the air and trotting into her office. She placed a bag on her desk and then came out to join us.

Jaylin opened his arms to embrace her. "Good morning, Miss Lady. I see that life is treating you well."

She pulled herself back and looked up at Jaylin. "Well, it must be treating you extremely well. Nokea knows better than to let you come to St. Louis alone. Is she crazy!"

Jaylin let loose of Felicia and smiled. He didn't say anything because he'd already known how to handle sexual advancements. They started as soon as he got off the plane. The reservationists tried to jump his bones, the chick at the rental car facility was trying to get fucked, and the receptionist in the lobby had thrown herself at him, too. The Jaylin I once knew, no doubt, would have handled his business and handled it well.

"So, how long will you be staying?" Felicia asked him.

"Not long. I'm gonna head back as soon as we get finished with the Mayor's Group."

"Negro, I thought we were having dinner tonight? And—" I cleared my throat.

"And what?" he said.

"And, I'm having a li'l somethin-somethin for my cousin, Trey, tomorrow night. Nothing extravagant, but I invited him and his friends to Davenports for a li'l celebration."

Jaylin held out his hands. "Well, why you ain't say nothing? I don't mind staying."

"Wait a minute," Felicia said. "Did you ask me if it was okay to invite those thugs over here?"

"Thugs? Trey and his friends ain't no thugs. And even if they were, I don't have to ask you nothing, Felicia. This is my place and yours."

She looked at Jaylin, "Do you see what kind of monster you've created? Shane is just . . . He's out of control. He talks to me like—

"Whoa—wait a minute," Jaylin said. "I'm out of it, baby. If anything, y'all need to learn how to get along. Every time I talk to Shane y'all fighting over some bullshit."

She smiled. "I know, but that's because we love each other, don't we boo?" She kissed me on the cheek.

I wiped my cheek and joked with her. "Get away from me. Don't be trying to butter me up, all right?"

She held her hand up to my face and trotted back to her office. She threw her hips from side to side, and didn't have to worry about Jaylin or me looking because our eyes were glued to her butt.

Once we came out of our trances, Jaylin leaned on my work table. "Man, how do you work with her everyday and not have the desire to fuck her?"

I laughed. "Because I've been there and done that. And, she hurt me. Once a woman hurts me as bad as she did, then I'm able to look at her in a different way. That doesn't mean I can't look at her ass, though."

We slammed our hands together. "I guess that makes sense. But, I honestly don't know how you do it."

I took a moment to gather my thoughts, trying to break the news to him about Scorpio coming to see him. It was already 10:15 a.m., and since she said she'd be here by 11:00 a.m., I knew my time was running out.

"If you don't mind," he said. "I'ma hit up your phone and tell Nokea I won't be back until Sunday. Then, I need to let out my leakage I've been holding since I got off the plane."

"Go do your thang," I said. Jaylin grabbed his Brooks Brothers suit jacket from the back of the chair and headed off to my office.

Felicia came out of her office and stood next to me with her arms folded. Her eyes were locked in on Jaylin through the glass windows in my office.

"He is still so fucking fine," she confessed. "Body all tanned, grey eyes glowing, goatee and beard neatly trimmed. All I can think about is those multiple orgasms he gave me and running my fingers through his thick curly hair when he screwed me."

She was in a daze.

I cleared my throat. "Felicia, I don't care to hear about your sexual experience with Jaylin. Do you mind?"

She reached over and rubbed the side of my face. "Don't be jealous, boo. You fine as hell, too, but that man is in a category all by himself." She gazed at him again. "Shane, look at that suit."

I shrugged my shoulders. "So, what about it?"

"It just—just clings to his muscles. And, the way he's showing off his chest with his button down crisp shirt, a tie would murder that outfit."

"Yes, Felicia. He has on a very nice suit. Now, would you please go take your mother her present so you can be on time for our meeting?"

"Damn, I almost forgot." Felicia stood for another moment, gazing at Jaylin until he hung up the phone. "Peep the square-toed shiny leather shoes," she said, underneath her breath. "If you don't learn nothing else from him, you've got to learn how to dress."

I smacked her ass hard and she laughed. "Girl, get your butt out of here. I got my style and he got his."

She rolled her eyes and walked off. Jaylin walked over and shook his head. He sat on the stool next to me.

"What's up with all the ass smacking, man? If I didn't know any better, I'd think you've been lying to me."

"Trust me, I ain't got nothing to hide. I'm satisfied with Sam, and I will not let Felicia or any other woman fuck that up for me."

"How's Sam doing anyway? Whenever we chat, you don't talk much about her."

"She cool. She just got back from handling this modeling gig in New York, and she's going back in a few more weeks. She's been talking about moving there, but I don't see that happening for me."

"Yeah, New York is a busy place. But, if you love her, then you'll do what you gotta do."

I nodded and wasn't up to talking about Sam.

Felicia told us she'd be back and Jaylin suggested that we go get something to eat.

"Yeah, that sounds good, but, uh, I need to talk to you about something."

"What?" Jaylin said, standing with his suit jacket thrown over his shoulder.

"I got a call the other day and it was from Scorpio. She asked me to meet her for dinner and I did."

Jaylin looked interested in what I had to say and laid his jacket on his lap before sitting back down. "So," he said. "What happened?"

"She wants to see you. I told her you were coming in town and she said that she wanted to see you."

"See me for what?"

"Honestly, I don't know." I looked at my Rolex. "She said she'd stop by around eleven. It's a quarter-to right now."

Jaylin gripped his hands together and looked down at the ground. He then raised his head and made direct eye contact with me. "I'm kind of uneasy about seeing her. Did you tell her—"

"Yes. I told her about you and Nokea being married and I told her about Jaylene. For the record, I told her you were a completely fulfilled man and had no desire to be anywhere else."

"How did she take the news?"

"For the most part, she did all right. She knows how much you love Nokea, but she still wants to see you."

Jaylin stood up and slowly walked over by the tall windows, gazing out at the view. He put his hands in his pockets and didn't say a word.

"Hey," I said. "If her coming here makes you uncomfortable, I'll call—"

"Naw," he said with his back facing me. "It's okay," he nodded, "it's definitely okay."

As soon as the words left his mouth, the door came open and Scorpio sauntered her way in. She looked at me first and smiled, and then looked at Jaylin's back since he was still turned.

"Hi," she said, walking up and giving me a hug. I squeezed her tightly, just to get a feel of her nipples that were hard and poking through her red fitted shirt. I rubbed my hand on her bare back and desperately wanted to remove the string that was tied in a knot.

Even while hearing her voice, Jaylin still hadn't turned around. Scorpio broke our embrace and walked over to him. I bit down on my lip as I glimpsed at her silky smooth fat-free back and ass that looked downright delicious in her hip-hugging jeans.

As she stood next to him, Jaylin turned his head and stared her up and down. Nervous, she moved away the bangs on her forehead that nearly covered her eyes. He said nothing, and neither did she. He then leaned forward, wrapped his arms around her and held her close to his chest. She placed her arms around his neck and tightly closed her eyes. When I noticed his eyes closed too, I knew there was some deep shit between them.

Scorpio broke their embrace, backed up a bit and smiled. I had never seen Jaylin look so nervous, but he managed to smile as well.

"What's up?" he said, in his deep masculine voice.

"Hi," she softly replied.

Trying to ease this uncomfortable situation, I intervened. "Why don't y'all come take a seat," I said, pulling up another stool for Scorpio to sit. She walked over to it and Jaylin followed closely behind. His eyelids lowered and zoomed on her backside until she took a seat.

I wanted to excuse myself so that they could be alone, but by the way Jaylin admired her, I didn't think the two of them being alone was a good idea. Jaylin quickly spoke up.

"How's my baby doing?"

"Mackenzie's doing well, Jaylin. She's grown into an even more beautiful little girl, and she still asks about you from time to time."

Jaylin stroked his goatee. "I'm curious. What do you tell her?"

"I told her the truth. That things didn't work out between us and you had to move on. You always said she'd someday understand and you were right. I know she misses you, but she's learned how to adjust."

Jaylin nodded. "And, what about the dog? Does Barbie miss me, too?"

Scorpio smiled. "She . . . we all miss you, but, I'm glad to hear that you're doing okay."

"Yeah, I'm doing fine."

"Shane told me that you had *another* baby?"

Jaylin looked over at me. "Yeah. I have a baby girl." He slightly leaned over on his stool and pulled out his wallet. He proudly pulled out a picture of Jaylene and handed it over to Scorpio. "That's my baby right there. That little girl means everything in the world to me."

Scorpio looked at the picture and forced out a smile. She told Jaylin how beautiful Jaylene was and quickly handed the picture back to him.

He looked at the picture, then put it back in his wallet. "So, what is it that you wanted to talk to me about? Shane said that you wanted to see me?"

I stood up. "I'm gon' allow y'all some privacy. Can I get y'all something to drink?"

Jaylin pulled on my arm. "Sit. We ain't looking for no privacy."

I lowered myself back on the stool.

"I . . . I really just wanted to know how you were doing," Scorpio said. "Lately, for whatever reason, you've been on my mind. I thought that something bad happened to you and—"

"Naw, I'm good, baby." Jaylin spoke with confidence. "Actually, couldn't be better. How about you? You're looking good and things must be going well."

"Yes. Things are going remarkably well. I finally got my business degree, and last year, I opened up Jay's. I haven't done much with my playwriting, but I hope to get back to it soon. For a thirty-two-year-old woman, I'd say I'm doing pretty well."

"Jay's?"

"It's my shop. You can get your hair, nails, and toes done there, along with a massage or facial."

Jaylin sat up straight and rubbed his chin. "That sounds intriguing, especially the name."

"Of course, I thought of you when I decided to name the place Jay's. I never really got a chance to thank you for all that you did for Mackenzie and I."

"And I never got a chance to tell you that it wasn't no problem. It was the least I could do."

I stood up again. "I'd say we give a toast to remembering the past, and focusing on the future."

This time, Jaylin didn't stop me as I walked away and came back with a bottle of Moët and three wine glasses. We lifted the filled glasses and clinked them together. Scorpio took only a few sips and then sat the glass on the table.

"I think I'd better get going," she looked at Jaylin. "Again, I just wanted to say hello and wish you well."

"Well, let me walk you out," Jaylin suggested. He placed his glass on the table, and before they moved toward the exit, Scorpio thanked me and gave me another hug. I watched as they made their way to the door, and even though I hated to admit it, they made a very attractive and sexy couple. It was a damn shame why some things don't work out, but there was no denying it hadn't worked out for a reason.

By the time they reached the door, Jaylin turned to me. "I'll be right back. I'm gon' walk Scorpio to her car."

I nodded and picked up our glasses of Moët to take them to the kitchen. On my way there, I stopped in my office to make sure my designs

"Shane, you'd better not ever repeat this to anybody, do you understand!"

I placed my finger on my lips. "Secrecy, dog. Your words are safe with me."

"I wanna fuck her so bad that I can taste it. I ain't never been one, nor will I ever be one to crave for something and not have it. Whatever I decide, you need to know that I love my wife, my kids, and I would never do anything to intentionally hurt them. Since I've been happily married, I have had no desire for another woman until today. Do not judge me, my brotha, and understand that I am human, and sometimes, the flesh gets weak."

I was silent because I definitely knew where the night was headed. A part of me felt angry for bringing them back together, and even though Nokea probably would never find out, I would always know the truth. I knew that if something went down tonight, I had to laugh in Nokea's face and pretend that everything was good. More than anything, I knew that this love affair between Jaylin and Scorpio would be an ongoing thing.

When 2:00 p.m. rolled around, I was pleased. Jaylin, Felicia and I sat in the boardroom with six investors from the Mayor's Group. After Jaylin threw down on his professional speech about how competent Davenports was to move forward with their project in downtown St. Louis, I knew the offer was in the bag. When he finished, I picked up where he left off and shared with them the ideas I had for bringing our city back to life. Many developers had already begun to do so, but my ideas added an exquisite taste of its own.

During my presentation, I noticed Jaylin drift off several times. I had to call his name three times to verify that he'd heard what I suggested. I knew he hadn't heard me, but he agreed with everything I said. Nobody else seemed to trip, but no doubt, I knew where his mind was.

By the time our meeting was over, it was almost 6:00 p.m. Felicia and I were overjoyed, as the Mayor's Group agreed to let Davenports be the designers for their five and a half million dollar project. Now, we wouldn't see all of that money, being the designers and all, but a large chunk of it was going to make its way into our hands.

After they left, we all sat around laughing and talking about what had went down. I thanked Jaylin repeatedly and so did Felicia.

"We are in debt to you forever, my brotha," I said, shaking his hand.

"Hey, y'all doing all of the work. I just made the introduction possible."

"Well, we really appreciate it," Felicia said. "If only you'd let me repay you."

"You can repay me by getting along better with Shane. I understand that there have been some squabbling matches between y'all."

"There are always squabbles within a partner-ship, Jaylin. Some things can't be avoided," she looked over at me. "Right, Shane?"

I shrugged my shoulders. "Hey, it's whatever. I'm just glad we closed that deal, and now we can move forward. If either of you would like to join me, I'm going to dinner with my marvelous woman, and after that, we're going home."

Felicia decided to go with me, but Jaylin said he'd pass. I'd guessed his mind was made up about tonight, so I didn't want to interfere any longer. Since he was staying at my place, I tossed my keys to him and told him I was most likely spending the night at Sam's place. He said that he wanted to chill for a moment, so I told him to lock up Davenports after he left.

# Scorpio

## 5

How or why did I do that to myself? Seeing Jaylin again gave me no peace at all. Actually, it brought out my true feelings for him no matter how hard I tried to convince myself any differently, I was still in love with him.

Thing is, he'd looked even better than the last time I'd seen him. His hair seemed healthier and Lord knows his body was even more intact. When he hugged me, I felt his nine plus inches of pleasure rubbing up against me. I didn't know if he was hard or not, but just the feel of it made me trickle in my panties.

I'd asked him to meet me for dinner tonight, and at first, he declined. I assured him that dinner was all I wanted, and then he said he'd think about it. Honestly, dinner was the last thing on my mind. I wanted him inside of me and I wanted him bad. I didn't care that he was married, and his kids weren't important either. The more I thought about how Nokea took him away from me, the more and more I desired to have him.

Tonight, though, was going to be my night. If I ever had to pull myself together and make magic happen, I knew it was all up to me. I told him where and how to reach me, and once he calls, I'll soon have my way.

When Bernie knocked on the door, I was sitting in my office envisioning tonight. She'd known I'd gone to see Jaylin, and once she finished with her customer's hair, she came to chat.

"By the look on your face, I can tell it must have been difficult."

"Have a seat, Bernie," I said. She took a seat in the chair in front of my desk. "Seeing him was unlike anything I'd ever experienced. It's like I was in shock or something. My words didn't seem to come out right and I got seriously tongue tied. And, that doesn't even account for the butterflies that roamed around in my stomach."

"Okay, so the worst part is over with. Now what?"

"Now, I'm waiting on him to call so that we can have dinner."

"Dinner? Where at?"

I shrugged my shoulders. "I don't know, but honestly, fuck a dinner. There's no way I can eat when all I can think about is him making love to me." I shook my head. "Bernie, I can't wait for you to meet him. Girl, he can put Denzel Washington, Shemar Moore, Blair Underwood, Idris Elba . . . all of those fine men to shame."

"Nah, I don't know about all of that. Shemar and Idris, uh, maybe, but Denzel? There ain't no man who's been capable of pulling that off but Obama."

We both laughed, and I somewhat agreed that I'd taken my comment too far.

"So, what time is this dinner supposed to be?"

"I told him to call me at eight. It's almost seven p.m. and I'm staying right here until this phone rings."

"I have never, ever seen you so giddy about a man. Jaylin must have really put something on you."

"That's putting it mildly. Once upon a time, we really had something special. I was supposed to be his wife, Bernie!" I yelled and slammed my fist on my desk. "It should have been me and not Nokea!"

"Damn, calm down. It's gon' be all right, you know."

We smiled and I rolled my eyes at her. "I know it's gon' be all right. As soon as I take back what is due to me, you damn right it's gon' be fine."

"I can't seem to figure out if you're out for revenge against this woman, or if you really want to be with Jaylin."

"Both. For me, this is personal, and I can't wait to feel him inside of me again."

"That's some deep shit, Scorpio. I don't want you to mess around and hurt yourself. You've already allowed him to do it once, and it'll be such a shame if you let him do it again."

Bernie went back to her work station and I stayed in my office waiting for my phone to ring. When I finally got my call, it wasn't until a quarter to nine and wasn't exactly what I expected.

"I'm kind of tied up tonight. We're gonna have to make plans for dinner the next time I come to St. Louis."

I took a deep breath and held my aching stomach. "You can't even take one hour of your time to have dinner with me?"

"Not tonight."

"What about tomorrow?"

"I have plans."

"What about lunch?"

"Damn, baby, I said I'll see you the next time I come back."

"Jaylin, you know that's a lie. We haven't seen each other in a long time and I don't understand why you're trying to avoid me."

"I'm not trying to avoid you, Scorpio. I'm a busy man, and besides, I'm married now. I ain't got no business having dinner or anything with my ex-fiancé."

"So, you don't trust yourself? Is that what you're saying?"

"No, what I'm saying is what I said before. I'm married—"

"That's bullshit and you know it," I yelled. I had to take a deep breath and calm myself. "You know damn well that you can make time for me if you want to."

"Well, I don't want to."

"And, why not? This time, though, I want the truth."

He was silent. I could tell that he moved the phone away because I heard him say something in the background.

I spoke softly, "Tell me why you can't have dinner with me?"

"Be . . . because I love my wife, my kids, and I am truly thankful for everything that I have. Being alone with you will cause me to jeopardize that. I don't trust myself, Scorpio, and I know that if I see you tonight, I'm going to have sex with you."

The feeling of what he said made me squeeze my legs together. I continued to speak in my soft, yet seductive voice. "So what, Jaylin. I'm dying to have sex with you, too. I've been feeling you inside of me all day long and I'm ready for the real thing. Tomorrow night, or whenever, you'll be back at home and no one will ever know what happened between us. Just allow me this one night, okay?"

"It's not that easy, baby. I'll know what went down between us and I can't face Nokea, knowing that after all we'd been through, I wound up right back in your arms."

I wasn't trying to hear him. "Do you remember how and when we used to make love everyday? How we'd wash each other in the shower, and I'd let you have your way with me anywhere, anyway, and anytime."

Jaylin was silent, so I continued.

"Well, I remember. I want to feel your dick Jaylin. What is so wrong with me wanting to feel and taste your cum again? You want to taste me, don't you?"

"Maybe," he said. I felt his voice getting weak.

"Then, come claim your pussy. It's always going to be yours, whenever and however you want it. If my memory serves me correctly, I'll be bending over by the time you get here. Jay's closes at midnight. I'm kicking everybody out by ten p.m., so tell me, Can I expect to see you walking through those doors shortly thereafter?"

He breathed heavily into the phone. "Listen, I'll call you back. I can't answer that right now, I'll just hit you back in a bit."

He hung up and I made my way up front to tell everybody to quickly wrap it up. I had a feeling he'd come tonight, and I didn't want no interruptions.

Bernie and Jamaica were the only two still doing hair. Yasing was on her last customer for the evening, so the pressure was not on her. Jamaica had just washed her customer's hair and it looked as if she had another hour or two to go. It was already after 9:00 p.m., so I had to make some other arrangements.

"I apologize everybody, but Jay's is gonna close in about five minutes. Again, I'm sorry for the inconvenience, and I'll give you all a free gift certificate to come back another time."

The last few customers tripped a bit, but not as much as Jamaica and Bernie. After the customers left, we quickly discussed it.

"Couldn't you meet him somewhere else," Bernie said. "Putting our customers out like that was kind of cold."

Jamaica put her hands on her hips. "You mean to tell me you kick them out over some dick? You can't be serious."

"Bernie and Jamaica, y'all please understand. This might be the last opportunity I have with him, and since he's so close by, I couldn't take a chance on asking him to meet me some place else. I know y'all felt like this for a man before, so don't be mad at me, okay?"

Both of them looked at me and broke off a half ass smile. Jamaica rolled her eyes, and Bernie walked to her work station to get her purse. "Call if you need me," she said. "And, don't do nothing I wouldn't do."

"Well, that means suck his dick, lick his balls, and if you got any whips," Jamaica said, looking at Bernie. "You might want to use those, too."

We laughed and Jamaica and Bernie walked out together going off on each other. Shortly after, Yasing left and I locked the door behind her.

I went back into my office and straightened up a bit. This would be Jaylin's first time in Jay's and I wanted him to see how my place had it going on.

After I finished tidying up a few of my stylists' workstations, I went back into my office. I put on a CD by Miles Davis that reminded me of Jaylin and poured myself a glass of wine. I lay back on the couch and slid a few pillows behind my head and back. Thinking more about him, I sipped the wine and looked at my hard nipples that were visible through my red shirt. I placed the glass on the table and removed my top. My hands roamed over my breasts and I massaged them together. I visualized the tip of Jaylin's tongue circling them and let out soft moans as if I could really feel him. Getting more excited, I unbuttoned my jeans and slid my hand down between my legs. I didn't have on any panties, so my hand grazed the smooth neatly trimmed hair on my pussy. Letting out more moans, I turned to my side and squeezed my legs tightly together.

I heard hard knocks at the door and listened to someone loudly call my name. When I jumped out of a deep sleep, I was still shirtless and my hand remained between my legs. Knowing that it was early morning, I was furious because Jaylin hadn't called back. I quickly put on my shirt and zipped my jeans. Before going to the door, I pulled my hair back into a ponytail, and just to confirm the time, I looked at the clock sitting on my desk. It was 7:45 a.m., and obviously, my opportunity had passed.

With a serious frown on my face, I hurried to the door to see who was outside banging. It was Bernie and she grinned as I slowly opened the door.

"Is he here?" she whispered.

I shook my head and tears welled in my eyes.

She locked the door behind her. She pointed her finger at me, as I was almost ready to lose it.

"Don't you dare!" she yelled. "I have watched you hurt yourself one time too many about the thoughts of this man! You need to stop, move on, and recognize what in the hell you got to offer somebody else! Do you understand?"

I closed my eyes to fight back my emotions and nodded.

"Now, got get changed. Let's go workout, and if you ever mention his name to me anymore, I'm gonna kick your butt!"

I managed to grin and went to my office to change into my workout gear. Bernie and I didn't talk about Jaylin, but I wasn't going to let him go that easily. I knew he was in St. Louis for one more night, and in knowing so, I had another plan up my sleeve.

# Shane

## 6

"Good for you," I said to Jaylin, as we sat at IHOP eating breakfast. "I gotta tell you man, I was a little worried."

"Well, you weren't the only damn person worried. I just don't see how I was able to shake off that feeling. When I got back to your place last night, I stayed in the shower almost all night trying to calm down my dick."

"I bet Scorpio is mad as hell this morning."

"I'm sure she's mad, but hell, I'm mad, too. I couldn't do it, though, dog. I—I just couldn't do it."

"I understand. And, like I said, I'm happy for you. Once you get through tonight, you'll be home free."

Jaylin scooped a fork full of cheese eggs in his mouth. "So, what kind of entertainment you got for Trey and his friends?"

"Man, it's gon' be funny. That fool turning twenty-one and I got this fine young tender coming to work his bones. You know the nigga a nerd, so I can't wait to see the look on his face. I be teasing him all the time about not getting no pussy."

"Twenty-one and he ain't getting no pussy? Something is definitely wrong with that picture. Shit, I was bone'en and own'en when I was twelve."

"Shit, man, me too. I hit my first gal when I was fourteen. She was twenty-six and titties and ass was out to here." I showed examples of how big they were with my hands.

"Shane, you don't even like women with that much titties or ass. The majority of your flavah has been tall and skinny chicks with nothing to work with. And, that's no offense to Sam, but it's the truth."

"I won't dispute that with you, my brotha, because you are certainly on the right path. It ain't about all that shit for me, though, Jay. I be looking for somebody who loves me for me, that's all."

"I feel you. Ain't nothing more special than loving a woman who definitely loves you back."

We finished up breakfast and I told Jaylin to meet me at Davenports by 9:00 p.m. I had a few errands to run, and since Sam wanted to help, I stopped by her place and picked her up.

She took all day getting ready, and when she came out she wore a strapless pink sundress with flowers and some flat sandals that matched. Her long hair was parted through the middle and hung along the sides of her cheeks.

"I'm ready," she said, while holding her straw purse in her hand.

"It's about time."

She walked over to me and buttoned up the few buttons I had undone on my white crisp Sean John shirt. I placed my hands in the pockets of my stone washed Sean John jeans and smiled as she tried to cover my chest.

"I don't want these other women looking at you while we're out," she joked. "Are you trying to get me into a fight?"

"I'd help if you did, you know. There's no way I'll let you get beat up."

She placed her hand on her hip. "There's no need to help me. I might be a thin woman, but I can fight."

I laughed and took Sam by her hand. By the time we made it to my Lexus, I had already undone the buttons on my shirt.

Sam helped me pick out a gift for Trey, and went to Davenports to help me decorate. She had

the place looking really nice, and when it neared
5:00 p.m., I asked her to hurry so we could have
dinner and I could get back here by nine.

When 9:00 p.m. rolled around, I was running late and rushed to get to Davenports. I'd
given Jaylin the keys so that he could get in
and he called to tell me the guest of honor had
already arrived. What held me up was, as Sam
and I broke off a quickie, she started in with her
questions about getting married. This time, our
argument got heated, and I left her place without
saying good-bye.

The few fellows I'd invited were already there.
Trey, his partners, Zeek, Jermaine, Cedric, and
Tony. On my end, I'd invited a cool client of
mine named Brandon, and of course, Jay. I kept
it simple because I didn't want to get Trey accustomed to the many wild parties that we'd thrown
in the past.

Everything seemed to be in order. For the
most part, we sat around drinking, talking
about women and our careers. I was completely
stunned when Trey told us how much pussy he'd
had. I couldn't believe it; I'd seriously thought he
was a nerd. I guess he'd acted that way around
his parents because they were in church all the
time.

By 11:00 p.m., we were all beyond fucked up. We'd been acting rather silly, and when Tony insisted he had to throw up, we all laughed as he crawled on the floor like a dog on his way to the bathroom. Trey was laid out on the floor with his arms stretched out while talking crazy underneath his breath.

"That cat is gone," Jay said with a major buzz. His eyes were red and so glassy that it looked as if they were filled with tears.

"He'll be all right," Brandon responded. "By morning, he won't remember a thing."

I walked over to Trey and smacked his leg. "Trey, get up man. Why you drink all that shit?"

"Cauuuuse," he moaned. "It's my muuutha-fuckin' birthday, that's why."

He grabbed my neck and held me in a choke hold. Slightly drunk, I fell to the floor and wrestled with him. During all of the commotion, the door opened and in walked Lady Ice. She was decent, but I'd seen better. Basically, had she been there for me, the party might have been over. Everybody's head turned, and when she dimmed the lights, I maneuvered myself off the floor.

"Y'all boys having fun without me," she said. She switched her hips from side to side and was searched from head to toe by wandering eyes.

"Get him now," I yelled, as Trey was still swaying back and forth on the floor. I handed Lady
Ice a bottle of wine and she gave me her CD to
start the music. She straddled her legs and stood
over Trey. He opened his mouth wide and she
poured the wine into his mouth. The wine spilt
all over the place and that caused him to act like
a serious maniac.

Lady Ice started dancing and her moves were
definitely to the rhythm. I looked at Jay and
Brandon and they were all into what she was putting on Trey. His other partners were too, and I
wanted to make sure that this was a twenty-first
birthday he'd never forget.

Jaylin seemed indulged and slid his hand
down over his thang. He kicked my leg, noticing
my attentiveness as well.

"You wrong, Shane. You are wrong for this."

I laughed at how fucked up he was. "Don't
blame me. You don't have to watch if you don't
want to."

"Damn, I wish I had my wife here! I have
never missed her so damn much!"

"Well, then, go home, fool. Get yo ass on the
plane tonight and jet."

"I plan to," he said standing up. He pulled out
his cell phone and held his manhood. Before
heading to another room, he took one last look

at Lady Ice and Trey fake playing with each other on the floor.

By the time Jaylin came out of my office, he mentioned that Tony was almost passed out on the bathroom floor. Lady Ice had two chairs sitting face-to-face by the windows that viewed the dark streets in Clayton. She asked me to sit in one and asked Jaylin to sit in the other. He declined.

"Naw, baby, you gon' and do your thang. I just want to watch," he replied.

She walked up to him and took his hand. "Come on, now, honey. I want the younger boys to see how their elders can really get down."

Jaylin hesitated, but I coaxed him into it. He plopped down in the chair and looked as if he were high.

Lady Ice reached in her bag for some handcuffs and willingly cuffed Jaylin's and my hands behind our backs. He didn't seem too happy, but he went with the flow. I, on the other hand, couldn't wait to see what else Lady Ice had to offer.

She kept the lights dim and turned off her music. She asked the other fellows to follow her, and after rescuing Tony from the bathroom, they all left the room. I didn't know what the fuck was going on, but I sat there thinking that she'd soon be back.

"I'on like this shit," Jaylin said. "Yell for her ass to come back in here and remove these cuffs."

"Yo, Lady Ice," I yelled. "Can brothas get some assistance?"

Nothing came of my yelling, until the door finally came open. I felt relieved that she was back because I knew Jaylin was moments away from getting his clown on.

We could barely see from the dimmed lighting, but when we were able to make out who had entered the room, it was Scorpio. She was boldly dressed in a black sheer strapless mini dress that showed her sheer bra and string tied panties underneath. Every part of her jaw dropping body was clearly visible and I couldn't help but sit there with my mouth wide open. I was too afraid to look at Jaylin because I knew his dick had to be thumping just as much as mine.

Scorpio stepped over to us clicking the sounds of her tall spiked heels. She looked at me first, and then we both turned our eyes to Jaylin. He didn't say one word until Scorpio placed the palms of her hands on his knees and bent her ass over right in front of me. She placed her face directly in front of his, touching her lips with his as she spoke.

"Why didn't you call me last night?" she whispered.

"Becaaause," he whined and moved his head to the left, then right. "Get these cuffs off me. Now!" he yelled.

I had to intervene. "Scorpio, game over, baby. Just take the cuffs off and—"

She stood with her front facing Jaylin and her backside facing me. I couldn't help but notice his name still tattooed on her butt. "I'll take them off as soon as I'm finished," she said.

With her ass staring me right in the face, I couldn't say shit. The back of her panties were sheer and silk and had me on a major rise. She backed herself up and sat on my lap. When she opened her legs, I could only envision what Jaylin saw. Her hands went down inside her panties and he closed his eyes. He dropped his head back in defeat. She politely asked for his attention, and I'll be damned if he didn't open his eyes and give it to her.

Once his eyes were focused in, baby girl turned around and went to work. Not on him, but on me. She lowered the upper part of her sheer dress and held her breasts together. Placing them directly in my face, I wanted so badly to suck the shit out of them, but I couldn't. She teased her nipples with her own hands and when she slid the rest of her dress off, she bent over and gave Jaylin the view I'd seen just moments ago. She had us both under her hypnotic spell, and after she popped off her bra, she reached for the button on my jeans.

"Uh-uh," I said. "That's taking it too far, Scorpio. Would you please take the cuffs off both of us?"

She ignored me, and when Jaylin yelled for her to remove them, she got more aggressive. She removed her panties, straddled his lap and forced her panties into his mouth. After they marinated, she pulled them back out and wrapped her arm around his neck.

"How did they taste?" she whispered. "Were they sweet enough for you?"

Jaylin didn't respond. He dropped his head back again, and she grabbed the back of his head and moved it forward.

"If you want me to stop, just say the word and I will."

"Stop," he said softly. "Please stop."

"Don't you want me to remove those cuffs so you can feel me?"

"Yesss," he moaned. "Yes, I want to feel all of you."

She grabbed his face and placed her lips on his. Unable to hold back any longer, Jaylin smacked lips with Scorpio as if kissing was going out of style. The juicy smacks got louder and heavier as they both seemed to be all into it. Moments later, Jaylin turned his head to the side and tried to avoid her.

"Stop this!" he ordered. "You've gotta stop this, baby. Don't make me do this, please don't make me do this."

Scorpio ignored every word he said. She reached for the button on his pants and I couldn't stand to see how weak my boy had gotten.

"Scorpio," I said, "Baby, don't regret what you're about to do."

She turned around and faced me. She straddled Jaylin's lap and gave me one of the sexiest looks I'd ever seen.

"Do you want me, Shane?"

I could barely respond, but trying to save all of us, I did. "Yes . . . Yes, I want you."

She stood up. "How bad do you want me? Cause, Jaylin sitting here like he don't want me."

"I want you," he said softly. "You just don't know how bad I want you."

Scorpio snickered and continued to stare me down. I'd hoped that he kept quiet until I got both of us out of this mess I knew we'd regret.

"He might want you, but not as bad as I do," I shot back.

She straddled my lap and placed her arms on my shoulders. We stared eye to eye without giving any blinks.

"If you want me so bad then why don't you take me?"

"I am, and I will, but just not right now."

"Well, I'm asking that you take what you want right here and right now. I might not offer it to you again, so you might as well take it while you can."

My heart was pounding and pounding fast. I could feel my hands dripping with sweat, and so was my forehead that Scorpio had taken upon herself to wipe.

Her performance continued as she turned on my lap and faced Jaylin again. This time, however, she removed my dick from my pants and it flopped out long, thick, and hard. At this point, I didn't have the courage or balls to stop her. Her wish was my command and there wasn't a damn thing I could say about it.

She sat directly on my hardness, but didn't let it go inside. Her wet slit stroked my pipe and I damn near had a fit. I tried to maneuver myself around in the chair to make it go in, but she wouldn't allow it to. She teased the fuck out of me and looked directly at Jaylin while she was doing it.

No doubt, fury covered his face. I could tell by the wrinkles on his forehead and the raising of his eyebrows that somebody was about to catch hell. As angry as he was, though, that didn't stop him from looking between Scorpio's legs. It was like watching the last two seconds of a tied football game with the St. Louis Rams getting ready to kick a field goal. His eyes were glued in, but I knew he was waiting to see if my dick would enter her.

The tip of my head touched her clit, and he knew that all she had to do was jolt down on it and it would be in. Knowing that, I begged Scorpio to stop. Jaylin gritted his teeth and looked viciously at her.

"Get these motherfuckin' cuffs off me, now! This is the same shit that ended our fucking relationship and you have the nerve to sit there and try to fuck my boy in front of me!"

She turned her head to the side. "Shane are you fucking me? If you are, then let me in on it, okay?"

"No . . . No, I'm not fucking you. But would you please get off me."

Scorpio rose up. She slid back into her panties, bra and mini dress while holding the keys to the handcuffs in her hand.

She sauntered back over to Jaylin and was face-to-face with him again. "I'm afraid to un-cuff you because I might die before I make it to the door. In the meantime," she said, squatting between his legs. She carefully unzipped his pants and pulled out his hard dick. Her mouth went into action and Jaylin's head dropped back again. "Umph, umph, umph," was all he could say. I couldn't believe this shit was happening right in front of me, and I couldn't help but wonder when my turn was coming.

Scorpio short changed Jaylin and cut it short. She stood and squeezed his cheeks with her hands. "I want that favor returned. Don't you ever tell me something you don't intend to do, and whatever happened to you being a man of your word? I waited for you last night, and you have to know how much it hurt me that you didn't show up. Until next time, Jaylin Jerome Rogers, I can only hope that we continue what I started."

He snatched his head away, and as fast as Scorpio entered the room, she put the keys down inside of his pants, zipped them, and left.

We sat staring at each other for a moment and let what had just happened settle. I was calling him a weak motherfucka to myself, and I'm sure in his vocabulary of words, he was calling me the same. Either way, I was the first one to open my mouth.

"How you gon' get the keys?" I asked.

"You the one who got us into this mess, so you figure it out."

"Aw, I know you ain't mad at me. If anything you should be mad at your damn self for standing her up last night," Shane said.

"I did not stand her up last night! I told her I couldn't go through with it."

"Nigga, you told her you'd call her back when you were on your way!"

"Did you hear what the fuck I just said?! I did not tell her I would call when I was on my way. I told her I'd call back so I could get her off the phone!" Jay yelled.

"Fool, don't be yelling at me!" Shane shot back.

"Nigga, don't be yelling at me!"

"What you want, Jay! You are not gon' sit there and blame me for your fuck ups!"

"Punk, I ain't blaming no damn body! I put my fucking self in this situation when I listened to you and overstayed my welcome. I should have taken my ass home to my wife and kids like I was supposed to do yesterday!"

"Well, you didn't, so now what!"

"Nothing!" Jay screamed.

"Then, stop complaining," I yelled and turned my head toward the window. I looked out and so did Jaylin. Things were quiet for awhile, as neither of us wanted to make a move for the keys or take the blame for what had happened.

As usual, I spoke up before he did. "I apologize, but had I known Scorpio would do what she did, I would have never agreed to her coming here."

Jaylin slightly tooted his lips. "You know damn well that you got a kick out of what just happened."

I quickly spoke up. "You were looking overly thrilled your damn self. Ain't no way you just didn't enjoy your dick in her mouth."

"And what if I did enjoy it?" Jay asked.

"Then, that's all on you. I'm not gon' lie and tell you she didn't just turn me the fuck on when we both know she damn well did." Shane replied.

"You are really angry about this shit, ain't you? What's with all the cussing and shit?" Jay said

"'Cause, man. I'on like to be teased like that. She fucked with my manhood and had a brotha kinda feeling like a wimp."

"Now you see exactly what I went through the few years we were together. Scorpio is a master at getting what she wants. And, I'll be damned, she almost got it. If not tonight, she'd damn sure earned herself a fast and furious fuck from me tomorrow."

"Tomorrow? Wha—"

"Tomorrow, I'm gon' give her what she wants. After that, I'm jetting. I'll write this down in my little black book as one of the biggest mistakes of my life and be done with it."

"Hey, fine. Do whatever you want to do. I am out of this shit and I do not want to know the details," Shane stated.

Jaylin was silent and then he looked down at the keys in his pants.

"Why don't you stand up, come over here, use your teeth and not your mouth, to get these keys out of my pants. Hold the key steady in your mouth and uncuff me," he said.

"Negro, please. I ain't about to put my face anywhere near your dick. Why don't you stand up, jump up and down, and try to get them to fall. Once they hit the floor, use your teeth to pick them up, and then hold your mouth steady and uncuff me."

"First of all, those keys aren't going to make it to the floor with this big ass hump in my pants. Secondly, my plan was a whole lot better than yours," Jaylin countered

"Your plan was shitty. That's the only thing it was," Shane claimed.

"Then, I guess we gon' sit here like this all night then," Jaylin said.

"Then, I guess so."

After hours of sitting, neither one of us budged. Every once in awhile we shot comments back and forth, but the keys remained in Jaylin's pants. The only thing that saved us was when Felicia came in on Sunday morning, claiming to have left some money in her drawer that needed to be deposited early Monday morning. She looked at us in disbelief.

"I am too embarrassed to ask y'all what happened at this party last night." She looked at my pants that were still unzipped. "This is ridiculous. And don't you ever have the audacity to tell me what a faithful friend you have." She turned to Jaylin. "Like I told him, once a ho, always a ho."

"Felicia, would you please get the keys from inside of Jaylin's pants and remove these cuffs," I asked.

She rushed to it, but took her time pulling them out. "This is an embarrassment to our company, and I pray like hell those hoochie mamas y'all invited here didn't have a videotape with them, especially for your sake Jaylin. If Nokea knew what kind of so called husband she's still got—"

I got frustrated with Felicia and so did Jaylin. "Just take the fucking cuffs off," we said in unison.

"Hold up!" she yelled while still roaming her hands down inside Jaylin's pants. "I know y'all ain't trying to disrespect me! It doesn't look like the two of you have many options here. Do I get an apology, or do I leave the keys in his pants?"

"Sorry," both of us said in unison again. We'd both been punked by a woman twice in one night and it wasn't a good feeling.

Felicia's hands stop roaming and she looked at Jaylin. "You should be disappointed in yourself for reserving something like that for one woman. There is much power in what you got and whenever you want to get things going again, just let me know."

Jaylin had a blank expression on his face and didn't say one word. It was so obvious how mad he really was.

Felicia removed the cuffs from my hands first and then from Jaylin. After that, we left. When we got back to my place, he asked if he could use it for the night to entertain Scorpio. All I said was I'd be over at Sam's place. I warned him about doing something he would surely regret.

# Scorpio

## 7

Since the shop was closed on Sunday, we sat around and celebrated Deidra's recent engagement. Leslie and the kids had even come with me and while the grown folks stayed upstairs at Jay's, the kids were in the basement playing.

Of course, Lady Ice and I were telling everybody the details of last night's events. Shane was so clueless when he provided me with her name during dinner. I knew she was my girl, Juanita, and we made plans to handle things exactly as they went down.

Everybody had known about Jaylin standing me up, so it was only fair that I made myself look good. When I described the look on Jaylin's and Shane's faces, the women in Jay's cracked up.

"Girl, I would have done anything to be in your shoes," Bernie said. "I can only imagine how things went down."

"You can't imagine it without knowing how fine both of them are," Leslie chimed in.

"Hello," Juanita said, giving her a high five. "If Scorpio didn't get there soon, I was gon' change plans and keep them for myself!"

"Scorpio made one mistake," Leslie continued, "and that was she didn't fuck'em. I would have pulled their dicks out and wore their asses out!"

The whole place agreed and passed around high fives.

"Naw, she did the right thing," Bernie said. "Sometimes, it's good to watch'em sweat. By screwin them, she would have given them what they wanted."

Nearly everybody nodded.

"Well, either way, it was a day I will never forget," I said, proudly.

"See, all this dick talk done made me horny," Jamaica said, standing up. "Either y'all feed me something or I'm gonna go home and get fed."

"I hope not by that crazy Negro who be busting you upside your head. The only thing you'll get from him is a black eye."

Bernie had touched a nerve with Jamaica. One thing she hated was for someone to talk about her abusive man.

"Bernie, mind your own business. At least I'm getting some. Your corrupted ass pussy so dry from not getting none, that even a rapist would turn it down."

"I guess some dick is better than no dick, huh? Even if it knocks you unconscious from time to time, you gotta have something, right ladies?"

Nobody responded because we could tell that Bernie had touched another nerve with Jamaica. She was heading her way before the bell on the door chimed and in walked Jaylin. The entire place was frozen in time. Our heads were in the same direction and not one person said a word! He was at his best, wearing a gray pair of pin-striped cuffed pants and a gray silk button down shirt that tightened around his muscular frame. The shirt matched his cattish grey eyes. They were covered with tinted glasses but everyone could see how gorgeous his eyes were. You could smell the money on him, and the silver and diamond watch that glistened on his wrist was probably a Rolex.

Jamaica pulled herself away from me. "Uh, you must be in the wrong place. Hollywood Boulevard is many, many miles from here."

Jaylin smiled and placed his hands in his pockets. He looked at me. "Can we talk," he said.

"Baby, sure," Jamaica said, looking around. "Do you wanna go somewhere private?"

Jaylin smiled again. I stepped forward to introduce him. "Everybody, this is Jaylin. This is the guy I named Jay's after."

"Girl," Jamaica shouted. "Shut your mouth! This the Jaylin we've been talking about—"

Bernie cleared her throat to stop Jamaica from talking. I told Jaylin to follow me and everybody's eyes followed. Somebody gave off a whistle and then everybody got started. By the time we made it to my office, the ladies were laughing and going crazy.

"You have to excuse them," I said, closing the door after Jaylin to drown out the noise. "They don't know no better."

"Yeah, that was pretty wild," he said. He stood for a while and looked around. "I'm kind of feeling Jay's, Scorpio. You done hooked up the place real nice."

"If you be good, I'll take you on a tour of the place later."

"Well, I'm not gon' be good." He took a seat on the leather sofa, leaned slightly to the side and rested on his elbow. He lowered his eyelids and looked between my legs. "You know you were wrong for last night, don't you?"

"Maybe," I said with my butt pressed against the front of my desk. "But, you were wrong for standing me up."

"I guess. But, either way, I want to make it up to you. Tonight. No strings attached—just me and you."

"What made you have a change of heart?"

"Do you have to ask?" he chuckled.

I knew my mouth could be persuasive. "Where would you like to meet? I would let you come to my place, but I don't want Mackenzie to see you."

"I wouldn't mind seeing her, you know. I think about her every single day. If you would allow me to see her for five minutes I'd be grateful."

"I'm sorry, but there's no way I can do that. Trust me, she'd be so happy to see you, and knowing she wouldn't be able to see you again would really hurt her."

"I'd explain to her that I live in Florida. All I want to do is hug her and let her know I haven't forgotten about her."

"Jaylin, no. I can't bring no hurt on her like that. Things are better off left as they are."

He disagreed, and no sooner than he did, I heard Mackenzie and li'l James coming down the hallway arguing.

I quickly stood up and panicked. "Please, you have got to hide. Jaylin, do not do this to her, please," I begged. I hurried him into a closet, and once he was inside, I closed the door. As soon as I sat in my chair, they came through the door.

"Mommy," Mackenzie said, in her sassy voice, while holding a Barbie doll in her hand. "James keeps pulling my hair." Her hair had a band around it that held back the long length and fluffiness of it. She looked so adorable in her pink Baby Phat skirt and jacket, and I knew Jaylin wouldn't be able to resist holding her in his arms. I hadn't paid much attention to what she said because my eyes were focused on the cracked closet door.

I shook my head from side to side as I saw it crack open wider. "Mackenzie, why can't you and James get along? Now, go play and, James, please stop doing whatever it is that you're doing to her."

They headed for the door, and when Jaylin opened the closet door, I swung my chair around and placed my hands over my face. How dare him go against my wishes?

"Daddy," I heard Mackenzie scream loudly.

He didn't say a word; I figured he must have been getting the hug he so desperately wanted.

I swung my chair back around and looked at the two of them tightly embracing each other. My heart hurt so badly; his eyes were closed and she held her arms around his neck when he picked her up.

He opened his eyes and moved his head back to break her embrace around his neck. Obviously, she didn't want to let go.

I was so upset with him that I got up to gather myself. I rushed to the bathroom and closed the door. I stood with my back against the door, closed my eyes, and dropped my head. I listened to him talk to her, but I couldn't make out what he said. When I heard her laugh, I took a deep breath, waited a few more minutes, and then opened the door. He sat on the couch with her on his lap.

Allowing them some time, I took James by the hand and walked him back downstairs with the other kids. I wasn't sure what it would do to Mackenzie after seeing Jaylin, but I knew she'd start bugging me about him again. I waited for about forty-five minutes before returning to my office. He'd had enough time with her, and now, his time was up.

I reached for Mackenzie's hand, as she continued talking while sitting on his lap. "Come on, baby," I said. "Leslie's going to take you all to Six Flags." I knew she wouldn't deny me because that was one of her favorite places to go. When she got off Jaylin's lap, I felt relieved.

"Daddy, can you go?"

Jaylin stood up. "Not this time, baby. My plane leaves today. I gotta get back to Florida, okay?"

She nodded. "Can I come to your house in Florida some day?"

I waited for his response.

"Hopefully, one day, yes. I promise to work on that, okay?" No doubt, he looked hurt. "Give me another hug before you go, and you be careful at Six Flags and have fun."

Mackenzie gave Jaylin another squeezing tight hug.

"I love you," he said softly.

"I love you, too," she responded, barely able to get the words out as his hold was so tight.

Slowly killing myself inside, I reached for Mackenzie's hand and she waved good-bye. I took her upfront to where Leslie was and gave her some money to take the kids to Six Flags. I asked her if they could go quickly, so Mackenzie wouldn't change her mind about staying with Jaylin. I wasn't sure what he told her, but whatever it was, her mind seemed to be at ease.

I made my way back to my office and Jaylin sat on the couch in a daze while rubbing his hands together. I closed the door, and he looked over at me.

"I'm sorry," he said. "I couldn't let that opportunity pass me by."

"Do you have any idea what you just did?"

"Yeah, I just made peace with something that's been bugging me for a long time." He placed his hand on his heart. "You don't understand, nor will you ever understand how much I needed that."

"And, what about us, Jaylin? How could you be so selfish to us?"

I walked over to my desk and sat my backside against it. I folded my arms in front of me and waited for a response.

"I can't answer that right now. All I know is seeing and holding her made me feel good. I apologize for not listening to you, and Mackenzie and I had an interesting talk. She—she'll be fine. I told you that she would and I kept my promise, didn't I?"

I knew Jaylin was talking about the money he and Nanny B had given us, but I also knew that I wanted more than his money. That being, of course, a life with him.

He stood up and came over next to me. He picked up a piece of paper on my desk and reached for a pen. He wrote something down on the paper, and then pushed his elbow on my hip.

"Get your butt off this desk," he said playfully.

I smiled and looked at the piece of paper he held in his hand. "This is Shane's new address. Meet me there around seven."

"Six," I said, anxious to be alone with him.

"Well, then six."

I reached up and rubbed the back of his curly hair. It was so soft, and I'd never forgotten the feel of it. When I stood up straight to kiss him, he backed away. He placed his lips on the inner side of his fingers and kissed them. Then, he slowly licked them, and placed them on my lips. "Let's save this for tonight. Ain't no need for us to get all hot and bothered up in here, so I'll see you tonight."

He walked toward the door. I got one last look at his sexy muscular frame and changed my mind.

"Five," I said. "How about I come see you at five?"

He turned around and smiled.

"Then, five it is."

I followed behind him as he made his way to the front entrance. As soon as everybody heard us coming, they all got quiet. This time, everybody held their fist in the air. Jaylin thought they were giving the sign of black power and told them to represent before he said good-bye. When he left, I had to ask what was going on.

"Now, that's the sign to alert others that there's a big-dick-Negro in the room," Jamaica said. "You've got to show your arm because that represents the length."

We all laughed and I was so excited about tonight. Now, everybody understood my enthusiasm about Jaylin and they joked about me being a happy-go-lucky-bitch.

# Jaylin

## 8

Now, why or how did I do that to myself? I wasn't sure but I know that holding Mackenzie in my arms was the best feeling ever. I dreamed of seeing her again, and even though it might not have been under the conditions that I wanted, for the time being it just had to do.

After Scorpio showed me what she was working with last night, I couldn't wait to get inside of her. My mind was fucked up and all I could think about was being in between her legs.

If anything, I couldn't believe these feelings I was having. And for the first time, I understood why women considered us dogs. I guess we just couldn't be right no matter how hard we tried. And believe me, I tried hard. Being unfaithful to Nokea had never been my motive. I promised to love and cherish her for the rest of my life, and there's no doubt that I will. Today, however, would be Scorpio's and my secret. Nobody would ever know about this, and once I leave St. Louis, I don't think I'm ever coming back.

Getting close to 3:00 p.m., I had Shane's bedroom laid out. I had rose petals spread out on the bed and on the floor. Sweet smelling candles lit up the room, and since I knew Scorpio liked chocolate covered strawberries, I stopped to pick up some, along with a bottle of Moët.

I put in a CD of Miles blowing his horn, and I laid my naked body on the bed, caressing myself in satin off-white sheets. I'd purchased those too because I wasn't comfortable with having sex on another man's sheets.

By 3:30, I was getting anxious. Scorpio said five o'clock, but I'd been rubbing on my manhood, thinking about her since her immaculate performance yesterday. I didn't see any harm in momentary satisfaction, especially when a woman made me feel as good as she did in the past.

Another thirty minutes had gone by, and I started to get a funny feeling in my stomach. The "what ifs" started kicking in. What if Nokea found out? What if Nokea walked in on us? What if Scorpio gets pregnant? I for damn sure wasn't gon' use no condom, so what if she called Nokea and told her she was pregnant? Then what? Feeling a bit paranoid, I reached for the phone next to me. I dialed home and Nanny B answered.

"Hey, Nanny B. Where my babies at?"

"They're outside, Jaylin. Where are you? I thought you were only going to be gone for one day."

"I thought I was too, but the Mayor's Group wanted to meet with Shane and me last night. I'm packing up right now and I should be home later on tonight."

"Okay, but have a safe trip home. We miss you around here. You know Jaylene and LJ—they've been asking for their daddy."

I smiled as I could hear Jaylene's da-da's in my mind and li'l Jaylin straight up asking for me. Nanny B put me on hold. She called for Nokea and she picked up the phone.

"Hi, baby," she said. "I miss you. When are you coming home?"

The sound of her squeaky, soft spoken voice damn near broke my heart. "I . . . I'll be there tonight."

"Okay, then I'll wait up for you."

"Say you will, huh?"

"Of course, I will. If I go to bed, we won't have an opportunity to work on our next child, will we?"

Nokea had been on birth control, and had made up her mind about not having any more kids—even though she knew how I desperately wanted a big family. "So, how we gon' work on this baby and you still taking the pill?"

"Shortly after our discussion, I stopped taking them. I'm willing to compromise what I want for what you want. After all, having another baby with you will only bring about more happy and joyous times for us."

I rubbed my chest. "But . . . but I want you to be cool with everything, too."

"And I am cool. Besides, anything for my man. I've done the math and if we get pregnant now, by the time we have our baby, Jaylene will be almost three."

I smiled and thought about my wife doing anything in the world for me. My babies . . . damn, my children. How dare me lie in bed naked waiting to fuck another woman. "You . . . you know I love you, don't you?" I swallowed hard.

"I'm not sure. With your willingness to be away from me for three whole days, I can't tell."

I was silent for a moment. "Three whole days that has been yet another wake-up call for me. When I get home, I promise to tell you about it."

"Is everything okay? You sound as if—"

"I sound as if I ain't got my head on straight."

Nokea was quiet. She could always tell when something wasn't right with me. "Jaylin, I don't know what's going on, but I hope and pray that you have not compromised our marriage. We have so much to be thankful for and there is nothing out here another woman can give you that I can't. I've proven that by marrying you and by giving birth to your children. If you mess up what we have, then you mess up a good thing. I'm not turning back the hands of time, and if you want to, then you're going to turn them back all by yourself. Never forget—the choice is always yours." She paused. "I love you, too."

Nokea hung up and our call had ended on that note. I took a deep breath and looked at my watch. It was a little after 4:00 p.m., and it didn't take long for me to figure out what I had to do. I rushed to put on my clothes and left Scorpio a note on the bed. I hoped she wouldn't be upset with me for changing my mind, but this was one risk I just wasn't willing to take. Hurrying, I packed my belongings at Shane's place, drove the rental car back to the airport, and waited on my plane's departure.

I arrived home at almost 10:00 p.m. that night. The house was peacefully quiet and from the looks of it, everybody was already in bed. Before entering my bedroom, I went to LJ's and

Jaylene's rooms and gave them a kiss. I then opened the doors to my bedroom and saw Nokea lying sideways in bed. The room was somewhat dark, but it always had a sliver of light inside when the doors to the balcony were open. A comfortable breeze from outside stirred around in the room. I dropped my luggage on the floor, took off my clothes, and eased in bed behind Nokea's petite frame. She tilted her head to the side, as I pecked my lips down her neck. I placed my hand over hers and squeezed it tightly.

"Daddy's home," I whispered.

Lying in her yellow satin panties that looked spectacular against her brown silky smooth skin, she turned around and lay on her back. She placed her hand on the side of my face, and I raked my fingers through her short layered hair.

"I'm glad you're back," she said in a soft tone. "I had a funny feeling that I almost lost you."

"Never. And even though I almost fucked up—"

She placed her fingers on my lips. "I don't want to know. As long as you didn't, that's all that matters."

"I didn't." I happily kissed her. "I promise you I didn't."

"Good," she smiled.

She rolled on her stomach and placed her head on her hands. I massaged my hands deeply into her back and lowered one hand down to her silky panties. Having just enough curve to her ass, I slid my finger underneath her panty line and tickled her butt cheeks with the tips of my finger. I softly rubbed it between her crack and then placed my finger in my mouth. Getting a tiny taste of her, I straddled her backside and scooted myself down to taste her even more. I sucked her panties and her butt cheeks into my mouth, and when she lifted her butt a bit higher, I was able to dive into the spot where I wanted to land. My lips felt the moistness through her panties, and I slid my tongue down the creases of her shaved wet pussy lips.

"Take them off," she ordered. "Please take my panties off."

Instead of taking off her panties, I used my finger to pull them aside. I plucked her clit like a violin and dipped my thick fingers inside of her. With her insides as wet as dripping rain, I fingered her to a rhythm that had her on the verge of cumming. Before she came, she removed my fingers from inside of her. I had turned over on my back, and she crawled up to my face to straddle it. My arms locked around her thighs, and she brought her sweet juices to my lips. I ripped her panties away from her pussy, as if I was opening a present. My gift awaited me when I opened my mouth and I was well rewarded.

Nokea worked me over, and then lowered herself to give me a ride. Her legs were straddled far apart, and as I plunged into her, I watched her polish my dick with juices. Like always, I was turned the fuck on! We had our routine on lock down because I definitely knew how to please my wife and she damn sure knew how to please me.

After at least an hour of lovemaking "Jaylin's way", we layed naked outside while swaying back and forth on a hammock. We covered ourselves with a thin satin sheet and Nokea had fallen asleep with her head resting on my chest.

I couldn't sleep thinking about the most tempting days since I'd been married. The last thing Nokea said stuck to me like glue. She said that I had a choice. And more than anything, she was right. I was responsible for putting myself in every situation I faced. I could have easily handled things differently by going to St. Louis, taking care of business, and coming back home. Instead, I chose to stay two additional days, I chose to walk Scorpio to her car, I chose to call her on the phone, I chose to stay for Trey's party, I chose to kiss her back when she kissed me, I chose to go see her at Jay's, and I even chose to meet her at Shane's house and most likely fuck her brains out. No doubt, the choices were mine. The only thing I hadn't regretted was seeing Mackenzie. I would never take back seeing her for nothing in the world.

I lay there thinking about being a married man. Sometimes, it was hard to make the right choices. Women are always gon' be women . . . some out for one thing, and some aiming for another. This time, I was glad that my *ultimate* choice was the right choice that led me back to the only woman I loved.

Nokea lifted her head as she felt the raindrops falling on her face. I'd already seen the rain coming and had no desire to go inside. Instead, I pulled the sheet off both of us and eased on top of her. She rubbed my wet hair back with her hands and stared into my eyes.

"We'd better come up with a name for our next child and fast."

I lifted her leg on my shoulder and the rain had already started to pour on my back. "First, we got to work hard at making it." My dick went deep inside; I gave her several lengthy strokes. "Then, we gotta work hard at having another—"

"No, baby, this is it," she stroked me back. "Three is my limit."

"You the boss, baby. Whatever you say goes."

Nokea snickered and we continued our love-making outside in the rain.

# Scorpio

# 9

After Jay-Baby left Jay's, it didn't take me ten minutes and I was on my way out as well. I told Bernie I'd see her tomorrow and asked her to lock up for me.

Within the hour, I sat on the edge of my bed and stared into my closet. I wasn't sure what I'd put on, but whatever it was I wanted to make sure it had easy access. I was sure Jaylin wouldn't care what I wore, because by the look in his eyes, I could tell my clothes would most likely be left at the front door.

With that in mind, I decided on a one piece strapless powdered blue jumper. No bra was needed, and neither were any panties. He could remove the jumper in two seconds, so I laid it across my bed and went to the bathroom for my bath.

The water was scorching hot as I dipped my toes in the tub to test the water. Steam formed all around me, and I laid my head back, promising myself that I wouldn't fall asleep.

By the time I finished my bath, it was a few minutes after 4:00 p.m. I rubbed my entire body with shimmering lotion and slid the jumper over my awesomely shaped figure. I looked in the mirror and turned slightly to the side. There was no way he'd reject this again, and if he did, he'd be a fool.

Not planning to do much with my hair, I teased it a bit with my fingers. It had a slight wild look to it, but it sure made me look sexy. I glossed my lips, looked for my purse, and jetted.

All kinds of thoughts roamed through my head as I drove. The thought of Jaylin making love to me was heavy on my mind, but also, the thought of him going home to Nokea ate at me even more. What if I'd never hear from him again? I knew that allowing him to make love to me would bring upon serious attachment on my part. Maybe, on his part as well. If anything, I'd have to wait for him to come back to St. Louis and love me all over again. The question was: would he even come back? As good as I'd be to him, he'd definitely come back. I'd make sure that this was the best loving he'd ever gotten. Since our previous intimate moments together, I'd had a few more tricks up my sleeves to show him. I'd learned some things that would turn him on in an instant, and my ability to make him cum frequently would certainly be in my best interest.

Then, there was the condom thing. Normally, I'd break one out with the quickness, but I decided against it. I was almost positive that he wouldn't have one handy either. I wouldn't mind having his baby and it was very possible since I wasn't taking any birth control pills. We'd planned to have a baby before, so maybe this was just another opportunity presenting itself. I smiled as I thought of how this one time could turn into something special between us.

I was almost at Shane's place and I could already feel the moistness between my legs. In my mind, his dick was turning me out and I could feel the pain of it in my gut. While stopped at a stoplight, I looked in the rearview mirror. Since the wind had blown my hair all over, I used my fingertips to straighten it. All of a sudden, my fingers stopped moving. I stared in the mirror at my beautiful eyes and didn't even blink. The light must have changed; I could hear a few horns blowing behind me.

*What was I doing?* I thought. I must be out of my mind to even go to Shane's place. If I did, when all was said and done, the only person who'd be hurt was me. Jaylin would go home to Nokea as if nothing ever happened. She'd be the victorious one because she'd still have the man I so desperately wanted. It was obvious that he'd already made his choice when he married her. The only thing I'd have was a wet and purely satisfied pussy. That feeling I'd only have for hours and then it would be gone. *Was it worth it?* I asked myself. Was being with Jaylin worth me hurting myself all over again? Not to even mention hurting Mackenzie if for whatever reason this *thing* between us turned out to be something more.

By the time I had my answer, I was already parked in my driveway. Knowing that Jaylin would be furious with me for not showing, I turned off my phone so I didn't have to answer it when he called to persuade me to come. I hesitantly walked inside and made my way upstairs to my bedroom. Having little sleep since he'd been in town, I lay in bed and held my body pillow close to me. I wished it were him, but some wishes, unfortunately, don't come true. I'd even envisioned the extent I'd known he'd gone through to please me. I figured that wine, soft music, and chocolate covered strawberries most likely awaited me. I looked at my watch and thought about changing my mind. Deciding against it, I didn't know if I made the right decision or not, but something deep inside told me I had.

# Shane

## 10

I was mad as hell at Sam. She decided to cancel all lovemaking until I decided what I wanted to do with our relationship. Now that was just downright stupid. How could she take the pussy, and then tell me to make up my mind about getting married? I could easily lie to her and say I want to get married, but fuck it. Going to that extreme wasn't worth my time.

Since I didn't want to interrupt Jaylin's sex session with Scorpio, and Sam had put me out, I found myself at the Marriott last night. I called my house early this morning and got no answer. I figured they most likely had left, and when I drove down the street and saw no cars, my suspicion was correct.

I couldn't believe that Jaylin had wrapped things up so quickly. I was sure that him and Scorpio would be here all day and all night—all morning, until the next morning. I guess he was in a rush to get back to Nokea and his guilt had probably kicked in.

I got out of my car a bit disappointed in him. Then, there was a side that knew what affect Scorpio had on him. After all, she had the same affect on me. I would have cheated on Sam in a heartbeat, so that's how I knew it wasn't time for me to get married. Being the man that I was today, I would be no good for a woman who was looking for a brotha to settle down and commit to marrying.

I opened my front door that seemed to be already unlocked, and made my way to my bedroom. Hoping that everything was cool, I stood in the doorway and looked inside. My bed was neatly made with satin off-white sheets. Red and pink rose petals were all over the place and burnt candles were visible, too. It for damn sure didn't look as if any fucking had gone on because the room would have been much more of a mess. I walked further inside and noticed an envelope on the bed. It had Scorpio's name on the front. Trying to figure out what was up, I opened the envelope, and pulled out the piece of paper inside. I unfolded the letter and it simply said: *Sorry, but I had to go. I couldn't do this to you or to myself. Whenever you find someone who loves you as much as you love yourself, then maybe you'll understand why. Love Jay-Baby.*

*Well, I'll be damned*, I thought. He couldn't even do it. How he found the strength to walk away this time, I'd never understand, especially after appearing so weak yesterday.

I sat on the bed and wondered . . . If the letter was in my possession, why didn't Scorpio get it? I reached for the phone to call Jaylin. It was still early, but I knew he'd always make time to talk to me. He answered on the second ring.

"Yeah, I know. I forgot to tell you I was outtie," he said.

"Well, it ain't like I needed a public announcement or anything, but a phone call would have been nice. Especially to let your boy know you made it home."

"Man, I was trying to get the hell out of there as fast as I could. My ass was tripping."

"Yeah, you were. Especially, by leaving my damn door unlocked."

"I thought Scorpio would have locked it on her way out."

"Well, if she was here she didn't."

"I don't know why she wouldn't, but maybe she was upset."

"Upset about the letter?"

"Yes."

"But, I don't think she read the letter. When I got it off my bed, it was still sealed."

Jaylin paused. "Say it was, huh?"

"Yep. By the looks of things, I think she had a change of heart, too."

Jaylin snickered. "Damn, that's fucked up."

"Naw, not really. I guess she thought about the consequences like you did."

"Pimp, I'm an irresistible man," he joked. "That kind of shit doesn't happen to me."

"I guess there's a first time for everything, bro, you think?"

Jaylin laughed. "I guess so and good for her. When you talk to her, make sure you tell her I said so."

"What makes you think I'll be talking to her? Our business is finished."

"Oh, I doubt that very much. By the way you were all into her, I'd say it's just getting started."

"Negro, please. I don't want your leftovers."

"My leftovers are good. And, you should be thanking me for serving them to you. I just might change my mind, though."

"Whatever, Jay. If or when I speak to her, I'll let you know what's up."

"You do that, my brotha, and keep in touch."

"Take care. Maybe I'll see you in a few months. This time, though, I'm coming your way."

"The door will always be open."

We ended our call and I lay back on the bed. I wasn't sure if he'd encouraged me to see Scorpio, but a huge part of me wanted to take our friendship to another level. I hated to go behind my boy like that, but I felt the same connection with her I'd felt in the past. I just didn't know if I wanted to pursue her right now.

# Scorpio

## 11

Almost a whole week had gone by and I hadn't heard from Jaylin. I was sure he was pissed that I opted not to show, but I hoped he understood I couldn't go on hurting myself anymore. I wanted to call his cell phone number I'd gotten from when he called me, but I decided to leave well enough alone.

Since then, I've been having a fucking festival. I'd invited Spencer back into my life, I was just with Maxwell last night, and this morning, Calvin, my workout instructor and I had plans to hook up tonight. Basically, I'd gone back to my old ways already. I thought seeing Jaylin would give me closure, but for some reason, it seemed as if things got worse. Neither of the men were to my satisfaction and it was as if I didn't have nothing else to do. I think I loved the attention they gave me. They all ate out of the palms of my hands and wanted so desperately to be with me. The challenge made them more eager, but I'd been dangling them on a string, as I'd been doing all along.

By all means, I had some powerful stuff to work with. I knew it, and they knew it, too. I'd heard brothas talk about bad, good, or just any ole pussy; but according to many, I was in a category all by myself. Basically, the total package with a li'l something extra-extra to go with it.

Other than dealing with Jaylin, I'd always been in control of my relationships. I said when, where, and how. Most of the time, I called the shots, and many of my companions didn't seem to mind.

I sat in my office and lightly blew my breath on my nails I'd just polished. I reminded myself to call Shane and apologize for how desperate I appeared to be; with some free time on my hands, I picked up the phone to call him. I hated like hell that when I called Davenports, Felicia answered the phone.

"Shane Alexander, please," I said, disguising my voice.

"May I ask who's calling," she said professionally.

"Scorpio—"

The phone went dead.

I couldn't believe that bitch had hung up on me, so I called right back.

"Davenports," she said again.

"May I speak to Shane Alexander?"

"No you may nottt," she said, hanging onto the *T*.

"And, why nottt." I replied, hanging onto the *T* as well.

She hung up again. I refused to play her childish games, so I waited until later to call Shane at home. Before that thought sunk in, my cell phone rang and it was Shane calling back. When he asked for me, he sounded a bit angry.

"This is Scorpio," I said.

"Did you just call for me?"

"Yes, I did. Unfortunately, your unprofessional partner still has a case of bitterness in her bones."

"I wholeheartedly apologize. And, trust me, it won't happen again."

"Sure," I said.

"Anyway, what's up? I'm sure there was a purpose for your call."

"Yes, there was. I wanted to apologize to you for the other night. It was so tacky of me to come off like that, and to involve you wasn't cool."

"No, it really wasn't. But, it's cool. I enjoyed myself, so it ain't no biggie."

"Are you sure? I mean . . . I'd like to offer you some kind of peace offering."

"Scorpio, I'm serious. There ain't no need."

I paused for a moment; I wanted to know if he'd talked to Jaylin. "So, uh, have you heard from your friend?"

"Yes, and as a matter of fact, he left something for you."

"Really? Something like what?"

"I'll bring it over to Jay's during my lunch break. Besides, I haven't had the opportunity to see your place. Jay said it was off the chain."

I smiled. "I try. And, I'll be here when you come. If I'm not up front, just ask the ladies to buzz me."

"Will do," he said, and then hung up.

I could hear all the hoopla going on and figured Shane must have walked through the door. Soon after all the noise, I waited for my phone to buzz and it did.

"Yes," I said, holding down the intercom button.

"Girl, God done blessed us again," Jamaica said, in a teary voice. "You should see what he just dropped down from heaven."

"Please ask him if his name is Shane. If so, send him back to my office."

I released the button because I knew Shane was on his way back. I looked toward the doorway, and soon, one hell of a man appeared. He wore a royal blue oversized shirt and a white wifebeater was underneath. His faded jeans fit nicely around his waistline and were held up by a thick black Gucci belt. Face wise, his flawless carmello skin was shining and his pearly whites had me melting in my seat.

"Hi, Shane," I said, standing to greet him.

I invited him in and closed the door behind him. I asked him to have a seat on the couch, and I took a seat beside him. I was wearing a khaki short linen skirt; it rose up a bit and showed my silky smooth legs. Shane couldn't help but look. He then reached in his pocket and handed an envelope to me.

"What's this?" I asked.

"It's a letter for you."

"From who?"

"Jaylin."

I shook my head. "I don't want to read it because I know he went off because—"

"Just read it." Shane spoke urgently. "This was on my bed when I returned home that day."

I took the opened envelope from his hand. I opened the letter and read it. My jaw dropped and I looked at Shane.

"Are you telling me that he left?"

"No, I'm not telling you. The letter told you."

I sat in disbelief. "I can't believe this! After bringing his ass over here to seduce me, he left?"

"Well, if you look at it like that, you seduced him—"

"Bullshit, Shane." I pointed my finger at him. "You knew from day one that Jaylin was playing fucking games with me! He was turning me on and off! Damn," I screamed. "Had I gone to your place that night I would have gotten the shock of my life!"

"So, why didn't you show up?"

"Be—because I didn't want to play the victim anymore. After I thought about the disadvantages of giving myself to him, I couldn't go through with it." I chuckled, "I can't believe he packed up his belongings and left. But, what else did I expect? That's the typical fucking Jaylin Rogers, ain't it?"

Shane was quiet and he allowed me to vent for about ten minutes. When he saw me getting teary-eyed, he pulled me close to his chest and wrapped his arm around my shoulder.

"No, I'm not having none of that. Both of y'all did the right thing and no one is to blame."

"Then, why does this hurt so badly?" I asked, unable to maintain my composure. I released my emotions while laying my head against Shane's chest.

"I don't know why it hurts," he said, holding me. "I never loved anybody to that extent. You and Jaylin had something really special, Scorpio, but it was better off left in the past."

Even though I agreed, I continued to express myself. Shane held me even tighter and placed his lips on my forehead.

"Shhh," he whispered. "Everything will be all right. You got a lot of good things to look forward to, okay?"

I lifted my face and looked at him with my teary-eyes. "Good things like what, Shane? Tell me what good things I have to look forward to."

Our eyes locked for awhile, and then Shane placed his finger underneath my chin. He lifted it and inched his face closer to mine. "Good things like," he placed his lips on mine. I inched my head back, only to see him move forward. His hand touched the back of my head to keep it steady. Our tongues intertwined with each other and the feeling was . . . good. So good, that I'd eased back on the couch and tried to pull him on top of me.

"I don't want you like this," he whispered, as I held a tight grip around his neck. I ignored him and released one of my hands from around his neck to remove his shirt. Even though he was saying, "not like this," he allowed me to remove his shirt. Our tongues continued in motion, while Shane rubbed his hands up and down my legs. He quickly pulled his wifebeater over his head, revealing his nicely cut upper body. I knew I was in business and my insides were on fire!

The moment was intense. We breathed hard and Shane's lips were getting wetter and softer. He eased his hands up the sides of my skirt to lift it. Assisting him just a bit, I lifted my butt off the couch so he could remove my thong. He held the string and looked down at what I was offering.

"I can't take you like this," he said again. "Under these conditions—this is wrong."

"No it's not. I want you to fuck me. I've been thinking about it for a long time."

He moved his head from side to side. "Not now, and not like this. I can't." He released his hand from the string on my thong and sat up. Frustrated, I continued to lay back on my elbows with my legs open.

"I must be losing my touch," I griped. "First Jaylin, now you. What's going on Shane? Is this a game y'all playing with me or what?"

His eyes dropped between my legs again. "Trust me, it's no game. The timing ain't right, Scorpio. I don't know what you're aiming for and I don't want to be part of your revenge for Jaylin."

"Revenge? I'm not out for revenge, Shane. I felt something and I acted on it. Forgive me for responding to *your* advancement."

Shane stood up and placed his hand in his pocket. He walked toward my desk and then turned around. "Okay, I'll tell you what—why don't you let me take you out on Sunday?"

"Why?" I sat up. "To make up for your rejection?"

"Naw, just to . . . kind of make shit right between us. Kind of develop a better friendship or something. Let me get to know you better."

"I already got plenty of friends," I said with attitude and then stood up. "I don't need no more."

"You can never have too many friends. That's, of course, if you mean true friends and not screwing partners. I ain't trying to be one of your screwing partnas, all right?"

"I'll call you later and let you know."

He walked over to the couch to get his shirts. I couldn't help myself from getting weak while looking at his body. After he put on his shirts, I straightened myself up and got ready to walk him out.

As we made our way through the shop, this time, the ladies shrugged their shoulders. I had an idea what that meant, but I didn't say a word until Shane left. I stood with my hand on my hip and looked around the room.

"I guess that means that y'all don't know, right?" I said.

"An A⁺ for you, miss thang. You're so right this time." Jamaica said. "Howeva, my dear, we got a feeling that you might know something you're not willing to share."

"I ain't telling y'all no more of my business. The last time I shared something with y'all, half of St. Louis knew about it."

"Come on, Scorpio. Please," Bernie whined.

Deidra chimed in. "I know, girl. You can't keep nothing like that a secret, especially with a brotha that fine. It's either the pinky or the fist, which one?"

I smiled, raised my fist and stretched my arm high in the air. "Hands off, though, ladies. This one is mine."

We all laughed.

"She gets all the good ones," Jamaica griped. "Can't you allow somebody to have just *one*?"

"If you want, you can have Spencer. I don't think I'm gon' be needing him anymore."

"No thank you," she said. "I need a postman that can deliver. Not one who don't even know how to lick the mail.'"

The ladies slapped high fives and I referred to them all as nasty girls. I guess they weren't any nastier than me because I had a feeling that within the next few days, Shane and me were about to get downright dirty and filthy nasty with each other and I sure as hell couldn't wait.

# Shane

# 12

Since Scorpio and I had a heated moment at Jay's, I hadn't been able to stop thinking about her. I told her to call me, but it was Monday afternoon and I still hadn't heard from her yet. I guess my suspicion was right, and that was, she was using me to get back at Jaylin.

If anything, I wasn't going to get caught up in her mess. It was obvious that she was looking for somebody to use and it for damn sure wasn't going to be me. Anyway, I couldn't focus too much time on it. The Mayor's Group kept Felicia and I busy, so my issues with women simply had to wait. I made that clear to Sam when she visited me the other day. She apologized for giving me an ultimatum, but I was still uneasy about working things out with her. Especially, since I'd known I had feelings for Scorpio. I wasn't sure what it would lead to, but I wasn't about to get into another relationship before closing the door on the previous one.

As always, Felicia had been working my nerves. She'd been questioning me about Scorpio and the shit drove me crazy. I couldn't get nothing done without her making snide comments. And, whenever I suggested Scorpio and I were just friends, Felicia couldn't control herself from calling her bitches and hos. Now, that was awfully ironic, especially when those two words fit her to a capital *T*.

After sitting around pouting all day, Felicia asked if I wanted to go to lunch. I wanted to tell her "hell no" but since my stomach growled I opted to go.

We made it to J. Bucks, but the line was almost outside of the door. The waiters quickly seated everybody, and when they took us to our seats, I was surprised to see Scorpio and another companion. The brotha looked to be much older than Scorpio, and since Felicia noticed my stares, that caused her to follow the direction of my eyes.

"She is such a tramp," Felicia said. I pulled the chair back for her to take a seat.

"Well, that's her business, Felicia. Why don't you chill out and enjoy your lunch with me?"

She gave Scorpio another devious look and then faced me. "Why you always taking up for her? Every time I say something, you're always defending her. I hope you realize, what Jaylin realized, and that was: She ain't good for nothing other than lying on her back."

I took a deep breath and gave Felicia a cold stare. "Stop, all right? If all we gon' do is sit here and discuss Scorpio, I'm leaving. McDonald's right down the street and a Big Mac sounds pretty good right now."

The waiter came over, and instead of waiting for our drinks, I told her I was ready to order. I didn't want to be in J. Bucks no longer than I had to because the situation was quite sticky. Not knowing who the brotha was with Scorpio, I found myself a bit jealous. I knew he was one of her *friends*—and by the way, he couldn't stop grinning while looking at her. If that wasn't enough, I noticed his hand touch her leg from underneath the table. She laughed and rubbed her hand along his beard.

Felicia cleared her throat. "Are you going to sit there and gawk at her? If so, then I'm leaving."

I didn't notice my stares. "The, uh, brotha she with . . . I think I know him from somewhere. I just can't remember." I lied.

"Yeah, right," Felicia said, taking another look at him. She sipped from her glass of water and cleared her throat. "I got a question for you."

"What's that?" I asked.

"If you don't want to, you don't have to tell me, but did Jaylin fuck her while he was here?"

"No. Absolutely not."

"You wouldn't tell me if he did."

"No I wouldn't, however, I did tell you he don't go out like that no more."

She threw her hand back. "Whatever, Shane. You know for a fact I know Jaylin better than anybody. It is just a matter of time that he's gonna be back to his old ways. Nokea has got to be one stupid woman if she believes a man that fine ain't cheating on her."

"Fine or not, people change, Felicia."

She lifted her index finger and moved it from side to side. "And, they can always change back."

So far, Felicia's and my lunch was strictly on other people's business. I tried hard not to go there with her, but the things she kept saying made me defensive. Either way, I had to do something to stay occupied, since Scorpio and her obvious lover held my attention.

Our lunch had been served, and when I noticed Scorpio and her friend stand up to leave, I purposely laughed out loud with Felicia so

Scorpio would turn her head. She'd been so indulged with her conversation, I wasn't sure if she'd even known I was there. At this point she did. She turned her head and waved at me from a short distance. Trying to play it cool and not look overly excited, I nodded and turned back to Felicia. She and I both watched as Scorpio and her companion made their way to the door. I was focused on her tall, pretty legs that showed because of the short skirt she wore. Her long curly hair was bouncing against her back, and always, she had the attention of every man in the place.

"You want to fuck her, don't you?" Felicia said. She broke my concentration.

Even though I did, Felicia wouldn't know about it. "Felicia, whether you want to admit it or not, that woman got it going on. Did you see the way her skirt gripped her fat ass and her silk blouse showed her hard nipples? If anything you learn from her, you should learn how to dress like her. Maybe you'll get as much attention as she does."

"Okay, that was cute. I know you said that just to get back at me for telling you how fine Jaylin is, but giving her props in front of me is a no-no. Besides, I dress a whole lot better than she does. Every piece of clothing I own looks better, and costs more than anything she can afford—so there."

"Well, miss, I bet that woman who just walked out of here can purchase her clothes from Kmart and still come out looking just as good as you do by wasting your money at Saks. It's not the clothes that make the lady, it's the lady who makes the clothes."

"Shut the hell up, would you? When you still get done talking, she is the biggest ho that I know in St. Louis. Some hos can clean up good, and she happens to be one of them."

"We need to end this conversation, okay? All you know, and all you've ever known, is that she had sex with Jaylin; and that's it. How or why that makes her a ho, you tell me?"

Felicia sat up straight in her seat. "Fool, not only did she have sex with Jaylin, but she had sex with his cousin, Stephon, too. And, by the way you're acting, I wouldn't doubt that she gave you a piece of her, let's-pass-it-around ass, too."

I thought about my sexual encounter with Scorpio many years ago. I'd just licked between her legs for a moment, she came, and that was it. Knowing that Felicia knew nothing of it, I fired back hard. "You, my dear, have shared your body with Jaylin, Stephon, and me. How can you sit there and dog out another woman, when all three of us had you any way we wanted you. I ain't trying to hurt your feelings, but you need to think about shit before you say it. Bottom line, you can't be no judge, and you need to take a look at yourself in the mirror." I stood up and laid my napkin on the table. I pulled my wallet from my pants and dropped a fifty dollar bill on the table. After that, I left.

I couldn't figure out if I was more mad at Felicia, or angry with Scorpio for trying to play me shady. She hadn't called and she could have kept that fake ass wave to herself.

When I looked outside of the restaurant and seen Scorpio holding hands with her lunch date and kissing him, that was right about the time I started arguing with Felicia. Maybe she was right though. Scorpio had been putting herself out there a bit, but I knew there was something good inside of her. I also knew that being hurt could cause a person to act out of the norm.

Since Felicia drove, I decided to walk back to the office and made my way up Forsyth Boulevard. There was a man on the corner selling roses, and the brotha who Scorpio was with stood next to him. I watched as he paid for the roses, and opened the passenger's side door to his gray Cadillac, handing the roses to her. I couldn't see her face, but I watched as he leaned in for a kiss. I didn't want her to see me, so I crossed to the other side of the street and slowed my pace until he pulled off.

This was a sign for me not to get involved. I knew it was a game she was playing with men and probably didn't give a damn about no one. She was out to get what she could and didn't have a problem breaking a few hearts along the way. At this point, I was glad she hadn't called. And, she for damn sure didn't have to worry about me calling her.

# Scorpio

## 13

In the middle of the day, there I was lying in between Maxwell's legs with my head on his chest. We'd previously encountered somewhat good sex, and for the time being, he was the best thing I could find, in the bedroom, comparable to Jaylin.

No matter how good he was, though, as soon as I'd gotten my satisfaction, I was always ready to go. Besides, Maxwell was married, so I knew I'd better get the hell out of his house before his wife came home. He said he'd leave her for me, but that's what they all said. I wasn't trying to be with him like that anyway, so there was no need for him to leave his wife and come to a woman who wanted nothing more from him but sex.

See, I learned the hard way by giving a man all my love. Mister you know who taught me that no matter how much I put myself out there for men,

I wasn't going to get the same in return. Those days were over with. I didn't give a fuck about love and love didn't give a fuck about me. All the love I needed was from Mackenzie, Leslie, and my nieces and nephews; that in itself, was more than enough.

Maxwell was sound asleep and the look of a satisfied man showed on his face. Other than him having a wife, he was pretty cool to kick it with. He didn't harass me as much as the other men in my life did, and since he was forty-nine-years-old, he was very mature. In addition, he was rather fine for his age. He had a tint of gray in his wavy hair and neatly trimmed beard. I adored being with a man who dressed well, smelled good, and had his own money. Most importantly, Maxwell was able to turn heads when he walked and that was a big plus for me.

I was ready to go home, so I eased my naked body off Maxwell and tried not to wake him. Sleeping and creeping was the name of my game; and after I quietly put my clothes on, I closed the door behind me on my way out.

I got inside of my car, and noticed my cell phone blinking, displaying four messages. Of course, Spencer was bugging, and so was Latrell, a new flavah I'd met the past weekend. Leslie left a message and told me to hurry home. Apparently, the kids had gotten into a fight, and according to her, Mackenzie's lip was busted. In a rage, I hurried home to see what was up.

I pulled in the driveway and was surprised to see the kids outside playing. Mackenzie ran up to me, and when I noticed slight puffiness in her lip, I asked what had happened.

"I kicked the ball and it hit li'l James in the face," she said, while holding the ball underneath her arm. "He got mad and punched me. When I cried he said he was sorry and now we're playing again."

I was mad. "James," I yelled. He was two years older than Mackenzie and for damn sure didn't have no business punching a girl. Seeing how angry I was, he slowly walked up to me.

"Yes," he said.

"Don't put your hands on my daughter. Do you understand?"

He nodded.

"I need a, 'yes ma'am,'" I said, pointing my finger at him.

"Yes, ma'am. I told her I was sorry."

"Well, sometimes, sorry just isn't good enough."

Just then, Leslie came storming outside. "Thank you," she said, placing her hand on her hip. "I already corrected my child, so I don't need you out here doing it again."

"When it comes to mine, I do what the hell I want to do. You allow your kids to get away with too much shit and I'm sick of it!"

"Don't make me disrespect you in front of these kids, Scorpio. I suggest you go back to wherever you came from and try me on another day!"

"And, I suggest you stop li'l James from becoming the product of his father. If you don't stop him now, I'd hate to give props to the person who will."

I rolled my eyes at Leslie and walked off. She followed behind me and the kids stayed outside. As I went inside, the aroma of delicious smelling food was in the air. I walked into the kitchen and noticed a big casserole dish of mac and cheese, a plate piled high with crispy chicken, and a few other side dishes.

"Don't you walk off and I haven't finished talking to you yet," Leslie yelled.

Hungry, I picked up a piece of chicken and placed it in my mouth. I chewed and looked at Leslie. "I don't care what you say, li'l James had no business putting his hands on her."

"And, I never said he did. I'm working on James, because he got issues. I can't blame him for me having a no-good fool in my life for years.

He often seen his daddy go upside my head, so what else is he supposed to know?"

"I—I know. I just don't like for nobody to mistreat my baby, that's all."

"Same here. But, kids gon' always be kids. I talked to James about hitting Mackenzie and he promised me he wouldn't do it again. If he does, then he knows there's going to be consequences."

"Big consequences," I said.

"Consequences that only his mama will deliver."

I smirked at Leslie and we embraced each other. After I fixed both of our plates, we sat at the kitchen table for a chat.

"So," she said. "You never did tell me how the other night went with Jaylin. I gotta admit, when he came into the shop that day—girl, I'd only wished I was in your shoes."

"Ah, trust me—no you don't. Jaylin needs to wear a sign on his forehead that says, I can fuck you well, however, your heart will break afterwards."

"So, y'all didn't hook up?"

"Nope. We were supposed to meet at Shane's place, but I didn't show and neither did he."

Leslie laughed. "Now, that's funny. I can't believe the both of you turned each other down."

"Hey, the man's in love. In love with a simple bitch who I can't stand. If she'd stayed married to Collins and went on about her business, Jaylin and I would still be together today."

"Well, he was with her first, Scorpio. They were together nine or ten years before you met him?"

"Nine," I said, gritting my teeth.

"That's a long time to be with somebody. It was just a matter of time, but he was destined to be with her. You need to thank your lucky stars that God didn't allow you to marry a man like him. That would be too much head and heartache for me." Leslie was in deep thought. "Can you imagine how much attention he probably incurs on a daily basis? I'm sure he has to fight pussy off everyday. I don't know of no man who can fight for that long."

"Well, that's Nokea's problem, not mine. When we were together, I had my share of trouble with women. Thing is, though, Jaylin knew how to handle his shit. Whenever you're with him, he makes you feel like the love of his life. It's when he's not with you, that's when you have to worry."

Leslie nodded and we finished our dinner. The kids came in and ate as well. I didn't feel like going back to Jay's because I was too tired. Leslie told me she'd go, so that allowed me to spend some time with Mackenzie and Leslie's seven kids.

By the end of the day, I was exhausted. I applauded Leslie for her patience, but having so many kids simply wasn't cut out for me. Mackenzie was enough. She was high maintenance and always had to have her way. I'd seen how bossy she was with Leslie's kids, and that brought on much frustration for them. I made it my business to have a talk with her before we went to bed.

The kids were downstairs watching TV and I was upstairs in my room while on the phone with Spencer. I said he'd be history, but a part of me still wanted to be nice. Besides, Shane hadn't called. My rule was never to call him first. If he wanted me as bad as he said he did, then there shouldn't be no problem with him picking up the phone. He looked so workable at the restaurant earlier today, and I would have stopped to say hello, but he was with skank-ass Felicia. I don't think I ever hated anybody in the world as much as I hated her. Nokea was on my shit list too, but not like Felicia. She intentionally did what she could to hurt people, and that was in no way cool with me.

"Scorpio," Spencer whispered, as my thoughts were on seeing Shane at the restaurant.

"Yeah, baby."

"Can I see you tonight or what?"

"I told you it was that time of the month."

"And. That means nothing to me. We can always work around that."

"Well, I don't like working around my period."

"Then just come over so we can chill. All I wanna do is hold you."

"I don't feel like cuddling tonight, Spencer. I'll call you in a week or two."

"A week or two, huh? If you plan on calling me in a week or two, then I'm left to assume there's someone else occupying your time."

"There always is, and there always will be. I'm not trying to be a bitch, but I'm not looking for anybody to settle down with."

"And, I'm not looking forward to sharing you with anybody either. When you're ready to come around, you let me know."

He hung up and I'd been there and done that with Spencer before. We'd been on and off, and every time he'd say he was through dealing with me, he'd be right back with me once I begged for forgiveness. Being in control was really working out for me. Call me a ho if you'd like, but many men reacted this way all the time. If I can play the game better than they do, then there ain't no need to be mad at me.

Hearing very little from the kids, I went downstairs to check on them. Most of them had fallen asleep, except for li'l James. He was lying on the floor while resting his head on a pillow. The TV was right in front of him, so I turned it down. I kneeled down on the floor next to him and gave him a kiss on his cheek.

"I apologize for yelling at you earlier, okay?" He nodded and gave me a hug. "You know your auntie loves you, don't you?"

He nodded again.

I tucked him underneath the sheets and gave him another kiss before I headed to my room to get some sleep. I dreamed about having dinner with Shane, but his woman came in and spoiled it for us. Maybe that was a sign for me to forget about him, but then again—maybe not.

# Shane

## 14

Felicia had been acting really whack. Scorpio's name couldn't stop falling out of her mouth, and she was pissed as hell about me leaving her at lunch the other day. I reminded her over and over again that I didn't want to hear it. She was becoming a pain in the ass and that required me to work at home, rather than going to the office.

Since we couldn't seem to get along, I packed up my stuff for the day and decided to go home. It was already getting late, but I wanted to stay late to get something done. So much for that, and as I was on my way out, I listened to her yell and scream behind me.

If she didn't know what her problem was, I damn sure did. She wanted to get laid. She was mad at Scorpio for getting all the goods and she'd been left without. I promised myself, and so did Jaylin when he was in town, that we would never ever go there with Felicia again.

It was almost 8:30 p.m. when I got home. I planned to wrap it up at the office by 10:00 p.m., but so much for that thought. Somewhat tired, I grabbed the mail from my mailbox and unlocked the front door. I flicked the light switch in my living room, but the lights didn't come on. Noticing a flickering light coming from my bedroom, I placed my keys and mail on the table. I took slow steps to my bedroom, and when I peeked inside the doorway, Sam was lying sideways on my bed.

"Home so soon," she said. She rubbed the spot in front of her. "Come lay down, but remove your clothes before you get here. I want to give you a massage."

I hated to mess up the mood, but I had to go there. "Are you sure there won't be no strings attached? I don't want to get all hyped and you—"

"Shane, stop being so stubborn and take off your clothes."

I hesitated, but did it anyway. I climbed in bed next to Sam and lay on my side to face her. She grabbed one of my fluffy pillows.

"Rest your head on the pillow and lay on your stomach."

No questions asked, I did as she'd requested.

Sam slid her thin, but firm leg across my back and straddled it. She rubbed her hands together and massaged my neckline and shoulders. When she got to my back, she rubbed something on her hands and had me feeling as if I was in another world.

"What's that on your hands?" I moaned. "That shit feels so good."

"So, I take it that you like it?"

"Love it," I confirmed. She lowered herself and rolled my ass cheeks around in her hands. She massaged my left side, and then my right. Continuing to have her way with me, she used her tongue to tickle my butt. I wanted to burst into laughter, but I let out a soft snicker and she moved on with her foreplay.

My dick got rock solid hard from her licks. I could barely lay on it, but she asked me to be patient until she was finished. I felt the tip of her finger gently rub the crack of my butt, but when she tried to go in further, that caused me to jump up and turn around.

"What the fuck are you doing?" I asked.

"I'm playing with you—that's what I'm doing."

"Well, sorry, I don't play like that." I quickly sat up and got out of bed. Sam grabbed my hand.

"Would you wait a minute? All I wanted to do was try something different."

I snatched my hand away. "Then, why don't you try something different with somebody else? I ain't the one." I walked over to the lights and turned them on. I blew out the candles and reached for my silk robe.

"Hey, this party is over. I think you'd better be leaving."

Sam sighed and raked her hair back with her fingers. "Shane, what is wrong with you? You have got some nerve trying to put me out. Every time you experiment on me, I allow you to do it. When I try a li'l finger action, you go berserk."

"Look, I don't know who the hell you've been experimenting with, but you can take that shit right back where you got it from. I hope you understand that ain't nothing going in my ass, baby. That shit is for them DL brothas, and nothing about that pertains to me."

"Okay, fine. Just get back in bed so that we can continue. I promise to keep my fingers where they belong."

"They belong right on my doorknob on your way out. I'm not in the mood right now and I'll call you later."

With attitude, Sam got out of bed and quickly put on her clothes. She was furious because I wasn't ready to "try something new" and left without saying good-bye.

To get my mind off what Sam had done, I went into my office and closed the door. I had a spacious office in my house that I'd go to when I wanted to concentrate on one of my projects. I'd been in my office many of nights, working on designs for the Mayor's Group. The room was dark and just to give myself a little light, I turned on the twenty-inch monitor on my desk. I placed a pad of sketch paper in front of me and grabbed a pencil. I started to draw and when I realized I'd been sketching a picture of Scorpio, I wanted to make the picture appear as beautiful as she really was.

My masterpiece was coming alive and I was almost finished. That was until the phone rang and interrupted me. I tried to ignore it, but the person called right back. Instead of ignoring it again, I picked up and it was Felicia.

"What?" I said.

"Now, that's no way to greet me."

"What do you want, Felicia, I'm busy."

"Do you have company?"

"No."

"Then you're not busy."

"Listen, I'm not in the mood tonight. State your business or else I'm gone."

"You're in love with Scorpio, aren't you?"

Frustrated, I took a deep breath. "No!" I yelled. "No, I am not in love with Scorpio."

"Then why do you defend her so much? During lunch, you stormed out like I had talked about your mama or something."

"Felicia, she's a good friend of mine and I don't appreciate you dogging her out like you do."

"I'm a good friend of yours, but you never defend me."

"That's a lie. I defend you all the time. As many horrible things that people have said to me about you, I always take up for you."

"Whoever said something horrible about me is just jealous. People hate women who are in powerful positions and they do everything they can to tear them down."

"I agree. So, can I get back to doing what I was doing before you called?"

"What were you doing?"

I lifted the sketch pad with the picture of Scorpio and dared to tell Felicia what I'd been doing. "I was drawing."

"Drawing what?"

"A picture of Sam."

"I'm sure she'll like it."

"I'm sure she will, too."

Felicia paused. There was silence before either of us said anything. "Good night, Felicia, I'm going to bed."

"Just make sure it's not with Scorpio."

"I'm convinced. You are obsessed with her, aren't you?"

"No, never. I've been thinking about a lot of things, that's all."

"A lot of things like what?"

"Get some rest and we'll talk about it tomorrow."

I hung up and dropped my forehead in my hands, occasionally rubbing it. I had a banging ass headache and before closing my eyes, I took two aspirins and laid my head on my desk.

By morning, I was leaned back in my chair, snoring my butt off. The trash trucks outside kicked up mega noise and interrupted my sleep. When I looked at the time on my monitor, it showed 10:00 a.m. I hadn't slept this late in awhile, so I hurried to the bathroom to shower. By the time I got dressed and got to work, Felicia wasn't there. She'd left a note on my desk that said I was fired and had a bagel laid beside it. The note had a big smiling face on it, so I knew she was bullshitting me.

I put the bagel into my mouth, and Felicia came walking through the door. She peeked her head into my office and smiled.

"Thanks for the bagel," I said.

"It was the least I could do," she said, and then took a seat. She held something in her hand, and when I asked what it was, she placed it behind her back.

"What's the secret?" I asked.

"Last night, do you remember I told you I wanted to talk to you about something?"

"Yes. So, what's up?"

"Well . . . I kind of got something on my mind. Before I tell you, I want you to put this disk into your computer."

Felicia stood up and walked the disk over to me. I looked at it and put it in my D: drive. I waited patiently for her document to open up, and when it did, I couldn't believe my eyes.

"What is this?" I said, looking at the events that took place at Trey's birthday gathering. By the looks of it, we were being taped.

"You mean, you don't recognize anyone," she said, sarcastically. She pointed at my monitor. "That's Trey, there's Brandon, there goes Jaylin, and . . . oh yeah, there you go. If you'd tune in a little longer, this gets so much better."

"Where in the hell did you get this from?"

"Well," Felicia said, walking back over to the couch. She crossed her legs. "It's like this—just in case you haven't noticed, Davenports is surrounded with hidden cameras. See, I have to protect what's mine, and I wanted to make sure you weren't up to no slick mess. Now, I was able to overlook your little sex scenes with the females you'd been bringing up in here, however, this latest incident, I can't let that one go."

I was stunned, and continued to listen while biting my bottom lip. I wasn't ready to act a fool just yet, but I had to respond. "You are out of your mind, Felicia. I can't believe you would stoop so low."

"Me? What's low is what's on that CD. Have you gotten to the part when Scorpio shows up, or are you still watching the other tramp do her thing?"

I glanced at my monitor and Scorpio was to soon enter the room. I kept quiet until I saw her stand between Jaylin and me. Shortly thereafter, I witnessed her wax Jaylin's dick.

"Look at your eyes, Shane. Those eyes show a man who craves for that woman. I can honestly say that even though I've watched this shit at least ten times, Jaylin showed less interest than you."

"So," I said defensively. "What the fuck is this all about?"

Felicia stood up again and came over to my desk. She placed the palms of her hands on the edge and bent down. "This is about me trying to figure out what to do with such valuable information. I have the capabilities of making shit hard for you, as well as for Jaylin. I'm not too thrilled about hurting you, unless you just happen to get with somebody I despise. But Jaylin, that's a different story. I don't like his wife, and how dare him come here and treat me like I'm nobody. I gave him four years of my life and I don't like to be treated in such a way."

I was numb. "After all Jaylin has done for Davenports, I can't believe the only thing you can think about is him dissing you for another woman. Felicia! Get your head on straight and quit tripping on me, baby. We have done something that not one damn African American business I know of in St. Louis has done! Within two years, thanks to Jaylin who came through for us when we didn't have shit, this company has earned almost a quarter of a million dollars."

"True to the fact or not, that motherfucka played me. Like I said, I don't like to be—"

I stood up and slammed my hand on the desk. "And, I don't like to be played either. I'm not gon' lose out because you ain't getting dicked down like you want to. Maybe if you'd stop passing around your worn out pussy, then maybe it would be good enough for some man to want to keep it. Either way, I ain't got time for your mess! I will have my things packed and out of here by tonight. When I'm gone, I'd like to see how far you get."

She clapped her hands together. "What an Oscar winning performance. Now, in addition to swagga, you and Denzel Washington got something else in common. But, you need to calm your butt down before I call security and have them escort you out of here for acting ignorant. There's no need for you to blow your top. I wanted you to know that I refuse to be partnered up with a man who shows interest in Scorpio. I had many of lonely, hurtful nights because of what she took from me. When she stepped into Jaylin's life she didn't give a fuck about me or Nokea. I know first hand what kind of impact she can have on a man, and I don't need you around here slipping cause she got your mind all fucked up like she had Jaylin's."

"So, I lusted for her at Trey's party. I lust for her when I see her. I'm a man, Felicia. And when I see a beautiful woman, shit like that happens. It doesn't mean I want to go off and marry her. It doesn't mean I want a relationship with her. All it means is I'm human, and when a woman turns me on, then she just turns me on."

"Then, promise me that you will not get involved with her. I don't want her to be nowhere near Davenports. It's bad enough she's already calling here, and next, she'll be bringing her tail over here everyday working my nerves."

"I can't promise you nothing like that. I do, however, promise to keep my personal business at home. For you to have cameras around here, and not share it with me—that was devious. If I wanted to, I could have you arrested for that mess."

She held her hands in front of her. "Cuff me," she said. "It's obvious you like to be tied up, so I'll be more than happy to play your game with you. Now, I know you're upset about this, but that's what you get for playing house. This is a place of business and any other employer would have fired you for carrying on in such a way. I'm being nice because I like you—I like you as my partner, and I see us going far together."

"We are not going anywhere, unless you get yourself together. You got a good thing going on, Felicia, and please don't blow it. Honestly, I don't give a fuck what you do with this CD. But, one more stunt like this, and I'm out of here."

"As of yet, I don't plan on doing anything with that CD. However, my rule stands, if you bring Scorpio anywhere near me, this CD gets mailed to Nokea and to all of our clients as my excuse for having to end this partnership."

I wanted to punch Felicia in her face for being so stupid, but I held my composure. "So, it's like that, huh?"

"I'm afraid so—it's like that."

I picked up my briefcase that sat next to my desk. I opened it and put the papers on my desk inside. "I'm outtie. You can't blame me for trying, but I can't work under these conditions. I will talk to our lawyer, Mr. Frick, tomorrow and make arrangements to end this so called ass partnership."

She folded her arms in front of her. "If that's how you want it, then fine. What I'm asking of you is simple. If you don't understand, then adios."

There was nothing much left for me to say to Felicia. She had her mind made up and so did I. This unstable partnership had gone on for too long and it was simply time for me to go.

# Scorpio

# 15

I was so glad Friday was approaching, which meant more money for me. Jay's always carried a full house on the weekend because for whatever reason, the weekend was a time to look good. Now, I'd made my share of money during the week too, but Fridays and Saturdays were always booming.

I needed a pedicure, and sat down to let Yasing do her thing. Her husband, Yen, stood next to her talking, and everybody's eyes roamed around the room. After they finished their conversation in Chinese, she gave Yen a kiss and I assumed he said good-bye to us when he spoke and waved.

Jamaica stopped working on her customer's hair and held a comb in her hand. "I ain't trying to be nosy, Yasing, but what were y'all saying?"

Yasing smiled. "Huh?"

"You know what I mean . . . I don't think it's fair that y'all can understand our language, but we can't understand y'alls."

Yasing laughed. "But, our languish is just as easy to learn as yours."

"Girl, please. You and your man could have been up in here calling all of us niggas and we wouldn't have known nothing about it."

"No, no niggas. We not call you niggas."

"Well, what y'all be saying then?"

"That none of yo business. That between Yen and me."

"Tell her, Yasing," Bernie said. "Keep that hoochie mama out of your business."

Jamaica looked at Bernie. "Now, Bernie, I haven't had to disrespect you in two days. We were doing just fine, until you had to open your big mouth. That's the same big mouth that's been spilling all of Scorpio's business up in here." Jamaica turned to me. "If I were you, I'd kick her butt out of your shop. We wouldn't know half of what you did, if she didn't tell us."

"Jamaica, Bernie only knows what I tell her. I have nothing to hide and if anybody wants to know anything about me, all you got to do is ask me."

"Okay," Jamaica said. "Let's get down with a li'l truth or dare then. Are y'all with me?"

We laughed, but everybody agreed.

"Fine, then I'm gon' start with . . . Bernie. Truth or dare?"

"I knew you would start with me."

"Truth or dare, skeeza; take your pick."

Bernie placed her hand on her hip. "Truth."

"Is it true that . . . you ain't had no dick in three years?"

"Dare?" she laughed.

We all teased Bernie about being unfair. "Okay," she said. "That is false. Actually, it's been four years and I ain't mad about it either. Until I find somebody who deserves what I got, then I'll make some arrangements. Until then, my legs are staying closed."

"I heard that," nearly everybody agreed, except Jamaica. She tooted her lips. "Four years is a mighty long time for a woman to go without sex. I feel deeply sorry for your vibrator because that thing probably getting one hell of a work out."

"Oh, you betta believe it is," Bernie confirmed. "And, I don't have to worry about it not calling me tomorrow, giving me a sexually transmitted disease, cheating on me, or finding out that it's on the down-low. You should invest in one yourself. Maybe, just maybe, it'll alleviate some of your problems."

"Next," Jamaica said holding up her hand. "Deidra Lasha Evans."

"Yes," Deidra said, while swinging around in an empty chair.

"Truth or dare?"

"Dare."

"You's a bold bitch, ain't you?"

We laughed.

"I dare you to go outside, drop your halter, and keep it down until a man gives you some money. Don't come back in here until you have at least ten dollars."

I interrupted. "Now, that's taking things too far. I don't want nobody to think we're running some kind of whore house in here, and Deidra don't need to be exposing herself in such a way."

Jamaica snapped, "From where I come from a dare is a dare! If y'all don't want to play the game—"

"Don't worry about it Scorpio," Deidra said. "Give me less than five minutes and I'll be back with some dough."

Deidra untied her top and covered her tiny breasts with her hands. After that, she headed outside. Several people moved over to the window to see if she had the nerve to flash her breasts. Jamaica continued on with her game.

"Miss Scorpio," she said. "You know I couldn't leave you out."

"I was sure of that," I said.

"Truth or dare?"

"I'd rather go with the truth since your dares are outrageous."

"Okay, then—is it true that you got butt ball naked the other day for the Hollywood Lover #2, and screwed him in your office?"

I pulled my head back. "What? Who in the hell is the Hollywood Lover #2?"

"The second brotha with the twisties who came in here and got lost trying to find his way to Hollywood."

"Shane?"

"Yes, *Shame.* It was a damn shame how good he looked."

Everybody laughed, and before I could tell my side of the story, Deidra came in waving a twenty dollar bill in her hand.

"Look what I got," she said, dancing around. "Look what I got."

Jamaica tooted her lips again. "Now, whoever gave you twenty dollars for showing those li'l tits was a desperate fool."

"Oooo, girl. You shouldn't talk about your man like that. That is so cruel of you."

"Please, my man knows better. He ain't got to pay you when he got all this to look forward to." She lifted a chunk of her left breast.

"Well, he did. He's outside parking his car. Within a few minutes, the door shall chime."

We all thought Deidra was playing, but sure enough, just moments later, Jamaica's boyfriend, Darious, came through the door.

"What's up, y'all?" he said, looking around with a toothpick dangling from his mouth.

"What's up?" Jamaica said. "I know you didn't just give Deidra no twenty dollars for showing you her breasts."

"Damn, why you trippin'?" he placed his hands in the pockets of his jeans that hung low and showed his underwear. "It what'en nothin' but twenty dollars. You act like it was a hundred dollars or somethin'."

Jamaica and her man started to argue. Every time he came in here, some shit always happened. Sometimes the chaos scared my customers away, but I wasn't having it today.

"Look, why don't y'all take y'all argument outside? There are people in here who don't want to hear it."

"Bitch, shut up," he said. "Don't interrupt me when I'm talking to my woman."

"Darious, you need to leave," Jamaica said. "I don't need you up in here disrespecting me or my friends."

"I agree," I said standing up. "Now, I'm asking you nicely to leave and I'm not going to be too many more of your bitches."

He stepped forward and grabbed Jamaica by her neck. Soon after, Bernie pulled out a silver pistol from inside of her drawer.

She aimed it at him. "Not up in here, and not today, fool. We asked you to leave and now you got a choice. Either you leave with holes in your behind or you gon' leave the same way you came in here—though the front door."

"She don't look like she playing," Deidra added. "Her husband quickly found that out, but he can't tell you cause he's six feet under."

Darious released Jamaica's neck and held his hands up as he walked to the door. He gave an evil stare at Jamaica and made his exit. When he was out of sight, we all slowly got back to our seats.

"You need to be really careful," Bernie said to Jamaica. "That fool is trouble."

"Don't worry about it. My brothers are coming from L.A. next week and Darious will be dealt with. His days of putting his hands on me are running out."

"Just be careful," I said.

After Yasing finished my toes, I headed back to my office to take a nap. I was tired from the late hours I'd been putting in at Jay's, as well as the late nights I'd been spending with my men. I had a date with Maxwell tonight, but he called earlier and cancelled our plans. For that, he would pay. I would be sure to place him on the back burner and make him wait at least two or three weeks before I saw him again.

I closed the door to my office, lay back on my couch, and within seconds, I was out like a light.

There was a light tap on my door, and when I woke up and asked who it was, it was Bernie. I pulled my hair back and stumbled my tired butt to the door.

"Hey," I said, opening it. Bernie came in and so did one of her customers.

"Scorpio, this is Eva. She wants to speak to you about her concerns with your place. She addressed them to me, but I told her you were the one to speak to."

"That's fine. Have a seat," I said.

Bernie left the room and Eva sat in a chair in front of my desk. She was an older short woman with a small frame so I didn't anticipate her coming in here to start any mess with me.

"Bernie was doing my hair when Jamaica's boyfriend came in. I was blown away when she pulled out a gun, but more so upset that you, as the owner, didn't do nothing about it. I thought it was bad enough that you allowed one of your workers to expose herself in the street, but the gun incident really took the cake."

"I'm sorry you feel that way, uh—"

"Eva. Bernie already told you my name but maybe you forgot."

"Eva, it's obvious that you have some legitimate concerns, however, it's difficult trying to keep things in order around here. I don't know if you've ever tried to manage a business before, but anything can happen at a place like this. Whenever there are a lot of women around, there's always gon' be men. We don't always see eye to eye on things, so sometimes that can mean trouble. Unfortunately, there are times that trouble finds it way to Jay's, and when it does, I have to approach every situation as best as I can."

"Well, I think you can avoid some of the mess that goes on around here by choosing stylists with a bit more professionalism. Bernie is cool, but Jamaica and Deidra, they are two of the most foul mouthed women I've ever seen. I should be able to relax at a place like this. Whoever the hell you have sex with is none of my business. Just within the last several weeks of coming here,

I can write your life story. And, all the cussing makes my bones rattle. I'm a Christian woman and—"

"Eva, maybe you should find a new stylist? I have never had anyone complain about their visit at Jay's, and as hard as I try, I'll never be able to please everybody."

She stood up and wrapped her arm around the straps of her purse. "Maybe I will find me somewhere else to go."

I gave her an "oh well" look and Eva headed for the door. After she left, I heard the front door close and Bernie peeped her head in the doorway.

"You all right?" she asked.

"Hey, I'm fine. We can't please everybody, right?"

Just then my phone rang. I reached to answer it and Bernie waved good-bye.

"Hello." I said. There was silence, and soon, I heard heavy breathing into the phone and hung up. The phone rang again, and whoever it was called again.

"Who is this?" I said, while listening to the heavy breathing again. "You're a stupid mother-fucka," I yelled. I hung up and waited for them to call back, but they didn't.

I gathered my belongings in my office and headed up front. I turned down the lights, then made sure all of the hot irons were off. I locked the front door and headed to my car. As I neared it, it looked rather odd. And when I got closer to it, I could see that all four of my tires were flat. My hands were shaking, but I quickly pulled out my cell phone and called the police. It didn't take long for them to get there, and when the officer asked if I had any idea who might have done it, I really couldn't give him a name. I wanted to say Darious, because of what had happened today, but then again, I wanted to say Spencer because he was mad at me for calling it quits. Since he hadn't done anything crazy like this before, I had to eliminate him. I couldn't decide who was capable of doing something so stupid, so for the time being, I told the police I didn't have a clue.

The officer offered to stay with me until Troy's Truck & Towing arrived. I needed a ride home, but when I called home, Leslie didn't answer. I figured her and the kids must have been asleep, so I didn't want to bother her.

Since it was almost 11:00 p.m., and I knew Shane worked late nights, I called Davenports to see if I could catch up with him. When the answering machine at Davenports came on, I called his cell phone. Surprisingly, he answered.

"Hi, Shane, this is Scorpio."

"I recognized your number," he said dryly. "What's up?"

"I was wondering if you could do me a favor."

"Depends on what it is."

"Somebody slashed all four of my tires and I need a ride home. I'm sorry to bother you, but—"

He paused for a long while, as if he had to think about it. "Where are you?"

"I'm still at Jay's."

"Give me about twenty minutes. I'll be there in twenty to thirty minutes."

"Thanks," I said, and then hung up.

In less than twenty minutes, Shane was there. He parked his Lexus and walked up to me. He placed his hands in his pockets, observing my car jacked up by the tow truck.

"I'd take a guess and say that somebody really don't like you," he said.

"It's obvious, ain't it? And as I keep thinking about who, my list grows longer and longer."

"Damn, you got that many enemies?"

"I didn't think so, but—"

The tow truck pulled off and we got into Shane's car. He reached for his rearview mirror to adjust it.

"So, where do you live?" he asked.

"I live in Lake St. Louis, but I was hoping that I could spend the night with you. In the morning,

you can take me to find some tires for my car—
that's if you don't mind."

"I got a job, baby. You want me to put my job
aside for you?" he smiled.

I pouted, "Please."

He winked and started his car.

Shane drove off and headed to his place. He
lived in the Central West End, so we were there
in less than fifteen minutes. He had a brick ranch
style house that was much better than the studio
apartment he'd had a few years ago.

When we got inside, his place was decked out
with contemporary furniture. The colors were
mostly gray, black, and white; his off-white
leather sofa in the living room was off the chain.
I followed behind him toward his bedroom. He
tossed his keys on a nightstand, but I remained
in the doorway.

"I had a long day," he said, sitting on the bed
and pulling his shirt over his head. "I'll get you a
few pillows so you can sleep in my guest room."

My first thought was Jaylin. I looked at Shane's
king-sized bed and thought about the magic that
was supposed to take place there. Then, I thought
about how I had no desire to be in the guest room
tonight. I wanted to be held by the muscular bare
chest, hunk of a man that was in my view.

"Aren't you going to show me around your place? Also, I'd like to take a shower before I go to bed."

Shane's eyes searched me up and down before escorting me to another room.

"This is where you'll be sleeping tonight," he said. "Unless . . ." He walked me over to another room close by, "Unless you'd like to sleep in here. This room is a bit smaller than the other, so I suggest you choose that one."

Both rooms looked cozy, so it didn't matter to me either way. He then took me through the living room and into his kitchen. It was beautifully decorated with contemporary burnt orange leather chairs and a square glass table. To add an even more exquisite taste to it, he had stainless steel appliances and huge rugs covered the shiny hardwood floors.

"You can tell I don't use the kitchen that often," he said.

I laughed and agreed because it was spotless.

After we left the kitchen, he took me further back into another room. This place, he said, was his office. He turned on the light and I walked in to take a look. It was nice too, for a home office, and was dressed with mahogany leather and black. His black wooden desk and bookshelves were cluttered with papers and books.

"I apologize for the mess in here, but when it's clean, it looks a whole lot better."

"No need to apologize. I can tell that you got it going on." I smiled and walked over to his desk, noticing a drawing that looked familiar to me. I picked it up. Shane tried to snatch it away, but I could already tell it was me.

"Did you draw this?" I asked.

"Who else drew it?" he said. "Now, give it here."

I stared at the picture, as it was awesomely drawn. "I didn't know you could draw like this. And furthermore, why are you over here drawing pictures of me?"

He folded his arms in front of him, and all muscle showed. "If you must know, Pretty Lady, I drew that picture be . . . because I was thinking about you."

"And, why are you thinking about me?"

"I think about who I want to think about. You got a problem with that?"

"No, no," I said, placing the picture back on his desk. "You keep your li'l thoughts to yourself."

I strutted out of his office and he followed behind me. On our way back to his room he stopped at the linen closet, grabbed two pillows, and some towels.

"I got three bathrooms, take your pick. Hallway, guest room, or my room?"

"I'll use the one in your bedroom. That way, you can think about me while you watch."

"No thanks," Shane said.

We went into his bedroom and he opened the double doors that led to his bathroom. He placed the towels on the counter and told me he'd put the pillows in the guest room.

"If you need anything else, let me know."

"I need something to sleep in."

"Will a T-shirt be fine?"

"Yes, that'll do."

He nodded, and shortly after came back with a white T-shirt. He placed it on the counter next to my towels, and glanced at me as I stood with the back of my dress partially unzipped. I pulled my hair over to the side and turned my back toward him.

"Can you help me with this zipper," I asked. "I think it's stuck."

He came up from behind, unzipping my dress to the middle of my butt. Since I didn't have on any panties, I was sure he'd gotten a peek.

"It didn't seem stuck to me," he said. He walked back over to the doors. "Enjoy," he said, and then closed them.

I knew Shane wanted me just as much as I wanted him. One of us was about to give in, but after what happened the last time we were together, it wasn't going to be me.

I got naked and walked to the doors to open them. Shane lay across his bed while paging through a magazine.

"It's a bit stuffy in here," I said. "If you don't mind, I'd like to leave the doors open."

Shane gazed at my naked body and I could only imagine where his mind was when I turned my back. I stepped up the three steps that led to the glass shower and stood inside. Before turning on the water, I looked to see if he was watching me. His eyes were focused on the magazine in front of him.

Warm water sprayed out and dripped down my body. I lathered soap in my hands, rubbing it all over my body. I looked up again, but this time, Shane's eyes connected with mine. We just stared, waiting to see who would make the next move. Without looking down, he turned the page to the magazine, and then lowered his head again.

I got back to cleansing my body and noticed Shane's eyes glued to me again. This time, I had even more lather on me and massaged my soapy breasts together. My nipples were erect, and as the water ran between my legs, I lowered my soapy hand and rubbed between my upper thighs. I figured I'd give Shane a little something extra to watch, so I turned around and bent over. I scrubbed my ankles and allowed the water to drip down and rinse me.

As soon as I turned around, Shane had slid the glass door over. He was naked and stepped inside to join me.

"You're a dick teaser," he said with a sponge in his hand.

"Since you're standing here, I guess I must be good at what I do, huh?"

"Damn good," he admitted. He touched the side of my face with his hand and moved my wet hair away from my eyes. Our lips met up and the water sprayed on both of our faces. I felt his hard dick pressing against my stomach and couldn't wait for him to get inside of me. We had already wasted too much time, so I reached down and stroked his goods with my hands. I could tell by his heavy breathing that he enjoyed my touch.

I waited until the water rinsed Shane's dick, then edged up on the tips of my toes. I placed his pipe between my legs, allowing him to separate me, and guide against my walls. I tightly grabbed his muscular ass, each time he backed up, slid back in, and pressed against my clit with the tip of his overly thick head. The feel of it had me going crazy and I was ready to cut the foreplay.

I backed away from his lips and looked into his eyes. "Lift me up and give me what I want," I whispered. He stared at me and backed his dick out from between my legs. He lathered the sponge with soap and water and turned me around to face the shower's wall. With warm water still dripping down my body, he used the sponge to wash me. As he worked my back with the sponge, he reached his other hand around to my front side and massaged my breasts. When he lowered the sponge to my ass and washed it, he lowered his hand down my front side and circled his fingers around my clit. I closed my eyes and held my hair up in my hands. I bit down on my lip because the feeling was right where I needed it to be.

"Spread your legs," he ordered. I spread my legs further apart and Shane dropped the sponge to the shower's floor. He continued to rub my clit and used his other hand to insert my kitty cat from behind. It purred for him and he fingered me good. So good that I was surely about to cum.

"Shaaane," I moaned. "I don't want to come like this. Please put it inside. Now." I demanded.

He removed his hand from my clit, but continued to work me from the backside. "How bad do you want it?"

"Really, really bad."

"And, how bad is really bad."

"So . . . so bad that I can already feel it."

"That's good," he said, removing his fingers from inside me. I bent slightly over and Shane stood behind me. He opened me up from behind, and finally, made his way in. I gasped from the feeling and we both needed a moment to regroup. The intensity made both of us want to cum quickly.

"See, this is what you get for teasing me," he said. "Now, don't move. Just give me a minute."

"You're the one teasing me. If you move, I'm cumming. I'm warning you."

Shane stood for a moment and calmed himself. I closed my eyes as he rubbed the dripping water up and down on my back. He slowly navigated in and out of me, gripping his hands into my hips. His pipe touched every corner of my walls and completely filled my insides. I could feel him in my abdomen and I let it be known by the sounds of my soft moans.

"Mmmm, this feels so good, baby. I've waited a long, long time to feel like this again," I said.

Shane didn't respond. He kept with his slow and smooth stroking, and my knees were about to buckle. He felt my insides grip on his dick and dug his fingers into my hips to hold my body in place.

"Take your time," he suggested. "Let it flow down so I can feel it."

Shane changed his rhythm and sped up the pace. Soon, our gushy juices made the exchange and he backed out of me. Both of us wanted more pleasure, so we rinsed ourselves and headed for his bed. I sat on the edge and he stood in front of me. He placed one foot on the bed and I welcomed his hardness in my mouth. I polished it well, leaving it shiny as ever.

Shane moaned with pleasure; a bunch of my hair was tied up in his hands and his grips on my hair got tighter and tighter.

"I ain't cumming like this," he said. He backed out of my mouth and reached for something in his dresser drawer. He pulled out a squeeze container of K-Y Jelly and rubbed it on his goods. Thinking that he was ready to enter me, I backed up on the bed. I lay on my back and Shane eased up to me and straddled my stomach. He placed his pleasure between my breasts and held them close together. He slid his pipe in between them, and while lightly rubbing my nipples with his thumbs; it turned me on even more. I damn near went crazy, and inserted my finger inside of myself to bring down more juices. Shane had no problem lowering himself and brushing his lips against my wet hole. He licked up and down my slit, and then his tongue made a strategic and fierce move.

My mind went back to our encounter several years ago. He'd made me cum in an instant by loving my insides, and I'll be darned if he didn't do it again. He vibrated his tongue deeply inside of me and received a healthy taste of me.

Our first sex session went on for hours. I was the one to call it quits, because my insides throbbed from the slight soreness his thick package had delivered.

"Shane, this is it for me," I said, as my heart beat fast. I lay on my stomach, with my butt hiked in the air.

"I'm almost there," he said, stroking me from behind. "And if you want to call it quits, then I suggest you get there, too."

Having a tingle, and wanting to *get there* for the last time, I backed my ass up to Shane and got on my hands and knees. I bounced hard against him and stretched my right leg up on the bed. That opened me wider and Shane was all into it.

"Daaaamn, I'm loving this," he whispered. "I'm about to lose my mind fucking with you."

Still in position, I reached for his hand and placed it on my clit. He turned it in circles while pumping into me from behind. Within minutes, we both fell forward to the floor.

"I—I'm wore out," I said heavily breathing.

"That's putting it mildly. Exhausted is more like it."

Shane stood up and helped me off the floor. He held my body close to his and kissed my forehead before we got in bed.

Having the best sex I'd had since Jaylin, I couldn't even go to sleep. Shane was knocked out and was cuddled up behind me with his arms wrapped around my waist. I was grateful to him for taking my mind off the person who slashed my tires, and before he went to sleep, he assured me that we'd find out who was responsible. In the meantime, I really wasn't sure where this relationship between us was going, but I felt safe and secure being in his arms.

# Shane

## 16

Now, that's what a man may refer to as "good pussy." Scorpio had it going on, and there was no doubt that she was capable of whipping that thang on a brotha to mess up his mind. I mean . . . Jaylin told me how spectacular she was in bed, but damn, just to feel it for myself was like the best feeling ever. I'd wanted her since the day I'd met her. I didn't know that she was kicking it with my boy until later. I always told him, if they ever stopped messing around, I would make my move. And since he was happily married to Nokea, now was the time.

After one amazing night, I was up at 5:30 a.m. Normally, I'd be getting ready to go to the office, but since things didn't work out between Felicia and me, I planned to handle my business from home.

Thing is, I wasn't even mad about how she played me. I always knew some mess would go down between us; Jaylin for damn sure warned me. That woman was just downright flat-out crazy. After seeing Scorpio's car, it was obvious. I had a feeling that Felicia's jealousy had overtaken her. She was so obsessed with Scorpio, I wasn't sure how far Felicia would take it. Until I knew what was up for sure, I hadn't planned on saying anything to Scorpio. In the meantime, I had to call my boy Jay to let him know what was up. I had a feeling that CD would somehow make it into Nokea's hands and I knew that seeing Scorpio's mouth in action would devastate Nokea.

It was still a bit early to call Jaylin, so I went back into my bedroom to check on Scorpio. She was still asleep so I pulled the covers over her naked body and bent down to kiss her forehead. I went into the kitchen, planning on making us some breakfast, but there wasn't much in the fridge to work with. If anything, I did have several pieces of bacon left in a package and some bread. I knew I'd had some jelly, and when I searched the cabinets, I found a brand new jar. I always kept cereal in the house, so I pulled a box of Frosted Flakes from the cabinet.

It didn't take long to fry the bacon and spread the jelly on four pieces of toast. I fixed two bowls of cereal and poured out two glasses of orange juice. Everything went on a tray that I carried to my bedroom.

Still in my black boxers, I put the tray on a nightstand and cuddled in bed behind Scorpio. I kissed her cheek, and even though the thought of entering her again had crossed my mind, I decided to wait until later. Instead, I kissed her lips to wake her.

Her eyes slowly cracked open and she planted a smile on her face. She slowly turned around and lay on her back to face me.

"Good morning," she said.

"It is definitely a good morning," I replied. "Are you hungry?"

"A little. Why?"

"Because I fixed you a li'l something."

She smiled and sat up. She pulled her hair away from her face and looked at the food on the tray. "Aww, that was so sweet of you. Nobody ever brought me breakfast in bed."

"I can't believe that, but I plan to go the extra mile and feed it to you."

We laughed and I reached for a piece of toast. She tightened her mouth and wouldn't accept it until she brushed her teeth. Afterwards, she climbed back in bed with me, and I put the toast up to her mouth. She opened wide and took a bite.

I put the second piece in my mouth and we both chewed. When I reached for the orange juice, she took it from my hand.

"I think I can handle this," she said.

I reached for the cereal to feed it to her. It looked awfully soggy, so I left the spoon in the bowl and looked at it.

"I don't think you want—"

"No, the toast, bacon, and orange juice are fine. Let's save the cereal for another time."

I laughed and put the bowl back on the tray. Just then I heard my doorbell ring and wasn't sure who it was visiting me so early in the morning. I got off the bed and told Scorpio I'd be right back.

"Shane," she said.

I turned, already midway to my bedroom door.

Scorpio raised her index finger and told me to come to her.

I walked over and kneeled down on the bed to kiss her lips that were already puckered.

"Thank you and hurry back," she whispered.

"Will do."

I hurried to the door to see who it was. When I looked through the peephole, it was Felicia. She was clearly dressed for work, and I figured she made it her business to stop by on her way to the office. Seriously thinking about not opening the door, I changed my mind and did. I cracked it, just so she wouldn't take a look inside.

"What's up?" I said, standing shirtless.

She could see I wasn't dressed. "So, I see you're not coming to work."

"Felicia, we discussed this yesterday. I'm gonna work, but not at Davenports anymore."

"I know what you said yesterday, but we need to talk."

"Not right now. I'm busy. I'll call you later."

"No, we need to talk now. I thought about some things and hopefully we can work them out."

"I'm not interested in working out anything with you. So, like I said, I'll call you later."

"Is Sam over here? I don't care how busy you are, this is important. I talked to Frick last night and he thinks we should try and work things out."

"No, Sam is not over here. And, when I talked to Frick, he seems to think it's time to go our separate ways."

Just then, Scorpio's voice interrupted. "Shane," Scorpio said. "Is everything okay?"

I slightly turned my head to the side and looked at Scorpio standing with my sheet wrapped around her naked body.

"Everything is fine. I'll be back there in a minute."

She turned and walked away.

Felicia folded her arms in front of her and snapped. "That voice was very familiar. I hope to God that wasn't who I think it was."

"That voice was none of your business. Now, I'm not trying to disrespect you, but my door is soon going to close."

"See, this is exactly what I was talking about. I knew the moment you started seeing that bitch, you'd be singing a new tune. Admit it. That was Scorpio, wasn't it?"

"Good-bye, Felicia."

I moved the door forward to close it and she pushed back on it. She quickly placed her pointed toe shoe at the bottom so it wouldn't close.

"We need to talk," she said. "Whenever you get done contracting the AIDS virus, you need to come see me. Our business is important, Shane, and to let a woman like her come between us is wrong."

I didn't feel like saying much else, but, "I'll call you later."

She slid her foot away from the crack and I closed the door. I peeked through my blinds and watched her until she was out of sight.

When I got back to my bedroom, Scorpio was nowhere to be found. I looked in the bathroom and she wasn't there. I stepped into the hallway and walked down the hall to my guest room. When I opened the door, she wasn't there either. I then pulled the door open to my other room and there she was. She was still wrapped in the sheet while lying on the bed.

"I—I kind of had a vision this morning," she said in the partially dark room.

I leaned against the doorway. "Oh, yeah. That's funny. I kind of had one, too."

"Why don't you come in and express your vision to me over here, instead of expressing it from over there?" Scorpio said.

I walked further into the room and eased my way onto the bed with Scorpio. I lay between her legs and was face-to-face with her.

"So, tell me about this vision you had," I said, inhaling her sweet smell.

"I visualize me leaving my mark in every room of your house. Every time you enter a room, I visualize you only thinking of me. Then, when I'm gone, your thoughts will encourage you to pick up the phone and invite me over again and again. . . ."

"Hmmm," I said. "That's not bad—not bad at all, but I visualize us spending the entire day to-

gether. It can start by us not doing anything pertaining to work, having sex in the shower again,
going to see about your car, going to your house
to check on the family, having dinner this evening, coming back to my place, and then, putting
our mark on every room in my house, including
the covered patio."

"The patio too," she smiled. "Since you got a
bit more creative than I did, I'd say we stick to
your plan."

"That's my girl," I said, and then planted a kiss
on her lips.

After we got down in the shower we put on
our clothes and left to see about Scorpio's car.
I drove her to get some tires first, and then we
headed for the tow yard. One of Troy's workers
put her new tires on and she was ready to go.
I wanted to go home with her, but she insisted
that I not go.

"It's not that I don't want you to meet my family, Shane, but I don't like bringing my friends
around Mackenzie and my nieces and nephews."

"Hey, listen, no need to explain," I said, while
leaning against her car. She was already sitting
inside and ready to go.

"Just call me when you get finished taking care
of business at home, and we'll hook up then."

"That sounds fine. Once I go home and check on everything, I'm going to stop by Jay's to make sure everything is cool. After that, Ricardo, I will see you later."

"Please, no Ricardo. Stick to Shane, pretty lady."

Scorpio smiled and I bent down to give her a kiss. She drove off and I headed back home, awaiting my eventful evening.

I went into my office to call Jaylin. I didn't want to procrastinate about telling him about my departure from Davenports, nor about the CD Felicia had. When I told him, he couldn't believe it.

"She did what?" he yelled into the phone.

"Yeah, dog. Ain't that a bitch?"

"What is wrong with her ass?"

"I'on know. She's been acting kind of whack lately. All I can say is it's time for me to move on."

"Yeah, I don't blame you one bit. As soon as you get a chance, though, you need to call the Mayor's Group and let them know what's up. I don't know how they gon' feel about it, but that is one account you for damn sure don't want to lose."

"You got that right, especially after all the time and effort I put into getting it."

"Just to be on the safe side, I'll give Mr. Mayor a call and let him know about the change. In the meantime, you need to get with Frick and set up a new business under your name. Go with something like—like Alexander . . . Alexander & Company."

"Alexander & Company? Man, who in the fuck is my company? I understand the Alexander but I ain't got much company to go with it."

"Negro, you got me and that's more than enough company. Now, I don't want no involvement with the shit because my wife, my kids, and I are staying right here. I will, however, do what I can to assist."

I took a deep breath and felt relieved. Whenever Jaylin had my back, I knew things would be all good. "You know a brotha appreciate you, don't you?"

He laughed. "I know he'd better appreciate me. Cause if he don't, I'm gon' come there and bust his damn head open."

We both laughed.

"But, look," he said. "I need you to do two things for me."

"What's that?"

"Within the hour, I need you to call Mr. Mayor and tell him what's up. Like I said, I'll call him too, but it's better for him to hear about the inconvenience from you."

"I agree."

"Second, you need to find out Felicia's plans for that CD."

"Oh, I can tell you what her plans are. Somehow, she's going to get that CD to Nokea. Yesterday, Scorpio's tires were slashed and I think Felicia had something to do with it."

"Quit lying."

"Straight up. I wouldn't lie about no shit like that. I'm telling you, man, she is wacko."

"Why would she do something like that to Scorpio? And, if that CD makes it anywhere near my house, I'm gon' kill that bitch, Shane."

"I wouldn't blame you one bit. She's been on this trip about me feeling Scorpio. I told her what I do is my business, but she keeps pressuring me about the shit, especially after seeing what happened that night. All I can say is, you do not want Nokea to see that CD. You and I both look like two whipped fools lost in a trance."

"Damn, that's fucked up, but that's the kind of impact Scorpio got, man. Ain't no denying that."

"Naw, there really ain't."

Jaylin paused and so did I.

"Have you seen her lately?" he asked.

I wanted to lie, but I couldn't. "Yeah . . . yeah I saw her."

"And?"

"And what?"

"And what did she say?"

"About who—you?"

"Who else?"

I hesitated and leaned back in my chair. I picked up the sketched picture of her, held it in my hand, and looked at it.

"Shane," Jaylin yelled.

"What?" I yelled back.

"You heard me, fool. What you over there playing with yo dick or something?"

I laughed. "Naw, man, I was just thinking about something."

"Is that right," Jaylin said suspiciously. "I'm almost afraid to ask what."

"Then, don't. I'm not prepared—"

"Are you telling me you done already hit that?" his pitch was higher.

I took a hard swallow. "Ja . . . Jay, I don't—"

"Don't go no further. Whether you did or didn't, I don't want to know nothing about it."

I could tell by his tone he was bitter. "Listen . . . you know sometimes—"

"Shane!" he yelled. "Let it go, man. I said I'm not interested."

"That's what your mouth says, but if you need a moment, I can call you back. I don't want the wrong things to be said, and the last thing I want is for a woman to come between us. I respect our friendship to the fullest, but I have no control over my feelings."

"Shut the fuck up talking to me, pussy. You need to take a moment and gather your thoughts for after I make this phone call to Mr. Mayor."

"So, are you cool? You sound like you cool."

His voice rose. "Cool about what!"

"This—this thing between Scorpio and me?"

"Motherfucka, hell naw I ain't cool about it! But, what the fuck you want me to do, huh? I ain't gon' cry about it and I damn sure ain't gon' lose no sleep over it. And even though my name still tattooed on that ass, that pussy goes wherever the fuck it wants to go. As long as this pussy over here, married to me, don't go nowhere— that's all I'm concerned about. And as long as my name is Jaylin Jerome Rogers, this pussy will never have another man's dick inside of it. You got that? Never!" He spoke with confidence.

"Even if Nokea see that CD? You still think she would remain faithful to you?" I joked, knowing that she most likely would.

"Do you have fool written across your face? First of all, nigga, I learned how to avoid confrontations in my marriage. Honesty has never been a problem for me, so I already told Nokea what went down that weekend. She didn't want to know, but I told her anyway. I was not gon' let that shit come back and haunt me. She wasn't happy about it, and as a matter of fact, she was damn mad, but she understands that sometimes the flesh gets weak. She's just happy that I made the right choice and so am I."

"Well, if you told her, then why you worried about her seeing the CD?"

"There's a difference between me telling her, and her seeing it for herself. I ain't trying to bring no hurt on her like that. And, when you hurt her, you hurt me. Like I said, Felicia just better make sure that CD don't make it nowhere near my house."

"I gotta go by the office later to pick up some more of my things. Maybe she'll be singing a new tune, I don't know. As of this morning, she was still out there. Especially, when she found out Scorp—I had company."

"Stop letting that shit slip out your mouth. We gon' be cool, and we'll remain cool if you keep your personal business to yourself. For the last time, I do not wish to know what goes on between you and her."

"I apologize for letting that slip. From this moment on, my business is nobody's business but my own."

"Smart move. I'll hit you back after I talk to Mr. Mayor."

Jaylin hung up and I sat back in my chair. I took a sigh of relief and was glad things remained cool with us. Still, I wasn't happy about betraying him. Since we'd squashed our fallout over Felicia many years ago, Jaylin had been nothing but a good friend to me. I knew that even though he hadn't, and wouldn't admit it; the thought of me being with Scorpio was eating him up inside. Married to Nokea or not, it had to frustrate him.

When Jaylin called back, he said that Mr. Mayor had some minor issues he wanted to resolve with me. When I called him, he said he wanted me to redo the design and make it completely my own. He knew Felicia had added her touch to it, but he wanted to see if I was capable of handling the project on my own. Since I'd done most of the work, it wasn't that difficult to remove her ideas and add more of mine to the design. In addition to that, I called Frick to see if he could meet with me as soon as possible. I was anxious to relinquish my partnership with Davenports and move forward with Alexander & Company. I had a feeling that it was going to be the best thing since sliced bread.

My visit with Mr. Frick took up more time than I anticipated. He called in another attorney who could represent me. Being loyal to Felicia because she was the president of Davenports,

Frick felt it was in my best interest to work with Mr. McCalla. Either way, we all sat in Frick's office until almost 9:00 p.m., trying to work out the details. I found myself gazing at my watch and looking at the clock on the wall. The thought of Scorpio was on my mind, but my business had to take priority.

Finally, we wrapped up our meeting around a quarter to ten. I thanked both Frick and McCalla, and couldn't wait to return the four missed calls I'd gotten from Scorpio while in my meeting. Mr. Mayor called too, so I called him first to get our business out of the way.

When I returned his call, he wanted the new design completed by tomorrow and asked for an early meeting with me. Knowing that it would be a bad move to tell him anything other than: I'd see him tomorrow—I told him just that. I got on the elevator, took it down to the lobby, and dialed Scorpio's number to call her back.

"Listen, I'm gonna have to take a rain check for tonight. I'll give you a call on Sunday, and hopefully, we can get together then," I said.

"Sunday? Yeah, I guess," she said. "Besides, I'm a little tired anyway."

"Yeah, me too. I have to reconstruct one of my designs for the Mayor's Group. It'll probably take me all night, but I gotta get it done."

"I understand. Just give me a call Sunday and we'll see what's up."

"Will do, baby. Until then, stay sweet, all right?"

"Sure," she said, and then hung up.

# Scorpio

# 17

Men. Now, that's the kind of mess that irks the hell out of me. You give them some pussy, and then, they come up with excuses not to see you again. Thing is, I had a feeling Shane was going to play me like he did. He got what the hell he wanted, so why follow through with the plan? I was sure him and Jaylin had a superb time comparing notes, but now, all they would have of me were memories.

No doubt, I was mad, but I sure wasn't going to trip. I'd just continue to do what I do best and that's make men crave for me like they're already doing. What Shane didn't know was he added himself to the top of my "dangle list". Meaning, I call the shots, not him. I'll dangle his butt on a string until I get tired, and whenever I do, I promise to cut the string and drop him like a hot potato.

I was so angry with Shane that I sat in my office with the phone resting in my hand. To hell with Sunday. As far as I was concerned, he'd never ever see me again. Furious, I picked up the phone and dialed Spencer's number. I had a feeling that he was the one who slashed my tires, so it was time I gave him a piece of my mind. When I called his house, a female answered. I wasn't surprised because I knew he'd move onto someone else, since he knew our relationship wasn't salvageable.

"So, I see you've already found yourself a new trick," I said. "I hope she can help you pay for the damage you've done."

"What do you want, Scorpio?"

"I want one thousand and fifty dollars for the tires you slashed. That was so immature of you, but what more can I expect from a man with such a little penis."

"Don't make me go off on you. I don't know what the hell you're talking about, but when I get to Jay's on Monday, you'd better be singing a new tune."

"You won't be coming in here anymore. I plan to call the post office and let them know who's responsible for my car, Spencer. I will also obtain a restraining order against you, and if you come near me again, I will have you arrested."

I hung up and didn't allow him to say anything else. Why would I listen to his lies anyway, when I damn well knew he was the one responsible for slashing my tires? Besides, who else would want to hurt me in such a way? Jamaica's man, Darious, came to mind, but when I talked to her about it, she told me he was with her that night. I really didn't suspect him because if he'd had it out for anybody, it would have been Bernie for aiming a gun at him.

As I was in deep thought, my cell phone rang.

"Hello," I said again, and got no response. The caller breathed heavily into the phone. I tried to distinguish the sound from a male or female, but I couldn't.

"You're one sad lonely fool on the other end of this phone," I said. "Spencer, I know it's you. I guess your li'l girlfriend is already exhausted from that pencil you just poked inside of her, and now, you have nothing else to do."

The breathing got heavier, and after I took a few deep breaths myself, I hung up. Whoever it was called back, and instead of listening, I turned off my phone.

I rushed out of my office to pay Spencer a visit. This shit was going to stop! I grabbed my purse and cell phone from my desk and headed out.

When I reached the shop area, I stopped to tell Bernie I wouldn't be back and I asked her to lock up for me when she was finished. She was waiting for Eva to come out of the restroom. I'd guessed since she was getting her eyelashes done, she'd obviously forgiven my ghetto fabulous establishment.

She came out of the bathroom and I gave her a fake smile. "I'm glad you decided to come back," I said.

"Bernie assured me I was in a safe place, so I'm cool with that. I still don't agree with how you conduct yourself as the owner, but that ain't my business."

I wanted to go off, but Bernie gave me a look that said "don't." Instead, I gave my good-byes to Yasing and Deidra who were still hard at work, too.

I was at Spencer's house in no time. Anxious to put him in his place, I hurried to the door and knocked. It took him awhile to answer, but he did. My eyes searched him over as he stood in the doorway with his cotton robe on.

"What do you want?" he said, while holding the door open.

"We need to talk." I moved forward, as if I wasn't leaving, and he opened the door wider so I could come in. It was hard for him to turn me away because I was dressed in a pair of hip-hugging white capris, revealing my thong. The peach tube-top I wore draped low in the front and showed my cleavage and ab-tight midriff. I saw him look down at my white strapped high-heeled sandals and work his way up to my face that he obviously adored.

"I have company, Scorpio. Can't this wait until tomorrow?"

Company or not, I strutted into his living room and stood by his couch. I folded my arms in front of me and pushed my breasts up to give them more boost. "You need to ask your company to leave. I don't understand how you could stoop so low and slash my tires like you did. And, the phone calls are annoying."

He walked toward me. "Look, I don't know what you're talking about. I didn't slash your tires, nor have I made any obscene phone calls to you. That's childish and I don't play those kinds of games."

I gave him a hard stare, and from observing Spencer, it didn't look as if he was lying. "It's not like you'd admit to doing it anyway, would you?"

"If I were that angry with you, hell yes, I would admit to doing it. As a matter of fact, I would want you to know I did it."

"Yeah, whatever," I said.

"Okay, now that we got that straight, do you think this li'l dick Negro can get back to his date? Since you didn't want me, I had to find somebody else. She's waiting for me in the dining—"

"Make her leave," I said, bluntly.

"I don't think so, baby. You got it, but you ain't got it like that."

I gave Spencer a seductive look and walked closer to him. I pressed myself against him and lowered my hand. It touched the outside of his robe and I rubbed my hand on his woodpecker that had already started to rise.

I then whispered in his ear. "Who do you see in your bedroom tonight? Her or me? You have five seconds to make up your mind and if I don't get a response I'm leaving." I helped him quickly make up his mind when I placed his hand between my legs.

He moved his hand back and smiled. "Give me five minutes and I'll be right back. Don't go nowhere, all right?"

I smirked, and as he headed off to the dining room, I took a seat on his couch. I picked up a workout magazine from the table and paged through it. Less than three minutes later, Spencer and "his date" came through the door. I stood up and gave her a back-off-bitch look as if I really cared that she was spending time with Spencer.

He spoke first. "Kayla, this is Scorpio. We kind of need to resolve some issues and I promise I'll call—"

I interrupted. "Spencer don't lie to her like that. Women don't like liars. All we ever want is the truth, and the truth is, Kayla, Spencer and I are about to have sex. Your being here will be an interference, so I told him to ask you to leave."

She turned to Spencer. "Do not call me ever again. And when I see you at work, don't say nothing to me, you got it?" she yelled.

Spencer didn't trip because he knew what he was about to get himself into. "Hey, no problem," he smiled. "I'm not an ass kisser, baby."

Kayla looked as if she was a classy lady and didn't even clown. I respected her reaction and watched as she made her way to the door. After she slammed it, Spencer walked over to the lights to dim them. He untied the belt around his robe and let the belt drop to his sides. His robe slid open and I glanced down at his dick that pointed in my direction. Again, what a huge disappointment. Playing this game wasn't worth my time, but I had to show him who was in control of things.

I gave off a fake smile and pulled my shirt over my head. Spencer came up and wrapped his arms around my waist. He reached for the zipper to my capris, and after he unzipped them, I pulled them over my big behind and they fell to the floor. I stood in my white thong, revealing all my goods. The thong was supposed to be for Shane's eyes only, but there I was with Spencer who I had very little desire for.

In my pretend mode, I rubbed his back as he lowered his head, and licked my nipples.

"I want to fuck you bad, Scorpio. Let's go to my room, okay?"

I smiled and lightly pushed him backward. "Lay back on the couch," I suggested. "Then, we'll go to your room."

Spencer backed up on the couch behind him and I eased my way on top of him. I placed my lips on his and our tongues danced a bit. I licked up and down his neck, and for a bit more entertainment, I lowered myself to lick his nipples. His hands were all over my ass, and to heat up things even more, I allowed him to feel the heat between my legs.

He attempted to enter me, but I backed up a bit and let the tips of my nipples touch his chest. He grazed them with his hands.

"Where you going, baby?" he asked.

"I—I forgot my condoms. And . . . I'm really not feeling this right now."

His jaw dropped. "What you mean, you ain't feeling this? And, you know I got some condoms."

I backed up again and stood up. I combed my fingers through my hair and continued to tease him with my almost naked body. "I mean, I just changed my mind about having sex with you."

He grabbed my wrist. "Hell, naw. You can't be changing your mind when we're in the middle of something like that. Come here and chill out."

I snatched my wrist away from him. "I said that I don't feel like it Spencer. At first I did, but now I don't. A woman has a right to change her mind, doesn't she? You know, just like you changed your mind about asking Kayla to leave. That was cold, and if you do that to her, what makes me think you wouldn't do that to me?"

He looked pitiful. "I would never do that to you." He held my wrist again. "Now come on and quit playing."

I snatched away again. "Does it look like I'm playing? I am serious as serious can get. I'll call you tomorrow," I said, already reaching for my capris on the floor.

He quickly stood up. "This shit ain't going down like this! How the fuck you gon' play me?"

"Spencer, you played yourself. I will never have respect for a man who did what you did. I don't care how desperate you were to get inside of me, if you had plans with somebody else, then you should have stuck to them. You very well could have fucked up a good thing, and for what?" I laughed. "For a piece of ass that ain't got no love for you." I reached for my capris and Spencer snatched them out of my hand.

"You fucking bitch," he said. "I should kick your ass for trying to play me. But, ain't no trip. Bitches like you come and go all the time."

"Good, Spencer. And if you have a gang of bitches like me in your life, maybe you need to start rethinking some things. It seems to me as if you might be getting played quite often. Now, if you wouldn't mind handing me my capris so I can go."

"I ain't giving you nothing." He reached for my shirt too, but I was able to snatch it from him and put it on. "Get the hell out of here. You'll have to fight me for your pants."

I guess he felt as if it was a problem for me to leave in my thong and a shirt. I'd once made my living as a stripper and showing off my body was never a problem for me. I reached for my purse on the table and tucked it underneath my arm. Still in my high heels, I swished my ass from side to side so that Spencer could get one last look at what he'd never have again.

"Fucking freak," he mumbled. "Whoever that mother-fucka Jaylin is tattooed on your ass, he must be a damn fool."

I opened the door and turned to Spencer. "It's men like you and him who make me do what I do best. Until you learn how to grow the hell up and be a real man, then only at that time will I show you some respect. Until then, if you want to see more of the power of my pussy, then call me again. I have no problem treating you like I do, and frankly, I enjoy it. In the meantime, stop calling my phone and stalking me. If not, you're going to wish that you never met me." I slammed the door and could hear Spencer yakking. By the time he made it to the door, I was already backing my car out of his driveway. I blew him a kiss and took off.

It was late, and I didn't want to go home dressed as I was. Instead, I called Maxwell to see if he wanted some company. I was still bitter about Shane so I needed something to tear into tonight. When I called Maxwell's cell phone, he told me to come on over. I suggested we meet at a hotel, but he insisted coming to his house was fine.

"Maxwell, I'm uneasy about coming to your house. Your wife is going to kill me and you, too."

"Scorpio, my wife left me. She's been seeing somebody, and she knows that I've been seeing someone as well. We decided to go our separate ways."

"Is that right," I said. I knew there were always two sides to every story, but since I was in the mood for a decent fuck, I really didn't care to hear it. "I'll be there shortly. I have minimal clothes on so don't be alarmed when you see me."

"Baby, I don't care what you got on. It's coming off as soon as you hit the door."

We laughed, but I knew Maxwell was serious.

When I reached Maxwell's house in the Hampton's of Chesterfield, it was way after midnight.

"Where are your clothes at?" he asked.

"It's a long story and I'll be happy to share it with you later. For now, just hold me."

Maxwell didn't have no problem accommodating my request. He walked with me to his bedroom where he had a blanket laid on the floor in front of an unlit fireplace.

I lay down on the blanket and he lay down to face me. I didn't want to hurt Maxwell, but a big part of me knew that eventually I was going to. By all means, he'd put me before his wife, and for me, that wasn't cool.

"What do you want from me Maxwell?"

"I don't know. . . .Why do you ask?"

"Because I don't know what else I can offer you but sex."

"Then, maybe that's all I want. With all that's going on between my wife and me, I'm not looking for another woman to take her place. I'm kind of looking forward to being free. We've been married for twenty-one years and I need something fresh and lively. I guess she feels the same way since she left me, but we need this time apart. Besides, being with you makes me feel rejuvenated. I've done things with you that I haven't even explored with her."

"That's unbelievable, but I want you to understand something. I—I don't want a relationship either. If you've ever thought about divorcing your wife for me, don't. This is strictly a sex thing between us, and whether we face it or not, someday it's going to run out. Meanwhile," I said. I rolled on top of him and pulled my shirt over my head. "I hope you enjoy my company as much as I enjoy yours."

Maxwell kept quiet. After I dropped a condom into his hand, I eased my pussy up to his face. As usual, he knew exactly what to do with both of them.

***

Sunday was here before I knew it. Leslie and I were at Tumble Drum with the kids, while sitting in a booth eating pizza. She seemed mad about something, and when I asked what was wrong, she played me shady.

"Fine," I said. "Then keep your funky attitude to yourself."

She rolled her eyes. "I don't have an attitude. I'm just ready to move out and get my own place, that's all."

"Well, Miss Brooks should be out by next month. Once I get the place all cleaned up and inspected, it's yours."

"I know, but I get tired of you doing everything for us. All I get is a damn welfare check and food stamps. I don't want to get a job because then I won't have nobody to watch the kids."

"Leslie, why are you stressing? I don't mind helping out, and as much as you help me out with Mackenzie, how can I trip?"

She smiled. "Be sure to remind me to hug you later. You're a decent li'l sister, when you want to be."

"And you're a decent big sister, when you want to be. Bottom line is, we need to help each other. I got your back and I know you got mine."

Leslie nodded and we continued to talk and eat pizza. The kids were having a ball and I loved to see Mackenzie's face light up with joy. As I watched her, my phone vibrated. I reached for it and immediately recognized the number. It was Shane. Waiting for this moment, I answered.

"Hello," I said.

"Hey. Did I catch you at a bad time?"

"No, not at all. I'm at Tumble Drum with Leslie and the kids."

"Ah, okay. Then, why don't you hit me back when you leave."

"I'm cool. What's up?"

"I want to see you today. You think you can make that happen?"

"Maybe. What time?"

"It's still early, so how about seven or eight?"

"Seven or eight sounds fine with me. If you don't mind me asking, though, what's on the agenda for the night?"

"It's whatever you want. I got a surprise for you, too."

I chuckled. "Can't wait. I'll see you soon."

"Bye, pretty lady," he said, then hung up.

I slowly closed my phone and looked over at Leslie.

"Who was that?" she asked.

"Shane."

"Girl, how many men you got? Don't you get tired of dealing with them damn fools?"

"Sometimes, but I only deal with them when I want to."

"Well, I hope you ain't sleeping with *all* of them. There are too many diseases going around and I hope you ain't putting yourself out there like that."

"Leslie, stay out of my business, okay? Like I said, I only deal with them when I want to and I do not have sex with all of them. I don't want to see Shane tonight, so he'll have to find somebody else to lay him."

"Then, why'd you tell him you were going to see him?"

"Cause I felt like it. Besides, I already made plans to meet my new flavah, Latrell, for a drink tonight."

"Girl, them games gon' get you in trouble. If you don't want to be bothered, then you need to say so. If you don't mind me saying, Jaylin has hurt you in so many ways that I don't think you realize it. You need to get over your hurt and move on in a positive way."

"Jaylin was nothing but some satisfying dick and a learning experience for me. Nothing more and nothing less. Never, ever will I give a man all that I gave to him. It's just not worth it."

Leslie kept quiet and so did I. She didn't understand, and as a matter of fact, nobody knew my pain but me. I was dealing with my hurt as best as I could, and standing up Shane for the night was just the beginning.

# Shane

# 18

Everything was progressing well. I'd finished my design for the Mayor's Group on time, and after I met with Mr. Mayor, he was more than pleased. The account was all mine, and even though I had my work cut out for me, it was well worth it. This one account was enough to get me on my feet and get things going. I hadn't made preparations to remove my other accounts from Davenports, but all of them would soon follow. Felicia had enough accounts to keep her afloat, and if anything, we were now considered competitors.

It was already 6:15 p.m. and I was on my way home from the mall. I took Scorpio's sketched picture to a brotha at the Galleria who could airbrush his butt off. He hooked it up for me, and once I had it wrapped, I couldn't wait for her to see her surprise.

When I got home, I took the picture to my closed-in patio and set it in the corner. I then slightly turned the vertical blinds to cut back on the sunlight that lit the room. Once I straightened the pillows on my wicker loveseat and chaise, I turned on some soft music.

I returned to the living room and picked up the package I'd dropped when I came in. I'd gotten some smell good oils and lotions to massage her body with and carried them back to the patio. I placed them neatly on the table, along with the soft towels I'd gotten to cover her up. I felt good about tonight, and wondered if cooking us something would be a good idea. Instead, I opted for Italian food, but I decided to wait until she arrived before I placed our order.

As Scorpio's arrival time neared, I took a shower and couldn't stop thinking about her. I couldn't wait to see her, and more than anything, I couldn't believe how my body craved for her more than any woman I'd been with.

My shower didn't take too long, and afterward I changed into a pair of dark blue silk pajama pants. There was no need for a shirt because I wanted her to see my cut body that she admired so much. I headed back toward the closed-in patio and took a look at the romantic atmosphere. All I had to do was light the huge round candle

I had in the center of the table and the mood would be perfect.

I lit the candle and it filled the room with a soothing strawberry fragrance. I sat back on the chaise and placed my hand behind my head. Trying to get my mind off Scorpio, I picked up the remote and clicked on the plasma TV on the upper wall.

For the next hour or so the basketball game kept me tuned in. Time had flown by, and as I checked my watch for the fifth time, it was almost eight o'clock. I mentioned seven o'clock, but I figured something must have come up and she couldn't make it that soon.

I continued to watch the next game, and as I got into that one, I didn't realize the time had ticked away. By now, my watch showed almost 8:45 p.m. and Scorpio was a no show. I wondered where she was, but before I could call her, she called me.

"Hey," I said, smiling while holding the phone up to my ear.

"So, I guess you knew it's me, huh?"

"Yeah, it's pretty obvious. The caller ID don't lie."

She gave a soft snicker.

"Where are you?" I asked. "I'm getting kind of lonely."

"I was on my way, but, uh, something came up. A friend of mine asked me to meet her at CJ's tonight, so I'm afraid I can't make it. How about we shoot for next weekend?"

Shocked by her news, I slowly sat up. "Uh . . . I guess that's cool. But, if you don't mind me asking, can't you meet your friend some other time?"

"I could, but I need to go handle some business at Jay's as well."

"Business? On Sunday? I thought Jay's was closed."

"It's closed, but that doesn't mean I don't have to work."

"Well, would it be asking too much for you to put it off until tomorrow? I really wanted to see you."

"I really wanted to see you too, but my business can't wait. Just like yours couldn't wait the other day."

I thought about it and she was right. "Go handle your business. I look forward to hearing from you next weekend, all right?"

"Sure. Sounds like a plan to me," she said. "Good-bye."

More than disappointed, I didn't even say good-bye. I had a feeling that Scorpio was bullshitting me, but I wasn't gon' trip. I lifted the candle from the table and blew it out. I stood for a moment, thinking about how I wanted to make love to her so badly. Hell, it had been on my mind all day, but there wasn't a damn thing I could do about it. I'd even picked up the phone to call her back, but I quickly decided against it. Instead, I tossed the phone on the chaise and went to my room to get dressed. I didn't want to be cooped up in the crib, so I left. I called Brandon to see what he was up to, and ironically, he told me he was at CJ's having a drink with a friend. I told him I was on my way.

When I arrived at CJ's, Brandon and a female companion were seated at the bar. He favored Malcolm X in many ways, and no matter where he went, he always wore a black suit. Brandon introduced his friend as Roshel, and I took a seat to join them.

"I ain't cock blocking, am I?" I whispered while leaning in close to him

"Naw, man, she's my sister-in-law. Her and my brotha having some problems and I've always made myself available for conversation."

Roshel looked at her watch. "I'd better get going. I'm supposed to meet Christopher at home and I don't want to be late. Thanks for the advice, Brandon. I'm glad I can always count on you."

"Anytime," he said, giving her a hug. "You be careful."

"I will," she said and told both of us good-bye.

Brandon watched her as she left the bar and so did I.

"She seems like a nice woman," I said.

"Very nice. It's my brother that got issues. Fool can't decide if he gay or straight."

"That's fucked up. But in instances like that, there really ain't much to decide."

"Yeah, I know. That's what I told her. She need to step while she ahead of the game. I love my brotha, but the shit he's put his wife and kids through makes me angry." Brandon took a swig from the shot of Hennessey in front of him. He looked depressed, as always. That was one reason I hated being around him and listening to his problems often made me feel down.

The bartender sat my glass of Rémy on the bar, and I took a swig from it.

"Why you out tonight?" he asked. "I'm surprised you and Sam ain't hanging out. What about Amber? You still hitting that, too?"

"Every blue moon, but Sam and I are over. During sex, she tried some crazy shit on me and I wasn't having it. I sent her flying faster than a jay bird."

Brandon laughed and we sat for awhile drinking and talking. I gave him the scoop on Sam, and told him about my departure from Davenports. He was shocked and said exactly what Jaylin said: He knew it was bound to happen.

As we continued on, I looked up and couldn't believe my eyes. It was Scorpio, along with a younger man who could have easily been 50 Cent's twin. He was even dressed in G-Unit clothing from top to bottom. He didn't seem to be her type, but what did I know? A bad boy seemed right up her alley, but what in the hell happened to this girlfriend she was supposed to meet? Brandon gazed at her, right along with me.

"Some brothas have all the luck. He got to be paid to have a broad like that by his side. She is fine, ain't she?"

I nodded and continued to check her out. She wore an orange sheer strapless jumpsuit that perfectly fit her waistline. The bottom of her pants flared out and moved gracefully with her as she walked to a table and took a seat. Her hair was slicked back into a neat ponytail, revealing every bit of her beautiful made-up face. No doubt, I had to let her know that I was there, so I stood up to do just that. Brandon grabbed my arm.

"Man, I know you ain't about to approach her. Her man looks like he'd bust a cap in yo' ass with no hesitation."

"I know her. I'm just going to say hello."

Brandon let go and I headed to the table where Scorpio sat. From a short distance, she saw me coming and dropped her head to look at the menu. I placed my hands in my pockets and walked up to the table. First, I addressed the brotha she was with.

"I ain't trying to start nothing, but do you mind if I holla at your date for a minute?"

He shrugged. "That's up to her," he said.

I looked at Scorpio. "Can we go somewhere and talk?"

"No. I'm with someone right now and I'll talk to you later."

Her response caught me completely off guard. It was as if she was a totally different person than the one I'd talked to earlier. "Let me get this straight," I said, as the alcohol was working me a bit. "You cancelled on me just to be with him? If you had plans to kick it with him, why didn't you say so? You could have saved me a lot of time and trouble."

"Shane, I don't owe you an explanation. Now, you're being awfully rude. We'll discuss this tomorrow, okay?"

I snickered and turned my head to the side. I could have messed her up for playing me, but I wasn't that kind of man. I looked back at her and shook my head from side to side.

"You are a piece of work. For whatever reason, I gave you too much credit, but you—" I paused and couldn't get the words to come out like I wanted them to. Instead of continuing, I turned to walk away. I took two steps, before turning back around. "Don't worry about explaining shit to me tomorrow. Make sure that my number doesn't exist in your thick head anymore and have a great fucking night."

Scorpio didn't say a word. She cut her eyes and looked at the fool sitting with her.

"Would you like to go somewhere else," I heard him say. I didn't know what her response was because my back was already turned. I went back over to the bar and finished off my shot of Rémy.

"I'm out of here," I said, slamming the glass on the table.

"You all right, man?" Brandon asked. "Do you need me to drive you home?"

"Naw, I'm cool. I'll holla at you later."

Before heading out, I gave Scorpio one last glance and left.

On the drive home, I couldn't believe how hurt I was. Damn, it was just some pussy and there I was tripping as if she was the best thing that had ever happened to me. My mind was all fucked up and I was starting to not only see what Jaylin had been through, but what Felicia said was starting to make sense to me as well. How could I let any woman have such an affect on me? I hadn't felt this way in a long time and this was a feeling that I dreaded more than anything. No doubt, I felt pussy whipped.

By the time I made it home, it was almost 1:00 a.m. I had a slight buzz, and of course, I was horny as hell. I reached for the phone on my nightstand and sat on the edge of my bed. I called my ex-girlfriend, Amber, who I'd been seeing on and off for some time. She knew my calls always came late at night and never had a problem answering her phone.

"Are you asleep?" I asked.

"I'm surely not up waiting for your phone call at this time in the morning. Hell, yes, I'm asleep."

"Do you feel like some company?"

She hesitated. "Shane, these late nights have got to stop. I have to get up for work by six and I be tired—"

"Then, don't worry about it," I said softly. "I'll catch up with you some other time." I hung up, and I guess after thinking about what I was capable of putting on her, she called right back.

"How soon can you get here," she asked.

"I'm locking my front door right now," I lied. "I'll see you in a bit."

She hung up and I looked around for my keys. I remembered tossing them on the couch in the living room, so I went there to retrieve them. Afterwards, I locked the door and headed to my car. No sooner had I looked behind me to back up, a car parked at the end of my driveway and blocked me in. When I looked to see who it was, it was Scorpio. We both got out of our cars.

"You need to move your car because I'm getting ready to go," I said.

"Go where?" she said, walking up to me.

"That's none of your business. Now, move your car and go home."

She got closer to me. "I can tell you are highly upset with me, aren't you?"

I reached for my car door to open it. "Your game has been played Scorpio. It's played out, and as a matter of fact, I suggest you take your seductive behavior back to the brotha at CJ's. That shit don't work with me." I hopped inside of my car and closed the door. Scorpio reached for the handle on my back door and opened it. She sat on the backseat and left the door open. I looked at her in the rearview mirror.

I was irritated. "What—what is it that you want?"

"I want to apologize for how I reacted tonight. I was wrong for coming at you like I did and it wasn't a good feeling."

"Okay, cool. Apology accepted, now get out."

"Why are you rushing me? You said that you wanted to talk to me and now I'm here. Besides, your bitch can wait. I know you're not leaving this early in the morning to entertain a man. I'd bet any amount of money that a booty call awaits you."

I opened my car door. "You're damn right it does. And she sure as hell don't play games like you do, so get out of my car." I reached for Scorpio's wrist to help her out. She snatched her wrist away and looked at me as I bent down and got loud with her.

"Don't make me get ugly out here. You are not in control of a damn thing over here. If you think you can disrespect me in front of another moth-erfucka, and bring your butt over here like shit all good, then you messing with the wrong bro-tha. I ain't never been nobody's fool and I never will be! Now, for the last time, get the fuck out of my car so I can go!"

Scorpio reached her hand up and smacked the shit out of me. "Who in the hell are you yelling at!"

Before I knew it, I grabbed her hand; she was about to smack me again. I dove on top of her and she fell back on the seat. I tightly held her wrist above her head and gritted my teeth as I spoke.

"Your hands better not ever make it to my face again! I'm not gon' play this same fucking game you played with Jaylin, Scorpio! If you're looking for somebody to fuck you and fight with you all the time, then you're barking up the wrong tree!"

My heart beat fast and so did hers. I released her wrist and she could still see how angry I was. Her eyes watered as she stared deeply into mine. She then placed her hands on my head and pulled it to her.

"Hell no," I said, avoiding her kiss. I removed her hands from my head and backed up. "We are not going out like this."

She quickly rose up a bit and grabbed the collar on my shirt. She pulled me to her and placed her wet lips on my ear. "Fuck me good, Shane. You know you want to feel me and I want you to bust this pussy wide open. I'm sorry for what I said, please forgive me. Let's put it in the past and I promise never to go there again."

Her soft spoken tone and words turned me the fuck on! And even though my mind was saying, "jet", my dick was saying, "get wet."

I couldn't believe I was thinking about giving into her. She continued on being persistent, and that's when I got rough with her.

"So, is that all you want to do is fuck?"

She nodded. "For now, yes."

I was so displeased with her response that I didn't even give a shit. I ripped down the middle of her jumpsuit and tore it apart. She was naked underneath, so it didn't take long for me to unbutton my shirt and lower my pants. Within seconds, I put my dick inside of her and gave her what she wanted—a hard fuck. I separated her legs far apart, as one rested high upon the backseat and the other touched the front seat. Her head knocked against the door as I made fast and quick entries inside of her.

"Are you getting what you wanted?" I said, pounding with anger. She didn't respond. "If you want me to treat you like a piece of meat, then I will. A slut? I can do that, too. And, while you're at it, just pretend that I'm Jaylin! That's who you want fucking you, don't you!"

She grabbed the back of my head and pulled on my neatly done twisties. She started to work her hips with mine, and when she gave me a hard kiss with her eyes closed, I figured she must have been thinking about him.

That angered me even more, so I picked up the pace and tried like hell to knock the thoughts of him out of her mind.

She was tense and held on tightly to my hips that were in fast action. "Stop this," she strained her words and squeezed her eyes tightly together.

I breathed hard, "Then what else do you want? You want me to fuck you from behind, in your ass, what? Or would you prefer that I start calling you bitches and hos?" I reached for her arm to direct her in turning on her stomach.

She looked up at me and tears rushed to her eyes. They soon fell from the corner. "You're hurting me," she said softly. "I don't like the way you're making me feel. I didn't mean for you to fuck me like this and this is not what I wanted."

I stopped my motion. "Then how do you want it? You tell me. All I want to do . . . all I ever wanted to do was make love to you, but you want to be fucked, you want to be disrespected, and you want a man who treats you like shit."

She moved her head from side to side. "No, that's not what I want."

My voice calmed. "Then, what do you want? Whatever it is, I can give it to you. A long time ago, I told you I was the man for you, but you wasn't trying to hear me."

"Well, I hear you now. I hear you loud and clear and I don't want to hurt anymore."

"You will never have to hurt as long as you do right by me. You gotta trust me and give me a chance, okay?"

She nodded.

I leaned down and kissed her. My dick had calmed down during our conversation, but it had made its way back up when she slid her tongue in my mouth. I reached for her right leg and wrapped it around my waist. She followed suit and wrapped both her legs around me. We continued to kiss and I rubbed my hand in circles while touching her soft hips, thighs, and ass. I went back inside and it was a different feeling for me. I closed my eyes and dropped my head on her chest. For the first time, I was making love to her. I wanted her to know what I was feeling, but my actions said it all. She lifted my face and made me look at her.

"Now, I love the way you make me feel," she admitted. "Don't you ever be so quick to give up on me, okay?"

All I could do was nod and hope that things would work out.

# Scorpio

## 19

I rolled over in bed and Shane was not there. We'd been at it all night, and finally settled things down in his bedroom. When he'd brought me into the house last night, he rubbed my body down with oils and lotions, and had me on fire.

Honestly, Jaylin made me feel good in so many ways, but being with Shane, something was different. I wasn't sure what it was, but he knew how to tease, knew how to please, and knew how to treat a woman.

I had to work hard on not comparing the two of them. It was hard not to, especially since they had so much in common. It was obvious that they must have shared notes because Shane knew a lot of my favorite positions. I was still trying to figure him out, and I had a feeling that the pleasure would be all mine.

When I looked at the alarm clock on his dresser, it showed five minutes to eleven in the morning. I hadn't called the house to check on Mackenzie so I looked around for my phone. I couldn't find it and realized I must have left it in the car. When I reached for Shane's phone to use it, I picked it up and listened to him talk to another female.

"But, you still could have called," she said. "I stayed up all night waiting for you, and now, I can barely keep my eyes open at work."

"Like I said, I apologize, but I fell asleep. Besides, it was kind of late and I didn't want to inconvenience you since you said you had to get up for work."

"You've inconvenienced me many times before. Why would you consider last night any differently?"

"I don't know, Amber, I just did."

"So, am I going to hear from you tonight? The least you can do is make it up to me."

"Maybe I'll see you later. We'll see."

"That's what you always say. You need to know that your booty call days are coming to an end. I'm going to simply stop making myself available to you in the wee hours of the morning. You act as if you can't call me at a decent hour. If you have a dispute with Sam, try to get into it with her early so I can stop getting phone calls late at night, all right? Damn!" she hung up.

I quietly placed the phone back on the receiver and got out of bed. I reached for Shane's paisley print robe and put it on. As I walked down the hall to find him, I seriously wanted to know who Sam was, and who the booty call chick was. It was obvious that she didn't have her head on straight because dick ain't no good when it's *only* available in the wee hours of the morning.

I went to Shane's office, but he wasn't there. I then headed through the kitchen and walked back to his covered patio. He was standing in front of the tall glass windows looking out. His hands were in the pockets of his 501 jeans that were unbuttoned and barely hanging on his butt. As I had a clear view of the side of him, his abs were solid as a rock and the muscles in his arms and chest showed mega bulges. I guess he sensed I was looking at him and he turned his head to the side. He'd trimmed his goatee and the look in his brown slanted eyes said he was happy to see me.

"How long have you been standing there?" he asked.

I inched my way forward. "Long enough to know that my man got it going on. You should've been a model."

He gave a soft snicker. "So, I'm your man today, huh?"

I wrapped my arms around his waist. He kissed my forehead and put his arms on my shoulders.

"You don't have to be my man, but I thought we cleared that up earlier today. You haven't forgotten what you said, nor did you change your mind, did you?"

"I remember what I said, but first, we need to talk."

A part of me didn't like where this conversation was going, but I took a seat to listen. Shane sat on the table in front of me and held my hands together with his.

"By now, I'm sure you know that I got some real strong feelings for you. I—"

"I know, and I—"

He placed his index finger on my lips. "Please, let me finish."

I nodded.

"Anyway, I need to clear some things up with you, okay?"

I nodded again.

"I hope you understand that I can not, nor will I try to replace Jaylin. We are two completely different men who view relationships entirely different. He's a changed man now, but the man who you remember can't be replaced by me or anyone else. I think you're very confused and I don't know if you're searching for something that you'll never get. If you are able to accept me for who I am, then I say let's continue to roll with it. If you can't, then hey, be honest and tell me I'm not what you're looking for. Again, I'm not gon' fuck you because I'm a man who likes to make love to his woman. I'm not gon' fight with you because a man and a woman ain't got no business fighting each other. And I damn sure ain't gon' go around disrespecting you because you deserve better than that. Do you understand what I'm saying?"

"I know where you're coming from, Shane, but I don't expect you to be like Jaylin. I—"

He didn't even hear me out before cutting me off. "Yes you do. You might not notice it, but the same shit—stuff you pulled last night is what you used to do with him. I'm not playing the fuck me, fight me game, baby. I've been there and done that shit before. I don't want to argue with you and then break out into a sweat fucking each other's brains out. That's crazy. It always feels good being inside of you, but the issues are still there once it's over. When we make love I want to go into it stress free. When I pull out, I still want to be stress free. Just allow me that and we won't have no problems."

"Like I said before, Jaylin is a man of my past. I was hurt, Shane, and seeing him again brought about more hurt. I dealt with it and continue to deal with it the best way I know how. I can't just open up and give to another man what I gave to him. I'm so afraid of getting hurt again. Nobody knows this, but when he left me, I damn near lost my mind. I couldn't think, I couldn't eat, I couldn't sleep, and more than anything, my child basically had a mother that didn't exist. He was my everything, Shane, and it was so hard for me to move on without him."

"Baby, nobody should be your everything, but God. I'm in no position to be your everything and neither was Jaylin, but you've got to trust me. My mama taught me that when things don't work out, that means there's something better in store for me. You might not realize it now, but something good is waiting for you. Eventually, if you want to be happy again, you've got to find it in your heart to trust somebody, so why not me? All men are not after the same thing. We are not all game players and some of us do know how to love a woman the way she deserves to be loved. Women mess up by always putting us into the same category. You are so blind not to see what's in front of you and I hope that you don't miss out on a good thing, like so many others—all because you don't want to open your eyes and see what's there for you."

I placed my hands over my face to cover my eyes. I hated being this emotional, but it had been a long time since I'd discussed the hurt from my relationship with Jaylin. Shane kneeled in front of me. He rubbed his hand along the side of my face and moved my hand away from my teary eyes.

"I want you to get all of your cries out now. After today, I don't want you to shed another tear over the past. I'm here for you now and that's all that matters."

I tightly wrapped my arms around Shane's neck and broke down as he held me in his arms. He had me figured out. I thought about all I'd done by giving my body to men who wanted nothing from me but sex. I'd been feeling as if I was the one in control, but in reality, they controlled me. I'd never left any of them feeling as fulfilled as I did with Shane. He had so much more to offer me and his compassion for me was a major plus.

I got myself together, and we lay on the chaise in his patio room. He lightly rubbed my arm, while I rested my head on his chest.

"Would you do me a favor?" I asked.

"Anything," he said.

"When you talk to Jaylin, please don't tell him what I told you. I never want him to know how much I'd gone through after he left."

"I had no plans to tell him. Besides, he doesn't want to know about us anyway."

"Good," I said. I closed my eyes and felt so much more at peace, now that I'd gotten some of the pain off my chest.

Shane and I took a lengthy nap on the chaise. He woke me up about an hour ago and said that he was going into his office to do some work. Still a bit tired, I continued with my nap. When I woke up, I saw the sketched picture he'd drawn of me that was now an airbrushed picture. It was off the chain and I hurried up to go look at the most well put together piece of art I'd ever seen. Wanting to thank him, I went to his office to do just that. When I walked in, his back was turned, and he looked to be indulged with the design in front of him.

"Ricardo," I said. He didn't answer. I spoke again. "Shane."

He quickly turned around and looked at me standing with the picture in my hand.

"Thank you," I said. "Was this my surprise?"

"Yes. I also had something else waiting for you, but you've already gotten plenty of that."

I put the picture down and sat on his lap. He wrapped his arm around my waist and swung his chair around to face his design.

"What do you think of this?" he said.

"I think . . . I guess it looks nice. All it looks like to me is several buildings connected."

"Woman, you don't know nothing about a creative design when you see one. One day soon, you're going to see this building in it's entirety in downtown St. Louis. And when you see it, I want all the credit that is due to me."

"Okay, I'm impressed."

"Are you sure? You don't sound too impressed," I said.

"Shane, I'm impressed with everything about you. I just hope I can get my act together."

"I hope so, too," he laughed.

"Now, you need to get some stuff together as well," Scorpio chimed in.

"Hey, my stuff is together."

I shook my head. "No it's not," I said jokingly, as I thought about the phone call I listened to earlier.

"Oh, yes it is."

"If it is, then what are you going to do with your booty call woman? It seems as if she makes herself available to you whenever you call."

"Who, Amber?" Shane said.

"Yes, Amber. Are there more I should know about?"

"Naw, it's just Amber. But, she knows what time it is. I've been wrong for running to her like I did, but it's so hard not to when she always makes herself available. Now, though, I'm with you so things . . . things will be different."

"So, are you sure Amber is the least of my worries? With a man as fine as you are, I can't believe she's been your only sidekick."

"Well, that's it."

I looked at my watch and gave him a hint. "You know, *Sam's* wholesale warehouse closes around ten, don't they?"

"I guess," he said, still not catching on.

I tried again. "Uncle *Sam* be taking all my money. How about yours?"

"Being self employed, yes, he does. He hits me hard every year."

I continued, "You know, I once knew this brotha name *Sam* who—"

Shane tightly grabbed my thigh. "If you want to know about Sam, all you had to do was ask."

"I asked if there was anybody else and you said no."

"I said no because she and I are O-v-e-r. Not because of me and you hooking up, but I really wasn't feeling her. She tried some freaky shit on me in the bedroom and I didn't like it."

"Who in the hell is freakier than me? I hope I haven't done anything to turn you off, but I noticed that you're a hard man to please. You'll have to tell me what makes your body quiver."

He laughed, and then gave me a silent stare. He leaned me back on the floor and kneeled in between my legs.

"How did you know about Sam and Amber?" he asked while looking down at me.

"I'll confess if you tell me what makes you tick."

"I'm about to show you, once you tell me what I want to know."

"I listened to your phone call with Amber earlier. You tried to break her down gently, but I didn't like the words, and I quote, 'Maybe I'll see you later.' I hope her later never comes."

"It won't," he said. He separated my legs and pecked down my thighs. When he untied the robe I wore, it fell to my sides. He rubbed his hand on my stomach and worked his way down to touch the minimal and neatly trimmed hair on my pussy.

He made a ticking sound with his mouth.

"Just touching me makes you tick," I asked.

"No, but tasting you does."

His ticks got louder as he lowered himself and opened me up wider with the tip of his curled tongue. He circled it around my clit and placed his thick fingers inside to juice me even more. As he worked me so well, it quickly came to an end when he vibrated my insides. I could never contain myself when he loved my insides, and he was so much better at oral sex than Jaylin. I backed away from the feeling, but my legs had goosebumps and trembled.

"You all right," he said.

"I am fine. You just gotta let me, you know—cool out after that. Besides, you made my body quiver. And even though your mouth ticked, I didn't make your body quiver."

"Is that what you think," he said. He got on his knees and stretched his jockey shorts down so I could see his pipe. It plopped out and revealed his juices. "Every time I go between your legs, I let go. When I close my eyes, usually, I'm bringing myself down."

"But you never say anything. You don't flinch, you don't moan, you don't scream, nothing."

"Is that what you want me to do?"

"Yeah, say something. I need to know how good my pussy is. I can't tell with you trying to play it down like it ain't do you no justice."

He crawled up to me. "Aw, don't you worry your pretty li'l self about that. Yo shit, girl!" he yelled. "Make a man wanna fu . . . make love all day long!

I can't eat, sleep, drink, work, or go to the bath-room without thinking about it. Just make sure you stay well within my reach, all right?"

"You can leave your thoughts about me out of the bathroom. If you do that, I promise to be at your beck and call so you can make love to me whenever or however you want."

Shane promised to take me up on my offer, after he finished his work—he had gotten so busy with it. I told him I'd catch up with him later and left to go spend some time with Mackenzie.

I was on cloud nine leaving Shane's house. Before going home, I stopped by Jay's to check on things. When I pulled up, I was surprised to see three police cars outside. I hurried out of my car and noticed my windows had been spray painted. From what I could see, the words bitch and ho were not only on my windows, but on the frame work as well. I panicked and ran up to one of the officers.

"When did this happen?" I asked. "Who did this?"

"Ma'am, move out of the way. We're trying to conduct business."

"I'm the owner. My name is Scorpio Valentino."

"Miss Valentino, we've been trying to get in touch with you for about an hour. One of my officers drove by and noticed your place had been vandalized."

"Is anything missing?"

"I'm not sure. You'll have to go inside and see for yourself."

I took a deep breath and went inside. As I looked around, nothing seemed to be missing. I went back to my office and opened my safe. My money was still there, so it was obvious that this was another opportunity for somebody to get at me through vandalism. I told the police exactly what I thought and mentioned my tires being slashed the other day. This time, I gave Spencer's name, as I seriously thought he might have something to do with it, especially after how I played him. I was sure he was upset with me, and he wasn't about to let things die down.

The police stayed for awhile, checking for fingerprints. First, I called Leslie to check on her and the kids, and then I called Shane to tell him what happened. He said he'd be right over to help so I waited for him to come.

# Shane

## 20

Felicia was getting carried away with the shit. I called Davenports, and since she didn't answer, I left a message for her to call me back. I figured she was even more upset since McCalla and I had worked out the details about canceling my partnership with Davenports, and this kind of shit was right up her alley.

By the time I reached Jay's, Scorpio was outside talking to an officer. She looked highly upset and I walked up to comfort her.

"Why does this keep happening?" she asked while hugging me. "I think I know who's responsible."

"You do," I said. "Did you tell the police?"

"Yes, I did. And I'm about to go to the courthouse to get a restraining order against him."

"Who is him?"

"This guy named Spencer. He delivers the mail at Jay's and I've been seeing him off and on. I kind of played him, and ever since then, he's been on a roll."

I wasn't sure if Scorpio was barking up the wrong tree or not. "Have you been home yet?"

"No." She sounded frustrated.

"Well, go handle your business at the courthouse. After that, go home and chill out for awhile. Let me take care of this mess. I got a friend who can fix you up in no time."

Scorpio took her arms from around me. "Are you sure?"

"Yes, I'm sure."

"Thanks a lot, Shane."

We walked to her car, and then she gave me the keys to Jay's and left. I went inside and talked with the officer about my speculations. Unfortunately, he couldn't do much without proof, so Felicia was off the hook for now. The officer left, then I called Craig to see if he could come by and take care of the windows for me. He said he'd come by to give me an estimate within the next hour or two.

I searched for something that might help remove some of the spray paint off the windows. During my search, my phone vibrated. I reached for it clipped to my jeans and looked at the number. It was Felicia.

"What is your problem?" I asked.

"I don't have one, but you do. I'm suing you for taking business away from Davenports that I helped you with. If you have anything else to say to me, you need to talk to my attorney."

"Do as you please and I've already talked to Frick. I mentioned the Mayor's Group to him and he said it's up to them who they want to go with. You can't be mad if Alexander & Company was their choice."

"Alexander & Company my ass! I know Jaylin's got his hands in the pot somewhere, doesn't he? The only reason you're doing this is because of him. I show you a fucking CD and you go ballistic. This could have worked out between us, but noooo, you had to go—"

I could tell she was about to cry as her voice kept cracking. "Felicia, calm down, all right? This ain't no big deal. It was time to move on and Jaylin didn't have anything to do with it. Your attitude and the way you treated our partnership is what tore us apart."

"I told you I was sorry."

"Well, sorry just don't get it all the time."

"It should, especially when you know how hard it is for me to admit I'm wrong. And, I was wrong, okay? You've heard me say it, so come back to Davenports and work this out with me."

"No can do. I accept your apology, but it's best that we leave things as they are."

"I gave you a chance and I guess we'll be competitors. I promise to steal every building contract from underneath your nose."

"You can't steal it if you ain't better than me. And, you know for sure, you can't touch my creativity with a ten foot pole."

"Bullshit. I'm going to prove to you what I'm capable of—you'll see."

"I hope you ain't capable of cutting tires and spray painting buildings."

"What?"

"You heard me. I know you don't like Scorpio, and if you're the one responsible for vandalizing—"

Felicia laughed. "Are you telling me that somebody is out to get your bitch? Is that what you're saying?"

"Watch your mouth. I'm saying—I hope you ain't responsible for what's going on over here."

"Shane, listen, I haven't the slightest idea what you're talking about. I don't have time to deal with Scorpio's issues. She caused me much wasted time in the past and I'll be damned if I let anything about her consume me. Whoever is doing something to her, more power to them. It ain't me."

"I gotta go, all right?" I truly didn't want to hear her bash Scorpio again.

"Why? 'Cause your feelings are hurt? Every time I say something about her, you get so bent out of shape. You know it's because I speak the truth. She's a whore, a tramp, and a skeeza. She is going to take your heart and stomp all over it. You thought what I did was bad, but just wait. I've warned you and you can do sooooooooooo much better."

"Felicia, shut up. I told you before that I don't want to hear it, didn't I?"

"Okay, fine, but can we meet for dinner this evening? I want to clear up a few things with Davenports and wish you well with Alexander & Company. Frick said it might be a good idea for us to reconcile our differences."

"I don't know if I'll have time to meet you yet. I'll call you later."

"Don't forget. If you forget, I'm calling you. We really need to get some things squared away, all right?"

"All right," I said, and then hung up.

I stood for a moment and thought about Felicia. Maybe she wasn't the one responsible. Scorpio said she knew who it was and I definitely knew how far some men would go over some pussy.

Craig came by and gave me an estimate to paint the frame work and clean the windows. He said he could come back later, as long as someone would be here. I called Scorpio to see what time she would be back.

"I want to spend some time with Mackenzie today. She misses me, and with all that's been going on, I don't know what Spencer is after. I'm kind of afraid."

"Just take all the time you need. I'll stay here and whenever you get finished, come on back. Trust me, you have nothing to be afraid of, especially if you're with me."

"Thank you. And if you have something to do, I can always call Bernie. She'll be more than happy to stay there until your friend gets finished. How much is he charging me anyway?"

"A whopping one thousand, four hundred, and fourteen dollars. He gon' take care of the paint job and your windows, too."

"I knew it would be expensive. I have about a grand in a safe in my office. If you wouldn't mind giving him the rest until I get there to repay you, I'd appreciate it."

"I got you covered. I already paid him."

"Shane, no. I can afford to pay for my own stuff. Besides, Spencer is going to reimburse me for everything. I'll make sure of that."

"Scorpio, you need to stay away from that fool. Did you get a restraining order?"

"Yes, I sure did. And I already called and told him about it."

"What did he say?"

"He's still in denial. Pretending as if he don't know what I'm talking about. And the sad thing is, I really can't," she paused.

"Can't what?"

"I don't know if he's the one responsible. Something inside of me is saying he's not the one."

"Well, why don't you hire a private detective to check things out for you? At least, that way, if he's responsible, you'll have some evidence to put him in jail."

"I just might do that. In the meantime, I'll see you later."

"Later, pretty lady."

"I love it when you call me that."

"I call it as I see it. Now, get off this phone and go handle your business so you can hurry back to me. I miss your butt already."

"Dang, already?"

"Yep. And I hate it, too."

"Why is that?"

"Because it's the first sign of being in love."

Scorpio was quiet. "Why would you hate being in love?"

"Because it ain't no fun being in love by yourself."

"No it's not, but just know that I miss you too, okay?"

I snickered. "See ya later."

"Bye," she said, and hung up.

I closed my phone and clipped it back on my jeans. At this point, I really wasn't sure how I felt about Scorpio, but I knew my feelings were strong. More so, I knew I hadn't felt this way about any woman I'd been with for a long, long time.

Craig was back in no time. While he handled his business, I went back to Scorpio's office to chill. She had a plasma TV on the wall so I turned it on and sat back in her chair. After flipping through the channels, nothing interested me so I found myself getting a tad bit nosy. I opened her desk drawers, and the first thing I saw was a cracked picture of Jaylin. I chuckled a bit and figured she must have thrown it against the wall or something. As I searched further, I came across a blue notebook that clear as day had My Daily Journal written on the front. I opened it and saw many pages of written entries. I wanted to read it, but I couldn't. I hesitated a bit, and then put it back in her drawer.

I tapped my fingers on her desk, and I couldn't help but have a quick change of heart. I got up to lock the door and hurried back over to her desk to get the journal. I tapped it against the palm of my hand, deciding if this was something I wanted to do. Finally, my mind was made up as I walked over to the couch to take a seat.

I opened the journal to the first page, and it started with the day Jaylin left her. Even though she'd explained to me how she felt, there it was in black and white.

> *I feel as if I'm losing my mind. I love him more than life itself. I don't want to live without him.*

There are times where she circled her tears that must had fallen on the pages. I felt so bad for her, but I was so into it that I had to go on.

> *Finally, I allowed myself to meet a man. His name is Andre. He's adorable, but he's nothing like my Jaylin. I hadn't had sex in awhile, so I gave myself to him at his office today. It was just okay for me, but afterwards, something funny happened. I wanted to run like hell and cry. So, I did. He's been calling me like crazy, but I've already given him the big X. So . . . . . . . . . . . . . . . . . . Next.*

As I read on, Scorpio wrote about one man after the next. Same story, different day. She hadn't kept a stable relationship for more than three weeks. I flipped through several pages until I saw Spencer's name. At this point, it seemed as if he'd been around for awhile, just as much as Maxwell. She complained royally about the size of Spencer's dick, but said he was, at times, good company. As for Maxwell, it was obvious that she was feeling something for him. She wrote good things about him and said if he wasn't married, maybe things would be different. According to her journal, he was sexing her quite often. Mostly at hotels, but they'd been doing it in awkward places like, at the movies, in the elevator, in a bathroom stall, at the park, in his office, in her office, damn—even at a nightclub? Reading this shit was kind of pissing me off, but of course, I continued.

By now, the memories of Jaylin were starting to affect her again. I skip through a few more pages and she wrote that she was in desperate need to see him so she contacted me. Her getting in touch with me and finding out that he was coming to town was the best thing that happened to her all year. I read on and found out what she thought of me during dinner.

*Shane gave me all the information I needed. If I know Jaylin like I think I do, I'm sure he'll stay for Shane's cousin's party and I'll be waiting. Since Shane informed me Lady Ice would be the entertainment, I plan to contact her and make arrangements to rain on their parade. As for ole Shane, he's looking even better these days. I might have to put him on my "to-do" list, but we'll see.*

I skipped through several more pages and was truly shocked by what I saw next.

*They both looked like sad puppies. I was in control and they knew it. If I had my way, I would have fucked them both. The thought of being between them, and both fucking me, can't stop crossing my mind. I'd want Jaylin's lengthy hard meat inside of me and Shane's tongue to turn me out. He was a master at eating pussy and my memories won't let me forget. I've got to make this threesome happen, I just have to. Especially, after feeling Shane's dick touch me today. It was so smooth and I couldn't believe how thick it was. Had a head on it that would surely wet my walls.*

*Had Jaylin not been staring at me, I would have put Shane inside of me and fucked his brains out. I knew he wanted me . . . I could tell. Either way, I couldn't go wrong. Jaylin and Shane? It was any woman's dream come true.*

Her words messed me up. Not only that, but at this point, I was turned on by her thoughts. I had no idea she was feeling for me, like I was feeling for her. Either way, I continued, as things started to get rough again.

*I couldn't go through with it. For whatever reason, I didn't want to burden myself with bad memories of him going back to Nokea. I know I'm not supposed to hate, but I do. She has the life I want. She has the man I want to be with. How in the hell can another woman have what I want? I swear I hate this feeling and I wish it would go away. I can't stop the tears. Maxwell . . . here I come.*

The next few pages consisted of her intimate moments with Maxwell. It was clear that she was hurt and he was where she could lay her head. And at times, so was Spencer again, and a name I hadn't seen before, Terrell. This shit was unbelievable that a woman could put herself out there so badly. Not only that, but why? Why did I have to feel so strongly for her? I wasn't sure if I'd be added to this journal and my page would run out, as many of the other brothas had. I continued on and the last thing she wrote about was the day after she and I had sex at my house for the first time.

> *Shane's dick was everything I imagined it would be, and then some. It was almost as good as being with Jaylin, but it fell a tad bit short. Maybe because a part of me still yearns for him. Damn, I still love him! Maybe being with Shane is going to change some things. The way he touched and teased me in the shower made me feel like a new woman. I can't get the thought out of my mind, and I sit here, craving for more of him. My pussy is thumping and it can't wait to feel him tonight.*

On the last page was.

> *I'll cancel that bastard and buy me a new one! How dare him cancel on me tonight, after I've been thinking about him all day. And, the lame excuse about doing some work, please! Adios, Ricardo, it was good while it lasted.*

I knew there had to be more, so I rushed over to her desk. I was anxious to find out if she'd had sex with the brotha I saw her with at CJ's. If she had, that meant she had sex with him first and then with me just a few hours later. As I rambled through her drawers, I saw a box of opened condoms. I hoped and prayed that with all the sex she'd had, at least she was smart enough to use them. We hadn't, so I was skeptical. I continued to search for another journal and came to a halt when my phone buzzed. It was Scorpio, so I sat in her chair and took a deep breath.

"Hey, baby," I said, answering.

"Hi. How are things going?"

"Cool, cool. Craig should be finished in a li'l bit."

"Okay. And, thanks again for staying there. I know you had some work to do at home."

"Naw, I'm all right. Like I said, he's just about finished, and afterward, I'm gon' head back home."

"So, what's the play for later? Is it okay if I spend the night with you again?"

"It should be. What time are you coming by?"

"I guess around eleven. Is that too late? I want to make sure Mackenzie's asleep before I leave."

"Naw, that's fine. Besides, I'm supposed to meet Felicia for dinner. We need to work out a few things pertaining to Davenports."

"Well, why don't you just call me when you get finished?"

"Most definitely," I said.

She said good-bye and hung up.

Now, I was feeling a bit guilty for reading her journal, but it was too late because the damage had been done. If anything, I knew it made me look at her in a slightly different way. I understood her pain, but some of the stuff she did was taking shit to the extreme. As much as I enjoyed making love to her, I had to seriously consider condoms. I'd always been one to protect myself, but stupid me wanted to feel the real deal.

When Craig knocked on the door and told me he was finished, we both headed out and I locked the doors. I called Felicia on her cell phone and told her to meet me at Cardwell's. She said she was on her way, so I headed to Forsyth Boulevard.

While in the car, I called and made reservations. I arrived shortly thereafter and the maître d' sat me at a table. I was pleased that he sat me near the door because as soon as Felicia started to make a scene, I would be on my way out.

I waited for her, and almost thirty minutes later she strutted in, talking on her cell phone. She was nicely dressed in a lavender pants suit and her braids had been removed. Her hair was styled with a short layered feathered cut and she wore it well. Her makeup looked as if it was freshly painted and so did her thin eyebrows that had a thinly trimmed high arch.

I interrupted her phone call and called her name so she could see me. She smiled and ended her call.

"That was Frick," she said. I stood up and pulled her chair back so she could take a seat. "He's pleased that we're having dinner to talk things out."

"Felicia, I didn't come here to talk things out. I came here to make peace with you so that this transition can go smoothly for us."

"Yeah, well, I don't know how smoothly you expect it to go. If you think I'm going to let you have the Major's Group, you're sadly mistaken."

"It's Mayor's and not Major's Group. That's just how much time and effort that you put into the project. So little, that you can't even get the name right."

"Whatever the hell it is, you owe me something for my time."

"Realistically, I don't owe you nothing. Jaylin was the one who landed that account and it now belongs to me. If you get anything out of the deal, it will be minimal. Jaylin said he's going to direct the Mayor's Group elsewhere."

"You must have told him about the CD, didn't you?"

"Yes, I did. And, he's not too happy about it either, Felicia. Simply because he don't understand, neither, how you can be so devious after all he's done for us?"

"Again, Shane, I'm not being devious. Don't blame me if you two got caught with your pants down. If you never—"

"Look, I didn't come here to talk about that. We need to stick to business and not focus on shit that really ain't none of yours."

Felicia rolled her eyes and picked up a piece of bread from the table. She broke it in half and put a tiny bite in her mouth. While chewing, she looked suspiciously at me.

"What?" I said.

"You haven't told me how gorgeous I look."

I laughed. "That's because you haven't given me a chance. As a matter of fact, I love the hair. It looks nice, as well as the outfit."

"The one thousand, seven hundred, and fifty dollar outfit—that is. I picked it up at Saks yesterday."

"Okay . . . and, it looks nice. So there."

She continued to look suspiciously at me.

I laughed because her stares were funny. "What is it?" I said again.

"You get cuter by the day. Your flawless skin, your thick lips, and I must say that your bedroom eyes make me sick. I hate that, once again, the Playboy Bunny has yet another victim wrapped around her finger. She needs to package-up her pussy and put it on the market."

I couldn't help but laugh. As I was cracking up, my phone rang. I looked down to see who it was, and to my surprise, it was Jaylin.

"I need to get this," I chuckled and placed the phone on my ear. "Hello."

"Negro, are you sitting down," he yelled.

"Uh, yeah. Why?"

"Because I am the luckiest man in the entire world!"

"Okay. Now, calm down and tell me why."

"'Cause I am finer than any motherfuckin' body you know, I got just as much money as Donald Trump—not quite," he laughed. "I have the most beautiful children in the world, my nanny loves me, and my wife . . . boy, do I thank God for my wife! She's having my baby."

"She's pregnant?"

"Yes, fool, yes!"

"Well, congratulations are in order, again."

"Thanks, man, you just don't know how I feel! My legacy is in the works once again!"

"I'm happy for you and I know how anxious you were to have another child. I'm gon' have to come down so we can celebrate."

"Yeah, you do that. As a matter of fact, since you'll be the godfather again, why don't you make arrangements to come down this weekend? Besides, you haven't visited in awhile and LJ and Jaylene are always glad to see you."

"I most certainly will do that. Is Nokea around?"

He spoke anxiously. "Yeah, she's sitting on my lap. Hold on a second."

"Hi, Shane," Nokea said.

"Congratulations. Jaylin tells me that you gon' be a moms again."

"Yes, I am taking my final journey. I'm not looking forward to picking up all this weight again, but I know it's all worth it, especially to see my husband with such enthusiasm."

"Yeah, he sounds pretty excited."

"Him and Nanny B, both. I don't know which one of them will turn flips first. You'd think we'd just won a three hundred million dollar lottery over here."

"It's better than the damn lottery," I heard Jaylin yell from the background. "And, this journey is just beginning."

I heard lips smacking. "Trust me, Shane, you won't be getting this phone call ever again. Three children are enough for me. Thanks for the congrats, and from what I hear, I guess I'll be seeing you soon."

"Yes you will. Until then, stay sweet and tell Jaylin I'll give him a call later."

Nokea said that she would and hung up. I apologized for being rude to Felicia, as her ears were wide open and her arms were folded in front of her.

"Don't tell me that bitch is pregnant again?"

"No, I don't know of any bitch pregnant, but Nokea is."

"How many times is she going to lay on her back! It's ridiculous how stupid some women are. I've heard of being barefoot and in the kitchen, but she's running out of kitchens. It angers me that Nokea has spent damn near her entire life trying to please Jaylin. It must be nice to lay on your back, twenty-four–seven, get pregnant, and pop out babies for a man who's a player. How lucky she must feel?"

I shook my head. "You are a cold person, Felicia. Jaylin and Nokea love the hell out of each other. This ain't got nothing to do with her laying on her back for him. She is his wife and I'm sure that having their children is the best feeling she could possibly have."

"Of course it's the best feeling ever. I'd be happy, too, if I was sitting on a gold mine by having three babies by his ass. She knows damn well what she's doing. If she walks today, tomorrow, or any other day, her ass is set for life. Her and them rug rats. If I'd had my head on straight, as much as he'd put me on my back, I should have popped out a baby or two for him. I would've taken him for every dime he got."

"Well, thank God for condoms. Besides, ain't nobody cutting into Jaylin's finances but him. So there."

Felicia's mouth hung wide open. "Are you telling me that . . . that stupid—I don't even know what to call her if she signed a prenuptial agreement."

"I didn't say that, you did."

"Shane, she didn't, did she?"

"No. As a matter of fact, I don't know because it ain't none of my business. Now, either we gon' get back to discussing Davenports, or else, I'm taking off."

"I know she did because I could see her with a pen in her hand going, 'It's okay baby—anything that makes you happy.'" Felicia dropped her head back and rolled her eyes. No doubt, I'd had enough.

"I'm out. Call me when you get all of this out of your system."

I did the usual and dropped a fifty dollar bill on the table. After that, I left Felicia there to discuss her issues with herself.

# Scorpio

## 21

Shane called and said he'd made it home. Mackenzie was sound asleep, so after I gave her a kiss, I went downstairs to tell Leslie I was outtie.

During my drive, I had the top down on my Thunderbird and listened to "Again" on Faith Evans' *First Lady* CD. Her song surely hit home, as I sung the lyrics out loud. By the time I arrived at Shane's place, I sat in the car and finished the final verse. I must have replayed it at least five times before heading to his door.

I heard Shane coming to the door, and when he opened it, he was on the telephone. All he had on was his gray jockey shorts and a pair of white socks. I could tell he'd just gotten out of the shower because his body smelled awfully fresh. He leaned down and gave me a quick peck on the lips. I followed him to his room, and he stood by his dresser.

"Yes," he said to the person on the phone. "I'll be paying by credit card." He read off the numbers, wrote something on paper, and ended his call.

"Sorry about that," he said. "I'm, uh, going to Florida this weekend. I had to make arrangements."

"Florida? Why?"

"I, uh . . . I'm suppose to meet Jaylin so we can take care of some things with Alexander & Company."

"By the way you hesitated, I would assume that was a lie. Besides, you told me Jaylin wasn't going to be as involved with your company. If you are making plans to go see another woman—"

Shane put his arms around me, seeing me get upset. "Look, I didn't want to tell you the truth because I didn't want to upset you, okay?"

"Upset me how?"

"I'm going to Florida to visit my godchildren, and . . . to celebrate the new baby they're expecting."

My heart dropped to my stomach. "Nokea's pregnant?"

"Yes."

"Well, good for her. I hope you have fun."

"I'm only going to be gone for the weekend. I'll be back late Sunday night."

"That's fine," I said, quickly changing the subject. No doubt, my feelings were hurt. "How much do I owe you for Craig's work?"

"I told you that you didn't have to repay me."

"I know what you said, but I don't mind paying you back. Besides, I learned a valuable lesson about letting a man take care of everything for me. It's best that I do things for myself."

Shane could tell I was a bit on edge so he tightened his arms around me. "Hey, I got an idea. Let's go to this li'l jazz club down the street. It's nice and quiet and they don't close until 2:00 a.m. It'll give us a chance to listen to some soothing music and relax."

I took his arms from around my waist. "Baby, I really don't feel like it. I'm kind of tired from running around with the kids all day and this vandalizing stuff is working my nerves. Can we just cool out tonight? We'll go some other time."

"If you insist. I'll run your bath water and find you something to change into."

"Thanks," I said.

While Shane got my water ready, I sat on the edge of his bed and slowly removed my clothes. I couldn't help it that my thoughts were right back on Jaylin. Why did him and Nokea have to be so happy together? I couldn't have his baby for nothing in the world, but Nokea was popping them out like crazy. I wished like hell that Shane would have never told me, but stupid me, I had to know the truth.

I finished removing my clothes and went into the bathroom where Shane sat on the edge of the tub testing the bubbling water.

"I hope it's not too hot," he said.

"I'm sure it won't be." I placed my foot in the water and it was perfect. I sunk down in the tub and leaned back until the water touched the edge of my chin. Shane kneeled down next to me.

"Can I get you anything else?" he asked.

"You can give me a kiss."

He leaned forward and sucked my lips into his. We kissed for awhile and then he backed up.

"I'll be in the bedroom. If you need anything else, just holla."

I nodded. Shane dimmed the lights and turned on some light jazz on the intercom. He then closed the double doors to the bathroom and left me at peace.

Warm water and bubbles was one way to put me to sleep. When I woke up, the water was cold and the bubbles had dissolved. I wiped my face with my hands and stepped out of the water. I reached for the fluffy cream towel on the counter and went into Shane's bedroom. He was lying in bed sound asleep. He looked so peaceful that I didn't want to wake him. However, since I wanted him to make love to me, I had to make him aware.

I quietly crawled on the bed, until I was face-to-face with him. I pecked his lips a few times and then pecked my way down his chest. That wasn't enough to wake him, so I slid my hand inside of his jockey shorts and rubbed the smooth hair above his dick. It flopped out of his shorts and I couldn't wait to taste him. I covered his goods with my mouth, knowing I was in business when I felt his fingers roam through my hair. I couldn't see his eyes because my head was low and my long hair was spread out on his stomach.

"Mmmm," he softly moaned. "Come . . . come here for a minute."

I gave him a few more licks and eased up to him. "Yes," I said. He cuffed my face with his hands.

"You are not required to have sex with me every time we get together. Some times, I don't mind just chilling."

I stared down at Shane. "Put your hand between my legs," I politely asked. He hesitated, so I took his hand and placed it between my legs. "Does that feel like I want to chill?"

He cracked a tiny smile and his fingers went to work. Just so he didn't feel cheated, I turned my body around, which put us in a sixty-nine position. I let him finish his business, and as always, continued on with mine.

The loud sounds of my cell phone constantly ringing awakened us. I reached over Shane and looked for my pants on the floor. When I found them, I pulled the phone out of my pocket and yelled into the phone.

"What is it?"

No one responded. Soon, the heavy breathing started. I quickly closed my phone. "I don't have time for this shit this morning."

"Who was it?" Shane asked, while rubbing my ass that was clearly in his view.

I lay back down next to him. "It was somebody playing on my phone. I know it's the same person who's been causing me grief. They've been doing it for quite some time now."

"Then, get your number changed. Have you talked to a private detective yet?"

"I had planned to get around to it today." Just then, my phone rang again. Shane reached for it this time.

"Hello," he said. He said hello again. After that, the caller must have hung up.

"Yeah, you need to get your number changed. How long has that shit been going on?"

"Since all this crazy stuff started happening. I don't want to get my number changed because so many people have it. It would be a real inconvenience."

"Baby, you gotta do what you gotta do. Don't just sit back and let nobody harass you like that."

"I know. And, trust me, I'm going to find out who is responsible for all of this mess."

I had to use the bathroom, so I got up to go tinkle. Shane watched me as I walked to the bathroom, handled my business, and came back. I got back in bed and cuddled with him.

"I have a confession to make," he said.

"What?"

"You have one of the nicest, plumpest, well shaped asses that I've ever had the pleasure of seeing."

"Damn, how many asses have you seen?"

"Plenty. Trust me, there's been plenty. And that's what lets me know I'm working with something original."

"Well, thank you. And I must say that you have a nice chocolate ass, too. It's one that's soft as a baby's bottom and squeezable as Charmin. And boy, can that sucker go to work."

We both laughed.

Shane rubbed his hand on my ass again and I could feel exactly where his fingers were at. They were scrolling across Jaylin's name tattooed on my butt.

"You got a problem with that, don't you," I asked.

He nodded. "It kind of throws me off sometimes. I be in the middle of doing my thang, and bam, his name flashes right before me. I'm puzzled . . . why'd you go do something like that anyway?"

"Because I was stupid. And, I thought we'd be together forever. I've been thinking about getting it removed, but I heard that it hurts."

"If it hurts, I'll help it heal."

"I'm sure you will."

My phone rang and Shane and I both reached for it. He got to it before I did, but this time, he said it was Bernie.

"Hello," I said.

"What time are you coming to the shop?"

"I'll be there shortly. I kind of got myself into something I don't want to get out of right now."

"Well, get some for me and hurry it up. I got a 10:00 a.m. appointment that's probably waiting for me."

"Bye, girl. I'll be there soon."

I dropped the phone in my hand and took a deep breath. "I have to go let Bernie in this morning. I'm sure some of the other ladies might be waiting for me too."

"Well, go handle your business. I'll be here all day and I'm not going nowhere."

"But . . . but I was hoping to put a li'l something on your mind until I get back."

"I need to work on getting you off my mind so I can get some productive shit done around here. Besides, I meant what I said earlier, baby. I don't want you to feel as if you have to always give yourself to me sexually. Nor do I want our relationship to be based on just that. When I get back from Florida, I got another surprise for you."

"Another surprise? I'm not sure if I can handle your generosity. And as for us being intimate all the time, I enjoy it just as much as you do. If I have sex, it's because I want to. I have no control over my pussy tingling. If it tingles, it just tingles. Just like right now, it's tingling again. You've got to help my tingles go away."

"You always know the right things to say, don't you?" Shane said, putting me into position.

When I pulled up and saw three of my stylists, and a few customers outside waiting, I felt kind of bad. I hurried to open the door for them. I took a good look at the windows and paint job, and was pleased by what I saw.

I was glad that Bernie was the only one who knew I was being entertained by Shane, but you'd better believe that as soon as we got inside, she let me have it.

"All I'm saying, Scorpio, is these customers need to come first. Now, I can deal with you being a little late, but waiting for an hour is ridiculous." We walked back to my office.

"Bernie, I had a rough day yesterday and I needed somewhere to relax. I apologize for being late and if you lost out on any money, I'd be happy to replace it."

She held out her hand. "Barbara waited for awhile and so did Diamond. Both of them left, so two heads will cost you two hundred dollars."

I stood by my desk and opened my purse. I pulled out two hundred dollars and walked it over to Bernie as she stood in the doorway. "Here," I said. "Now, I don't want to hear your mouth anymore."

She snatched the money from my hands, then walked over to my desk. She laid the money on top and rolled her eyes. "You need to save that money for Mackenzie. I was only kidding, but I'm not kidding when I say that people don't like to be standing outside waiting. That's poor business, and in this economy, I can't afford to lose more business."

"I'm sorry. My vandal got my mind kind of tripping. And, being addicted to Shane ain't helping me one bit either. I'll feel so much better when I find out who's responsible for all this mess."

Bernie threw her hand back. "Girl, you know it's Spencer. It used to make his day when he came in here to see you. Now that you've cut that off, that Negro probably going crazy."

I agreed with Bernie and we walked toward the door. I looked over to my right and was shocked to see my journal on the table in front of the couch. I knew I hadn't left it out, so after Bernie left, I closed the door behind her and locked it.

Thinking hard about how it got there, I picked up my journal and flipped through it. I had an idea as to who'd left it there, so I went over to my desk and opened my drawers. Surely enough, someone had been rambling through my things. Question was, if he would lie to me about it? I picked up the phone and dialed Shane's number.

"Hey, baby," I said, "While you were here yesterday, did you do anything to keep yourself busy?"

"No . . . I mean, I watched TV. Why'd you ask?"

"The television must have gotten awfully boring."

"It was cool."

"But, I bet it wasn't cooler than my journal, was it?"

"Huh?"

"Shane, don't 'huh' me. You know what I'm talking about. You read my journal, didn't you?"

"What journal? I didn't see—"

"I can't believe you would lie to me about something so tedious."

"Look, I don't know what you're talking about. You might want to ask somebody else if they read it. It wasn't me."

I was silent and we both held the phone without saying anything. He was the first to open his mouth.

"Okay . . . I confess, but I kind of found it by accident."

"By accident? So, you just accidentally opened my drawer, pulled out my journal, and forced yours eyes to read it?"

"I didn't read *all* of it. I only read some of it."

"But, baby, those are my thoughts. My personal thoughts. I didn't want to share any of that with you. Let alone, make you aware of all my business."

"I'm sorry. I was wrong and I apologize. Why you making a big deal about it and you even said yourself that it wasn't that serious."

I got mad and hung up the phone. When he called back, I didn't even answer. And after reading through my entries that I hadn't read since I'd written them, I was embarrassed. I dropped my head on my desk and laid it on my arm. Shane knew a whole lot of things about me and I wasn't too thrilled to be with a man who knew that much.

After I read the entry about my desires to have a threesome with him and Jaylin, I tossed my journal to the floor. And Maxwell . . . Shane knew about the wild and freaky things I'd allowed him to do to me and vice versa. I could have cried. How dare him come into my office and invade my privacy like that. Then, lie about it? Disgusted, I got my journal off the floor. It was no longer for my eyes only, so I ripped out the pages and searched for my shredder. I sat at my desk, shredding the pages one by one. My phone interrupted me, and of course, it was Shane.

"What?" I spoke in a dull voice.

"Are you really that upset with me?"

"Hell, yes, Shane! I can't believe you would read my stuff like that."

"Damn, what's the big deal!" he yelled. "It ain't like it was a surprise or nothing. Besides, I didn't get all bent out of shape when you listened to my phone call the other day."

"This is totally different. I picked up your phone by accident. You deliberately went through my drawers and read my journal. I hope like hell that you found what you were looking for."

"Hey, I'm gon' say this one more time. I was wrong and I'm sorry. I can't take back what I did, but I really didn't expect for you to trip like this."

"What makes you say that? If that were the case, when I asked if you read it, you wouldn't have lied. And then, you have the nerve to ask me to trust you? How am I supposed to trust you and you over here going through my shit and lying to me when I ask you about it?"

"Look, stop acting like a drama queen. It's really not a big deal."

"So . . . you know about every intimate detail that I've experienced in the past two years and you're telling me it's not a big deal?"

"Hey, all I know is you're a freak." He laughed.

I sat up straight. "What did you just say?"

"I said . . . some of the shit in there was kind of freaky. Which makes you a freak. I'm a freak, too, and I for damn sure won't deny it. So there— we both some freaks."

"Okay, Mr. Freak Ass Motherfucka, don't call me no damn more. Since I am such a freak and a drama queen, why don't you pretend that I never came back into your life?"

"If you continue to talk to me like that, I will have no problem ending this," he spoke casually. "I told you before that I'm not up for a bunch of—"

"Kiss my ass," I said and hung up.

I nearly broke the phone into pieces by slamming it so hard. I couldn't believe all this was happening over a journal that was none of his business.

I got back to shredding my pages. I cleaned up and took my trash bag to the dumpster behind Jay's. As I made my way back inside, I noticed a white Maxima parked close by with tinted windows. I squinted to get a look at the license plate, and as soon as I did, the Maxima quickly sped off. I tried to catch up with it, but whoever was inside didn't want me to see them. I didn't see a face, but I for damn sure knew what kind of vehicle the person who was after me drove.

I hurried back inside and asked everybody in the shop if they knew of anyone who drove a white Maxima with tinted windows.

Jamaica pressed her finger against her temple and closed her eyes like she was in deep thought.

"Uh, uh, damn! What's his name . . . he played in *Boyz in the Hood* with Morris Chestnut."

"Ice T?" Bernie said.

"Bitch, it was Ice Cube and he wasn't driving no white Maxima in that movie either," I said.

"Ice T, Ice Cube, whatever," Jamaica said. "Bringing up their names done made me kind of thirsty. I'm gon' have to go to the kitchen and get me some Ice Water."

Everybody cracked up.

"Y'all I'm serious," I said, unable to contain my laughter. "I want to know if anybody personally knows somebody who drives that kind of car?"

"A white Maxima?" Deidra asked.

"Yes," I replied. "With tinted windows."

Everybody shook their heads, except Jamaica. She, of course, had another vague memory.

"Now I remember," she said, holding her forehead. "Damn, how could I forget? It was Nettie in *The Color Purple*. When she went back to that house at the end and reunited with Celie, she drove a white Maxima with tinted windows."

The whole place just burst into laughter, and Jamaica kept at it, rocking herself back and forth. "All my life I had to fight," she said, sounding just like Oprah.

"Girl, stop," I laughed. "You need to bring Tyler Perry up in here so you can audition for one of his movies."

She cleared her throat and laughed. "You know darn well that if I brought Tyler Perry up in here, I wouldn't even have time to audition because you'd be in here trying to screw him."

"Ooooooo's, and daaaang's," echoed throughout Jay's.

"Ha, ha, ho," I said. "I ain't mad at you for speaking the truth and don't hate on me cause I got it like that."

I broke out the high-fives with everybody in Jay's.

"I'm sorry, but I have to back up Scorpio on that one," Bernie said. "She has certainly had herself some fine men."

"As much as I hate to admit it," Jamaica said. "I must back her up, too, anytime she can bring Hollywood #1 and #2 up in here. And, I'll be damn, here comes Hollywood #3."

All heads turned to the door as it opened. In walked a tall, dark, thicker than thick brotha with a dirty white T-shirt on and some greasy looking jeans. Sweat dripped from his forehead and he wiped his oily hands across his lips.

"Anybody got a Coke soda?" Jamaica said. "We must be in that commercial." I gave her a shove.

"May I help you?" I asked in my professional mode.

"I've been working construction out front. I cut my hand on some glass and wondered if I could get a band-aid or something."

"Somebody get her out of here right now," Jamaica said, pointing to me. She looked at the brotha still standing by the door. "Baby, just hang on a second. I'm gon' get you a band-aid, some ice, some water, and possibly some of these chicken wings I fried for my lunch today. I'll fix you up real good, okay?"

He couldn't help but laugh and planted a wide smile on his face that showed his pearly whites.

Jamaica rushed off to the back. When she came back, I was standing next to the brotha while observing the cut on his hand. She pushed me out of the way.

"Let me see how bad it is, sweetie," she said, taking his hand.

I folded my arms and let her show continue. She wiped his cut with a towel and placed the bandage over it. She then gave him bottled water and offered him some chicken wings she had in a greasy brown paper bag.

"No, no thank you. I appreciate your kindness."

"Anytime," she said.

He reached for the doorknob. Before opening the door, he turned to his side and looked directly at me. "What did you say your name was?"

Jamaica and I introduced ourselves to him at the same time. She looked over at me. "He wasn't talking to you. He was talking to me."

I kept quiet.

"Nice to meet you both," he said and walked out.

"See," Jamaica said. "You done scared that man away wit yo ugly self."

"Girl, I'm not going to argue with your silly butt. You just mad because he couldn't keep his eyes off me. Everybody up in here knows that while you were back there playing the little housewife, he was up here flirting with me. He asked what my name was and I told him Miss Valentino. He couldn't remember it, so that's why he asked again."

"Jamaica, I think you'd better try and try again," Bernie said. "Hollywood #3 will soon be giving Scorpio a key."

Jamaica rolled her eyes at me. "I can't stand yo ole light skinned gorgeous hoochiefied self. Next time, just stay yo butt in the back."

"If or when, Miss Hater, he comes back in here. I'll be sure to let him know that you're interested. As for me, I'm not. I already got enough served out on my plate that I can't handle."

I lifted my hand in Jamaica's face and walked off. I chuckled on my way to my office and had forgotten about my disagreement with Shane. Just that fast—I was feeling bad, so I picked up the phone to call him. The first time, he didn't answer, but when I called back again, he picked up.

"Yeah," he said. I assumed he knew it was me by his dry tone.

"What are you doing?" I asked.

"I'm busy right now."

"So, I guess you're going to stay mad, huh?"

"You know what? You play too many damn games for me. Did you or did you not just cuss my ass out and hang up on me?"

"Yes, I did. And, you deserved it for calling me a freak and a drama queen."

"I got a feeling that you've been called a whole lot more than that. But, when it comes to me, you want to constantly play your damn games. I'm not the one, Scorpio, so you told me not to call you no more and I won't."

His stubborn ass hung up on me. Fine, I thought. If he wanted to call this off, that was dandy with me. We'd see how long this lasted.

# Shane

## 22

I was all packed and ready to go to Florida. I needed a break because I had so much on my mind. Mr. Mayor had me busy all week, so I really didn't have time to do much else. I'd even gotten another call from one of my previous clients who needed some ideas thrown out to him pertaining to building a new restaurant. I worked minimal time on his design and promised myself I would get to it as soon as I could.

I was so indulged with my work that I hadn't had much time to think about Scorpio not calling me or me not calling her. It really didn't hit me until I sat in my office on late Thursday evening and doodled around with my new design. I kept pausing and thinking, thinking and pausing until I got up enough nerve to call her. I dialed the first few numbers and put the phone back down. As I held the phone in my hand it rang. Not even looking at the caller ID, I quickly answered.

"Hello," I said.

"Hi," a voice said.

I didn't recognize it. "Who is this?"

"How soon do we forget? It's Sam."

"Aw, hey, what's up?"

"Nothing much. I haven't heard from you in awhile and I wondered what you were up to."

"I've been busy. Busy trying to sort things out with my new business."

"So, that's why you haven't called?"

"No, I haven't called because the last time we were together, things didn't work out too well. Now, how soon do we forget?"

"You sound bitter about something. Would you like for me to call you back?"

"How about I call you?"

"If you had thought about calling me, then you'd know that my number has been disconnected. Several weeks ago, I moved to New York. If you'd like my new number, I'll be happy to give it to you."

"What is it?" She gave it to me. I told her I wrote it down, even though I hadn't. "I'll call you back later."

"Don't forget."

I didn't respond and hung up. This on and off shit with women was driving me crazy. One minute, everything was cool, and the next it's like . . .

"nigga, don't call me no more." Then when they call, all is to be forgotten. Fuck that, I've said it before and I'll say it again, games are only for people who wish to play them.

Knowing that I had to get up early to catch my flight, I finally shut down about midnight. I poured myself a shot of Rémy and carried it to the bedroom with me. I sat on the edge of my bed and placed the glass close to my bottom lip. After I shot the Rémy down my throat, I put the glass on the dresser in front of me and fell back on the bed. My eyelids drooped, and within seconds, I was out.

I could always count on the phone to wake me. I jumped up and reached over to answer it. It fell to the floor, so I had to search the dark room to feel for it.

"Yeah," I said, squeezing my tired eyes together.

"Shane it's me, Amber. Did I wake you?"

No doubt, I was disappointed that it wasn't Scorpio. "Yeah, I'm really tired, though. Can I call you back tomorrow?"

"I wanted to know if I can come over. A few of my friends and I went out tonight and I'm not in the mood to go back home."

I yawned. "Listen, I'm a bit tired. I have to catch a plane early tomorrow morning so I need all the rest I can get."

"You can rest on the plane. As many times as you've called me in the middle of the night and I'd gotten up for you, I'm sure you can get up for me."

"Amber, you want to fuck and my dick is too tired to wake-up. If you come over here, you will be disappointed."

"And the next time you call my house in the middle of the night, you'll be disappointed, too."

I wanted to say, "I doubt it" but I kept my mouth shut. Amber told me to have a safe trip and said she'll be in touch soon.

After her call woke me up, I couldn't go back to sleep for nothing. I tossed and turned. Turned on the TV and flipped through the channels. I even went for a jog and lifted some weights. It was obvious that I was trying to keep my mind off Scorpio, but I wasn't doing too much of a good job of it.

I was delighted to see the sun come up. I showered, ate breakfast and headed for the airport. By 7:45 a.m., my plane was on the way to Florida.

# Scorpio

## 23

Well, I'll be darned. Here goes this miserable and sick feeling again. Every time I allow myself to fall for a man, and things don't work out, why do I always get this feeling? After what happened between Jaylin and me, I promised I would never feel this way again. But there I was, sitting up in my bed, thinking about Shane.

I hadn't talked to him all week and I for surely thought he'd call and say good-bye before he left on Friday. But, so much for that. I knew he was gone and I wasn't going to sit around the house feeling sorry for myself until he got back. At this point, I wasn't even sure if I'd ever hear from him again.

On Saturday, Leslie had gone to Jay's for me so I could get some rest. So much for that, as all I could hear were the kids downstairs screaming and hollering. I could tell they were playing so I stayed in bed and cooled out. I'd broken the bad news to Leslie the other day; Miss Brooks who lived in my apartment building wasn't moving out. She changed her mind and I didn't have the heart to tell her she still had to go. Leslie wasn't too thrilled about it, but I reminded her that she could stay here for as long as she wanted. I told her how much I appreciated her helping out and I called a travel agent to purchase tickets to Disney World. Her and the kids were pretty excited about going and they couldn't wait until next weekend. Having so much on my plate, I opted not to go. There was no way I could leave Jay's for seven whole days, and considering the problems I was having with my stalker, now wasn't the appropriate time for me to go anywhere.

At least I can say whoever's been responsible, they'd kind of chilled out. Nothing out of the ordinary had happened, and they hadn't called my phone since Shane answered it that day. I found that quite odd, and I wasn't sure if it meant anything or not.

By 6:00 p.m., I was ready to go to Jay's and trade places with Leslie. I took the kids to the mall and they cut up. I must have yelled at least a million times but it was as if nobody heard me. When lil James took it upon himself to stuff candy in his pocket, as if nobody was watching,

I'd had enough. The lady at the store treated him like a straight-up criminal. She called security and they came to the store and lectured him. Lectured him so hard that it made him cry. Damn, it almost made me cry and that's when I went off and almost got myself arrested. I knew he was wrong, and by all means, all he had to do was ask me to buy the candy and I would have. I told him exactly that and he said he was sorry.

No doubt, Leslie had her hands full, but so did I with Mackenzie. She was a prissy child who had to have everything she saw. And if I didn't get it, she'd throw a tantrum. She'd been doing that for years, but it was one more thing I could thank Jaylin for. He gave her any and everything she wanted and I was sure she hadn't forgotten.

Jay's was packed. There was nowhere to park, so the kids and I had to park on a parking lot further down the street. When I walked inside, it was noisy as ever. Gossip, gossip, and more gossip was going on. Jamaica was being her normal self and she and Bernie were at it again. Yasing was even arguing with one of her customers who claimed she'd lost her money and didn't have enough to pay. When Miss "this place is too ghetto" Eva walked in, I hurried to my office. Eva yelled out loudly, asking if anybody wanted to purchase tickets to a concert. Apparently, she couldn't make it and everybody was trying to get them.

I made the kids go to the lower level and play, and then headed for my office. The door was open and Leslie sat at my desk while paging through a stylist magazine.

"Don't you hear all that noise out there?"

She nodded. "Yes. That's why I'm back here."

"Girl, you have got to get some order in this place. Not only that, but you need to get some order with your kids."

She closed the magazine. "What happened? I'm sure you didn't make it through the day without any drama."

I told Leslie what happened at the mall and she was furious. So furious that she barely said good-bye. All she said was the kids and her would see me at home.

Since I'd gotten to Jay's, things had calmed down a bit. By now, it was almost midnight and I went back to my office to call Maxwell who'd been calling me like crazy. It wasn't like I was trying to play him off, but since things were going pretty smooth with Shane, I saw no need to call Maxwell anymore. Either way, I called and he wasn't thrilled about me avoiding him. He spoke in a deep, smooth but stern voice. It was like Leon's voice from *The Five Heartbeats* and always had a way of turning me on.

"Baby, you know it wasn't cool for you to just cut me off at the snap of your finger. We've been through too much for you to do that."

"Maxwell, I've been busy. I wanted to call, but every time I picked up the phone, something always came up and required me to put it back down. Don't take it personal, okay?"

"I'll try not to. What do you have going on for the rest of the evening?"

"Nothing, but it's getting kind of late."

"Then, why don't you bring your sweetness to me? I'm at the Marriott downtown. I just finished up a business dinner and I got myself a suite."

I hesitated, but then thought, what the hell? "I'll be there shortly. What's your room number?"

Maxwell gave me his room number and I waited until nearly everyone had left. Deidra and I left together, and just so I didn't have to walk down the dark street to my car, we got in Deidra's car and she drove me to mine. I got out and told her to have a safe ride home.

On my drive to the Marriott, I thought about having sex with Maxwell and felt uneasy about it. Even though I had a disagreement with Shane, I was positive that it wasn't over between us. And as much as I convinced myself I would never call him again, I knew I was lying to myself. I had my cell phone in my hand and dialed his number. The phone rang two times and when his voice mail picked up, I almost had a lost for words.

"Hi . . . uh, it's me. I hope you're having fun in Florida and call me whenever you get a chance. Bye." I paused. "I . . . I miss you. Hurry home so we can make up, okay?"

I closed my phone and made my way to the hotel.

When I entered the room, Maxwell was down to his robe. He was wrapping up a phone call and had already placed me on his lap while he talked. I could tell how happy he was to see me because he kept smiling and rushed to end his call. Whoever he was conversing with, kept running their mouth, and at times, he held the phone away from his ear and pecked my lips.

Anxious to get this over with, I stood up and removed my clothes. It was my attempt to get him to hurry up with his call so I walked over to the tall glass windows and looked outside. Still on the phone, Maxwell came up from behind and wrapped his arm around me. He pecked down the side of my neck and lowered his hand to touch between my legs. I closed my eyes and leaned my head back, thinking of Shane. I wondered what he was up to. Had he been thinking about me, too?

Maxwell continued to rub me, and I looked outside at the many people walking around. What quickly caught my attention was a man standing down below with a camera in his hand. He seemed to be focusing it in my direction, but I wasn't sure. I moved Maxwell's hand and backed away from the window. I then reached for the curtains to close them.

"John," Maxwell said. "Listen, I need to end this conference call. I'll call you on Monday and we can go over this more in detail. It's late and I'm really beat." He paused. "Okay . . . all right . . . sure." He tossed the phone on the bed. "Baby, I am really sorry about that. He called right before you came and I couldn't get him off the phone."

"It's okay," I said. "Business is business."

I knew exactly what Maxwell wanted to do first so I sat on the edge of the bed and widened my legs. He smiled and kneeled in front of me. He placed my thighs on his shoulders and I fell back on the bed. Normally, I'd sit up and watch him, but today, I didn't feel like it.

As his tongue entered me, I looked up at the ceiling and then closed my eyes. What would Shane do if he knew I was here once again? Would he even care? He said to hell with me, but I know he didn't mean it. So what I'm about to let Maxwell fuck me. And, fuck me good too, especially since—my cell phone rang. I looked at it on top of the dresser and quickly sat up.

"I need to answer that," I said, interrupting Maxwell.

"Not now," he said. "Get it later."

"I need to get it now. It might be important."

Maxwell backed up and I got off the bed. My phone had stopped ringing, but whoever it was left a message. I dialed my voice mail number and listened to the message. It was Shane: "I got your call, sorry I missed it. I guess you're not answering because you're busy. You'd better be good and I'll call you when I get back. I miss you too, pretty lady."

A wide smile covered my face and I was so ready to get the hell out of there.

I closed my phone and grabbed my skirt from the floor. "Maxwell I . . . I have to go. That was my sister and she needs me right now."

"Aw, come on baby. Is it that important?"

"More important than some dick? Yeah, I would say so. Maybe we can hook up tomorrow."

Maxwell sat on the bed with an attitude as I put on the rest of my clothes. I said good-bye, but he didn't respond. Oh well, I thought, and closed the door behind me.

***

When Sunday rolled around, I was anxious to hear from Shane. I didn't know what time his plane was coming in, but I hung around all day and waited for his call. By days end, I was disappointed. I'd even called his phone but got no answer. Maybe, just maybe, he decided to stay another day. If so, at least he could return my phone call to say so.

Monday came and went and so did Tuesday. Still, no Shane. By now, yes, I was letting it bother me. I had an attitude with everybody at Jay's and Leslie didn't even want me around. I couldn't help it, but how dare him not call me. My last message to him was yesterday, and after that, that was it for me. I didn't want to appear desperate to see him, but I sure as hell missed being around him. I thought he'd missed me, too, but what did I know? Him and Jaylin were probably having the time of their life. I would bet some money on it that Shane had him a thing or two in Florida going on. And, how stupid of me to play Maxwell like I did for nothing? He'd been calling me, but I was discouraged and didn't want to talk to him at all.

It was already 9:00 p.m. on Wednesday and I was so ready for Jay's to close. I was looking through some financial papers on my desk and Bernie buzzed into my office.

"What's up, Bernie?" I asked.

"Your assistance is needed up front."

I huffed. "I'll be up in a minute."

I placed my glasses on my desk and wiped my tired eyes. As I headed up front, I noticed the few women in the shop all staring outside. There was a black stretch Lincoln limousine parked out front and a chauffer stood beside it.

"Who they—"

Bernie shrugged her shoulders. "I don't know. The chauffer came in and asked for you."

"Who's inside?"

Everybody said they didn't know. I walked to the front door and pulled it open. The chauffer smiled at me.

"Miss Valentino," he said.

I nodded. "Yes."

He opened the back door. Somewhat afraid to see who was inside, I inched my way forward to see. As he was leaned back in the far corner, my eyes started from the bottom and saw the shiny black leather shoes, the black pants, white crisp button down linen shirt that was unbuttoned, and his pearly whites when I reached his face. His cologne was enough to make me go crazy and his index finger was placed gently on the side of his temple.

"Are you coming inside to have a seat or not?"

I hurried inside of Jay's, tossed Bernie the keys, and told her to lock up. Then, I slid in the backseat of the limousine, far away from him. The chauffer closed the door.

"What is this?" I asked. "And why haven't you returned any of my calls?"

"This is the surprise I told you about. I didn't call you back because I didn't know you called. I lost my phone after I left your message on Saturday night. Did you get it?"

"Yes, I got it."

"Good," he said.

There was silence as he stared at me from the other end of the limousine.

"Why do you always look at me like that?" I asked.

"Because you are a very beautiful woman to look at. And—I'm wondering why you're sitting over there when you should be sitting over here next to me."

"I'm sitting over here because the last thing I can recall, you were highly upset with me. Are you telling me all is forgiven and forgotten?"

Shane gave off a soft snicker. He touched the intercom button to talk to the chauffeur.

"Cedric, you're moving a bit too fast. I need you to drive real slow to our destination."

"How slow is real slow, Shane?"

"I mean, so slow that I don't want to feel us moving. And if you can't drive that slow, then drive around the Lou for awhile. Either way, make this about a . . . two hour ride. Lastly, turn up your music so you can't hear anything."

Cedric laughed. "I got it, boss."

Shane looked at me again, and I folded my arms in front of me. He unbuttoned the few buttons on his shirt and leaned forward to remove it. He then slightly leaned back and unzipped his pants. He didn't slide them down, but he got on his knees and scooted over to me. He knelt between my legs and rubbed his hands on my hips.

"I am really, really sorry for reading your journal and lying to you about it. Had I realized the consequences would cost me days and days without you, I never would have done it. I missed the hell out of you and I'm so glad to see your pretty face once again."

I offered no response. I'd been missing him so much that my mouth couldn't utter one word. All I could do was hold his face in my hand and plant my lips on his. Our tongues danced and I was so glad to have my man back.

Shane broke our kiss and backed up to remove my shoes. He tickled my feet and tossed my shoes over his shoulder. He then eased his hands up the sides of my hips, reaching for my panties. I rose up a bit and he pulled them down. Anxious for him, I stepped out of my panties and hurried to remove my top. Before I could even lower it, Shane had my breasts cuffed in his hands. He gave my breasts much pleasure with his mouth, and to speed things along, I reached out to lower his pants.

"Turn around and kneel down in front of me," he asked.

No questions asked, I got on my knees and faced the backseat. He moved in closer and I felt his hard dick lying against my butt.

Continuing the foreplay, he squeezed my breasts together and pecked down the side of my neck. His lips went to my back, and when they touched my butt, I bent further over on the seat so he could have easy access to me from behind.

Shane reached for the bottle of champagne next to him on the floor. I heard the cap pop and he took a healthy sip from the bottle.

"This will be cold," he said, lowering the bottle to my spine. He tilted the bottle, and it flowed down the cheeks of my ass, giving me a chill. I dropped my face in my hands and I surely knew what was about to happen next. Shane lifted my bent knee on the seat and lowered himself. He licked the champagne off my butt and teased me with his tongue from front to back.

His tongue was something that I realized I simply couldn't handle. I started to tremble, but he begged me to stay calm. So much for that, as I moaned out loudly and released myself in his mouth.

Shane allowed me no time to recuperate. He put his dick in me from behind and started with slow strokes. Teasing me even more, he pulled out to the tip of his head, then went in from different angles to stretch me wider.

The feeling was more than I expected and all I could do was close my eyes and keep my face in my hands. When I finally got myself together, I began to work so much better with him. Our rhythm was in tune and all you could hear were the sounds of our juices making much noise together.

We were never so eager to call it quits. Shane finished loving me from behind, and we changed positions. I gave him somewhat of a break from working so hard, and directed him to sit while I straddled his lap. He scooted himself down low and held my ass cheeks in his hands. I inserted him again, leaving not one inch of him behind. All he could do was close his eyes with pure pleasure, as I made my way to the tip of his head and slowly back down to his shaft. I kept an arch in my back and wouldn't allow him to forget this moment anytime soon. He pressed his fingers deeply into my butt and I knew what time it was. His body jerked and he squeezed his eyes together. Out of nowhere, he quickly opened them, grabbing my face in his hands.

"I love your motherfuckin' ass, do you hear me?" he yelled. "Don't you ever, ever forget that, do you understand?"

His heart raced and so did mine.

I nodded and he let go of my face. We stared at each other, as this was one awkward moment for me. Did he just say he was in love with me?

"Shane, I . . . I don't know what it is that I'm feeling—"

He placed his index finger on my lips. "Shhh. Just let what I said sink in and don't reply because you think I need a response. I might have been caught up in the moment, but now that my moment is over, I have no problem saying it again. I love you, Scorpio, and no matter what happens, I don't want you to ever forget it."

"Why do you keep saying that? Do you expect for something to happen?"

"I just know how relationships can be. And, we need to be honest with ourselves and admit that this relationship may be a difficult one. I hope we'll be able to work through our differences and the backlash of your relationship with Jaylin may have some affects."

Shane was more man than I'd ever had before. And even though I still had some feelings for Jaylin, Shane was causing me to forget about him. For the last several weeks, I had. I also realized that had Jaylin's and my love-hate relationship somehow managed to work itself out, I would have never known what it felt like to be with a man of Shane's caliber. He was the bomb.

Cedric buzzed back and informed Shane that we were only five minutes away from our destination. We hurried to put on our clothes and laughed about the mess we'd made. As Cedric parked the limousine, I was sliding up my panties and Shane was stepping into his shoes. When the door came open, I was fully dressed and waited to see what else the night had in store for me.

Shane stepped out first and reached for my hand to help me. As I looked around, I hadn't a clue where we were. There was nothing but a brick building to the left and a whole lot of land with a fence around it. I couldn't see what was further out in the grassy covered area because it was too dark.

"What is this?" I asked.

Shane reached in his pocket. He pulled out a blindfold. "You'll see in a minute."

I didn't want my eyes covered, but trying not to be a pain, I went with the flow. Shane took my hand and told Cedric we'd be back within an hour or so. We walked off and I felt nervous about not being able to see. Soon, I heard another voice and Shane asked the other person if everything was ready. We walked for about ten minutes and then came to a stop. The wet grass had my ankles itchy and my feet were uncomfortable.

"Step up," Shane said, directing me to the step in front of me.

I stepped up and he continued to hold my hand. He said thanks to the other person and he replied, "You're welcome."

I could feel Shane standing close to me.

"Are you ready," he said. "And when I remove the blindfold you've got to keep your eyes closed."

I nodded and he removed the blindfold. I kept my eyes tightly closed.

"Okay, now open them."

I opened my eyes and all I could see again was grassy land surrounding me. I looked up and saw that I was standing in a hot air balloon with Shane and a white man.

"Hell, no," I said. "This thing ain't going up with me in it, is it?"

"I'm afraid so, baby," he said. "In a few minutes, we will be on our way up."

My mouth hung wide open. "Shane, I am afraid of heights. If this thing goes up, I swear I am going to cry and scream."

"Just relax, all right? I know you're afraid of heights, but I want you to overcome your fears. I'll be right here to hold you, but you've got to trust me on this."

I closed my eyes and placed my hands over my face. "I can't believe I'm even considering letting you do this. I've been afraid of heights since I was a little girl and fell from a balcony."

"I know. Jaylin told me the story." Shane wrapped his arms around me and squeezed my waist tightly. He whispered in my ear. "After we take this ride together, this is one less fear you'll have in life. You're going to feel safe with me and you'll know that I got your back. Now, can we get this thing going?"

I removed my hand from my face and nodded. Shane gave the other man the go ahead, and shortly after, the balloon slowly lifted from the ground. He squeezed me tighter as he could already feel my body trembling.

The higher the balloon got, the more my body trembled. I couldn't even open my eyes and Shane begged me to take a peek. When I did, I could have fainted. I quickly turned around and grabbed Shane around his neck.

I panicked. "Please take this thing down. I'm so, so nervous."

"Don't be," he said, still squeezing me tightly. "Take a few deep breaths to calm yourself down. You'll be all right, trust me."

I took a few deep breaths and continued to hold his neck. I buried my face in his chest, while he rocked me back and forth.

"You are missing this amazing scenery," he confessed.

"Yes, you are," the other man said.

I wanted to tell both of them to go to hell but I couldn't.

"Baby, I can see your condo from here, look," he said.

I hesitated, and then snapped my head to the side. I took a peek and peeked again. It did look as if we were above my neighborhood, but I couldn't tell because down below looked awfully tiny.

"Are we in Lake St. Louis?" I asked.

Shane and the other man said that we were. After Shane wiped the tears from my eyes, he turned me around and held me close. My eyes were open, and I had to admit, the scenery and atmosphere were amazing.

"I see somebody's enjoying this," he whispered in my ear.

"I won't say all that, but it is nice. What made you come up with something like this?"

"I already told you. Besides, you and I are going to explore the world, baby. This is only the beginning."

I smiled and truly felt as if it was the beginning of something *different*. All I could think about was the many of nights I'd fallen asleep in tears, asking the Lord why this didn't happen or why that didn't happen in my relationships. I wasn't sure about my future, but I couldn't deny my desire to keep Shane in it.

# Scorpio

## 24

Life was good. I confessed my love to Shane the other day and our relationship was going strong. Leslie and the kids had been gone since last weekend, and since they had so much fun at Disney World, they decided to stay for another seven days.

That, of course, provided me a lot of free time. I spent most of it with Shane, and tried to get Jay's in order. I had a few issues with the stylists at times, but whenever there was a bunch of women together, nothing went smoothly. We all were well aware of that, so we tried to keep as much peace as possible.

As for my stalker, surprisingly, they'd kind of taken a chill pill. I guess because my number had been changed and everybody knew I'd been thinking about getting a bodyguard. I talked to a private detective about Spencer, but after keeping an eye on him for two weeks, the detective came up empty.

Around noon on a hot and steamy Saturday evening, the air conditioner decided that it no longer wanted to work. Jay's was burning up and many of the customers didn't feel like waiting. I'd called a heating and cooling company to come fix it, but the technician was supposed to be here hours ago. Even Shane said he'd send one of his friends over, but as of yet, he hadn't showed up.

Either way, the fans were blowing, hands were waving and sweat was dripping. I wanted to close Jay's, but the stylists complained about it cutting into their money. To take our minds off the heat, we all did what we knew best and kicked up a conversation about men. Of course, Miss Evil Eva didn't like that. She felt as if we were overstepping our boundaries by sharing too much information.

"All I'm saying," she griped. "Is y'all need to learn how to keep your business private. This is not a place for therapy."

"Like hell," Jamaica blurted out. "This is a place to talk about whatever you wanna talk about. I am a woman who offer good advice, so why in the hell would anybody pay hundreds and thousands of dollars to somebody who gon' go home and tell all of your business to other people anyway? Hell, I'll listen for free."

Eva rolled her eyes. "Bernie, hurry up with my hair. I have a funeral to go to."

"Yes," I said. "As a matter of fact, everybody needs to hurry up. I can't take this heat anymore, so once everybody in the chairs are finished, I'm locking the doors."

All of the other customers griped, and so did the stylists. But, I basically had no choice. It was hot enough for somebody to pass out and I'd be facing a lawsuit if they did.

Within the hour, everybody wrapped it up. Bernie and Eva were the last two out. I closed the door after them and went back to my office to call Shane and tell him to meet me for a late dinner at J Bucks around the corner. He didn't answer so I left a message.

I grabbed my purse off my desk and headed for the door. As soon as I turned off the lights, I bumped into somebody standing in the doorway to my office. I hit the lights and it was Eva.

"Did you forget something, Eva?" I asked. She had a disturbing look on her face, almost frightening.

"Yeah, I did. I need to talk to you."

I didn't feel like listening to her gripe about how unprofessional my place was. "Eva your concerns will have to wait until some other time. I—"

I paused when I saw the gun she had in her hand. She aimed it at me.

"This can't wait 'til no other time. Now, get your butt over there and take a seat on that couch!"

Seeing how unstable she was, I went over to the couch and took a seat. I spoke softly. "What's this all about, Eva?"

She came close to me. "It's about my twenty-one-year marriage that you helped destroy. You sit around here with your girlfriends and talk about how you've fucked my husband so well and joke about it! Bitch, do you have any idea what you've caused me?"

I was stunned. The only married man I'd been messing with was Maxwell and I couldn't believe she was his wife. "Eva, I—I never talked about Maxwell out there. Nobody knew about us but Bernie."

"That's a lie. The last time I was in here, you had your trifling-ass back here and I had to listen to everybody out there go on and on about how you, Miss Thang, was capable of stealing anybody's man away." She laughed and paced around in front of me. "Girl, they bragged on you as if you were some kind of queen or something.

And then when I talked to Maxwell about you, he said he'd met the woman of his dreams. Told me to pack up my shit after twenty-one years and get the fuck out."

"Eva, but he told me that you left him. He said you'd found someone else. I never would have kept it going if I had known—"

She snapped and shook the gun in her hands, still aiming it in my direction. "You knew damn well that he was lying. Of course he gon' tell you that, stupid-ass horny bitch! But it doesn't surprise me that you believed him. You, my dear, have caused me headaches." She pulled the trigger and the bullet went into the wall behind me. I ducked, covered my face and screamed out loud. "Many hurtful days and nights!" She pulled the trigger again and not knowing where it went, I fell to the floor and continued to scream. "And the loss of a man that I've loved my entire life!"

She lowered the gun by her side and looked at me crying hysterically on the floor. "Eva, please don't do this. I am sorry if I hurt you. I never meant to—"

Just then, Shane appeared in the doorway.

"What's—" he paused and looked at the gun in Eva's hand.

"Well, isn't this just dandy," she said. "Shane, right?" she asked. He cooperated with a nod. She held the gun steady in my direction and lifted her shirt. She pulled out a large envelope and told him to come get it. Shane cooperated again and eased the envelope from her hand.

"What's this and what's going on?" he hesitantly asked.

"Open it up," she said. "While you were away, your bitch decided to go entertain my husband again. She's been entertaining him for quite some time and I wish like hell you'd get some control over her."

I watched Shane open the envelope and I dropped my head when I saw his eyes look at the pictures in disgust. I'd known the pictures were taken from the person I'd seen outside of the hotel's window.

Shane didn't even look at me. He dropped the pictures on the floor and one of them slid right in front of me. I looked at it and saw Maxwell's arm wrapped around my waist with his finger inside of me.

"Please, give me the gun," Shane said to Eva. "As far as I'm concerned, they can have each other. He ain't even worth it, baby, and neither is she."

Eva looked at Shane from the corner of her eye and then looked at me. Tears began to pour down her face. "I loved him with everything I had! I raised his children and not once did I argue with him when he came in late at night. I would have stayed with him no matter what, but he didn't want me no more." She wiped the snot that dripped from her nose. "I hope you're proud of yourself. It's women like you who destroy what God puts together, and for that, heifer, you will pay."

Seeing that she was about to pull the trigger, Shane rushed up to Eva and grabbed the gun. It lowered in her hand but the bullet still went off. I thought it entered him, but it didn't. He held her tightly and eased his hand down to take the gun from her hands.

"It'll be all right," he said comforting her in his arms. "Trust me, everything will be fine."

"But how?" she said, sobbing on his chest. "I shot him yesterday and killed him. How in the hell is everything going to be all right?"

I gasped and took a hard swallow. Shane closed his eyes and shook his head. "Let's just hope and pray that everything will work out for you."

I cried even harder. It barely crossed my mind as to how much damage sleeping with Maxwell would cause. Never in my wildest dream did I expect for something like this to happen.

I sat up and wiped the flowing tears from my face. Shane continued to comfort Eva, and when he finally looked at me, he whispered for me to call the police. As I got up to do it, he walked slowly out of my office with Eva in his arms.

The police were there in no time. After Shane told them what had happened, they handcuffed Eva and placed her in the backseat of the police car. I was numb and shaken up, so I sat in Bernie's styling chair and watched.

Once the policecars cleared out, Shane came back inside and closed the door. His hands were in his pockets, his forehead was wrinkled, and he looked over at me with more disgust.

"I can't do this with you," he said. "What you did was wrong and I am fucking tired of you using your body to manipulate people."

"But—but it was over between Maxwell and me."

"Yeah, now it's over because he's probably laying somewhere shot up and dead! It wasn't over, though, when I was in Florida, was it?"

"I thought it was over between us. I didn't know that you were going to call me that night, and after I got your call, I left."

"Was that before or after you fucked him?"

"That never happened. I swear to you it never ever happened."

"You expect me to believe you, and I just looked at some pictures with his hands touching on you like that? You must really think I'm stupid. Not only that, but look what you put that poor woman through." He took a hard swallow.

I got up and stood in front of him. "Shane, you have got to believe me. You asked me to trust you, and now, I need for you to trust me. I am truly hurt by what just happened here and I am saddened by what I did to Eva. I'll have to live with that for the rest of my life, but I don't want to lose you. I need you now more than ever. Please don't walk out on me. Please."

He stood for awhile, and then, reached for the doorknob.

"I need some time alone," he said.

"How much time?" I sadly asked.

"For as long as it takes."

"Takes for what?"

"To get you out of my system."

He pulled the door open and walked out.

I couldn't do nothing but break down again and cry.

# Shane

## 25

Two weeks had gone by and my life was still in shambles. Business was good, but my heart had been broken into many pieces. Why or how did I ever get myself in this situation? Especially, after I watched Jay go through his ups and many downs with Scorpio and her games. When the crazy shit unfolded with them, I'd always sit back and shake my head. I'd ask myself, why wouldn't he just leave her alone or vice versa? If they were causing each other so much grief, then why? I knew he'd put her through a lot, too, but damn, what in the fuck did I do? Bottomline, I guess my dick just wasn't enough for her. If it was, then she never would have run to Maxwell so easily. And then to suggest that they'd never done anything that night. I guess my phone call had that much of an impact on her, huh?

The whole messed up thing about it was, I didn't even have nobody to talk to about this shit. Brandon was catching hell from his brotha's wife and he already had too much shit to deal with. In the past, I could always count on Stephon, but since I hadn't spoken to him in over a year, I wasn't sure if rehabilitation had done him any good or not. Jay, of course, was my best friend, but I couldn't even call him and talk about the shit because he refused to discuss Scorpio with me. I'd enjoyed myself so much in Florida, and after seeing the kind of love him and Nokea had for each other, that made me want to experience the same thing.

My body yearned to have a woman who loved me like Nokea loves him. She was his joy, his pride, and without her, Jaylin would be lost. He for damn sure knew what she was worth to him, and during my visit, he expressed that to me over and over again.

On the other hand, I deserved to share my life with a woman who loved me, just as much as she loved herself. Someday I wanted a family, too, and was it impossible to have a life free from a bunch of bullshit and drama. I'd never been a cheater to any woman that I knew for a fact I loved. She basically had everything: my heart, body, mind, and soul. How could any woman want anything less?

I'd been telling Scorpio that I needed time. She was being too persistent and called me almost every single day. I hadn't spoken one word to her because when I asked for time, I expected to get it. She showed up the other night without calling, and I was forced to leave her outside. It broke my heart to see her so upset, but it was time that she learned from her mistakes. In the past, she and Jaylin would argue, fuck, and make up—argue again, fuck again, and make up again. I knew she thought that routine would go down between us too but she was sadly mistaken.

It was obvious that the only thing she'd learned from Jaylin was how to manipulate people with sex, and how to use it to make them forgive you. And as much as I wanted to answer her calls, I couldn't. That would make me so much like him and I knew damn well that we were different. Eventually, as long as I continued to be the man that my mother, Ethel Alexander, raised me to be, then something good would come along. And if I had to wait another month, another year, or another lifetime, then I was willing to wait until I got exactly what I wanted from a woman.

# Scorpio

## 26

Shane had given up on me—on us, for that matter. For the past month or so, I'd been going at him with everything I had and my many efforts had failed. There was no way possible for me to prove to him I hadn't slept with Maxwell that night, and as far as trusting me again, there was no way in hell he would.

Somewhere in my mind I kept making excuses for what I'd done by saying that Shane called it off with me that week, so it was okay for me to move on. I knew deep inside that based on our strong feelings for each other, something as stupid as him reading my journal wasn't going to keep us apart for long.

So, our time apart gave me a chance to think about my mistakes. Never, ever would I date another married man. I cost Maxwell his life, and even though he was a cheater, he didn't deserve

to die. I even felt bad for Eva. What she'd done
was more than wrong, but losing her marriage
over somebody like me sent her over the edge. I
was just so caught up in my satisfaction, that it
was a thrill for me to be with Maxwell. I loved the
challenge and just to know that I could have any
man I wanted was the best feeling ever. Even if
he belonged to someone else.

Now, because of my stupidity, I've lost out
again. I think it hurts more this time around
because there was something different about being with Shane versus being with Jaylin. Shane
allowed me to be me. He cared more about what
I wanted, than what he wanted. He knew how to
make love to me without even being inside of me,
and he helped me overcome my feelings for Jaylin. That in itself was a good deed, and I refused
to let go of a man that was capable of opening my
eyes so I could see.

I was laying on my bed in deep thought. Mackenzie and Barbie were lying next to me asleep.
We had a long day after coming from the water
park so everybody was exhausted. It was still a
bit early, and since I was accustomed to going to
bed late, I was up watching TV. I reached over to
my dresser drawer and pulled out the pictures
that Eva had given to Shane. I looked at how they
surely revealed something hot and heavy must

have gone on with Maxwell and me that night. Whoever Eva hired to take the pictures, they had taken pictures of me from other days too. It was obvious because she'd known who Shane was in one of the pictures. At the bottom of a picture of us together, I noticed the date and time. I looked at the other pictures and they revealed the same thing. I found a picture of me entering the Marriott, a picture during the time I stood in the window with Maxwell, and one that showed me leaving. There was a fifteen minute time difference between the second and third pictures. I didn't know what it would mean to Shane, but at least I could prove to him that I wasn't lying. It wasn't much, but I had something to work with and I was desperate.

I pulled the covers back and got out of bed. I slid into my button down khaki dress and stepped into my white tennis shoes. My appearance was the last thing on my mind, as I grabbed a rubber band and tied it around my frizzy hair that had gotten wet earlier. After that, I grabbed my keys and jetted.

It took me less than thirty minutes to get to his place, and when I did, my heart sank into my stomach. A silver Mercedes was parked in his driveway and by the pink, and purple beads that hung from the rearview mirror, I knew the car belonged to a female.

I sat in my car for a moment to gather myself. I wanted to let him know I was outside, but since I'd been calling so much, he had my number blocked. Unable to walk away from the situation, I went to the door with the pictures in my hand. I lightly knocked, and soon after, I heard footsteps come toward the door.

"Shane," I said. "It's me. I need to show you something. Please open the door."

There was silence. I saw a light go out in the living room and I banged harder.

"Just five minutes," I said. "I swear to God that if you don't open this door, I'll stay here until you do. I really need to talk to you about something important."

Still, nothing. I banged again, and this time, he spoke up.

"Didn't I tell you I needed some time?"

"Yes. But I can't allow you time to be with somebody else. Please open the door."

Surprisingly, he did.

I stepped inside looking a mess, but right about now, I didn't care.

"I won't stay long," I said. "Can we go near some light so I can show you something?"

Shane headed back toward his covered patio and I followed. When we got there, I couldn't believe his visitor was Felicia. They had papers all over the place and Chinese food boxes were on the table. She was fully clothed, but Shane was in his red Calvin Klein boxers. I wasn't sure what was up, but I wasn't about to blow it and make a scene.

"No introduction needed," Felicia said, standing up. "Do you need me to come back or can we finish this tonight?"

Shane rubbed his hands on his face. "Why don't you come back tomorrow or Monday? Either day is fine with me."

"Shane, we really need to get this done. I don't need any setbacks—you understand what I'm saying?"

"I understand what you're saying. And there won't be no setbacks."

She snatched her purse off the table and tooted her lips at me. She said something underneath her breath, but I wasn't even trying to go there with Felicia. Shane walked her to the door and I heard the door close. Without taking a seat, I waited for him to come back. He ignored me and started picking up the papers around the table.

"I have something I need to show you. I'm not sure how you'll feel about it, but I hope it will clarify a few things."

"What?" he said. He looked disinterested. I laid the three pictures on the table and pointed to the first picture.

"This picture was taken when I entered the Marriott that day, the second picture was taken while I was in the room, and the third picture was when I left. If you look closely at the day and times on the pictures, there's a fifteen minute time difference from the second to the third pictures. There was no way I wrapped up sex with Maxwell that fast. You know me well and I am not one to finish up so quickly. Your phone call came as soon as I lay on the bed. I listened to it and I realized that I didn't want to be there. I knew it before, but at that moment, it confirmed it. I don't know if you'll believe me now, but it's all I got. I'm desperate for your love and I don't know what else to do."

He didn't even look at the pictures. He ignored me and continued picking up his papers. I didn't intend to start no crying festival, so when I felt myself about to lose it, I turned to leave. I took a few steps up from his patio and turned to him.

"I do love you. My heart aches badly for you. I didn't know what it meant to really love somebody until you opened my eyes so I could see. Maybe that was our purpose for being together, but my heart tells me there's more to it. If I'm wrong, then I guess I'm wrong."

I walked off and took a hard swallow to hold back my hurt. When I pulled on the doorknob, the door cracked open and Shane pressed his hand above it to close it. He stood closely behind me and I could feel his heart beat.

The room was dark and there was silence for awhile. I could feel his lips touch the back of my head.

"I'm a fool aren't I," he said. "A damn fool for love."

I shook my head. "No, no you're not."

"Then, why do I feel like one? What if you're lying to me? What if you're feeding me all this bullshit and you walk out of here and go be with somebody else? You've always done it in the past, Scorpio, so why is this time so different?"

I turned to face him. "I haven't been with anybody else. I did not lie to you about Maxwell and this time is different because I don't need any man in my life but you."

"I want to believe that so badly. But I hear this echo that says I'm a fool for loving you like I do."

"You tell that echo to go to hell. That's nothing but the devil, and whenever something good is about to happen, he's always poking his business where it don't belong."

I could see Shane's eyes feeling me out in the dark. He rubbed my messy hair back with his hands as we continued to stand by the door.

"I asked for time alone, in hopes that I'd get over you, but that never happened. I knew it wouldn't, but I was hoping to get rid of this feeling that sticks with me everywhere I go. Since you came through that door, that ill feeling is gone. I feel relieved and—"

Shane reached out for me and we tightly embraced each other, quietly standing for a long, long time.

That night was all too special to me. Shane held me in his arms on the living room couch, until I fell asleep. My heart no longer ached, and if anybody had learned from their mistakes, I surely had. I was going to do everything possible to never lose Shane again.

# Shane

## 27

Everything was all gravy. I woke up the next morning and cooked Scorpio and me some breakfast. She was still knocked out on the living room couch and I knew it was a matter of time that she got a whiff of the bacon and woke up.

Nearly ten minutes later, she came into the kitchen, looking just as pretty as she did last night.

"Good morning," I said, with a towel thrown over my shoulder.

She yawned. "And a good morning it is. Why'd you let me sleep so late?"

"Because you probably needed it."

She took a seat on one of the stools to watch me cook. "Do you need any help with that? That bacon is getting awfully black."

"I like my bacon burnt. Don't you?"

"No. Not that burnt."

I took a fork and picked up the bacon from the skillet. It was burnt to a crisp. "We can't eat this, can we?" I asked.

"I don't know about you, but I can't."

I turned off the stove and popped out the burnt toast from the toaster. When I took the pieces out, I burned the tips of my fingers. "Damn," I said, and then placed my fingers on my lips to lick them. "I'll have to find us something else to eat."

I headed for the fridge and Scorpio grabbed my arm. She took my burnt fingers and placed them on her lips. "If you're looking for something to eat, I can always serve you something tasty. Since you didn't get a chance to make love to me last night, do you think we can spend the day making up for a month of lost time?"

"Maybe," I said. "But, why should I be so generous to you today. You knew I wanted to have some fun last night, but you fell asleep."

Scorpio stood up. "Because, Mr. Shane Ricardo Alexander #2, I was tired last night, but today you owe me big time." She unbuttoned her khaki dress and dropped it to the floor.

I looked at her naked body. "You wrong for that because I am not an Alexander the second. I'm the first and the only."

"The #2 was meaning Hollywood #2. It's a secret between the stylists and me at Jay's. Now, getting back to why you owe me—"

Scorpio turned around and the tattoo that said JAYLIN'S had been removed from her butt.

I placed my hand on my chin. "Now, that's the kind of ass I'm talking about. Whoever got a chance to remove it must have been grateful."

"Not as grateful as you'll be today."

Scorpio sauntered off toward my bedroom. I watched her from behind, and not wanting to appear too anxious, I waited until she disappeared from my sight. I then stepped out of my shorts in the kitchen and made my way to my bedroom. When I got there, she had already positioned herself on the bed. I closed the curtains and didn't expect to open them for quite some time.

It was always the damn phone that broke me from my sleep. I slowly removed my arm from around Scorpio and reached over her to get it. I wasn't sure what time it was, but since the room was pitch black, I knew it was late.

"Yeah," I said in a sleepy voice.

"Hey, man," I heard a soft voice say. I couldn't make out the voice, but it sounded like Jaylin.

"Jay, is that you?"

He cleared his throat. "Yeah."

"What's up, man, is everything cool?"

He continued to speak with a soft voice. "Naw, Shane, everything ain't cool. I . . . I'm at the hospital. Nokea lost the baby."

I quickly sat up. "Jay, I'm so sorry to hear that. Is she all right?"

"Yeah, I guess. She . . . she kind of upset with me."

I was afraid to ask why, but I had to. "I hope you didn't cheat—"

"Naw, naw. She's upset because she saw that fucking CD!" His voice got louder. "After she looked at it, she fell backward down the steps and lost my motherfuckin' baby!"

I sat in disbelief. I couldn't believe what Jaylin had said to me. "Man, you gotta be thankful that Nokea didn't lose her life. And y'all can always have another—"

"Shane, I am thankful!" he yelled. "I am very thankful that I am not in St. Louis right now to kill that bitch! Nokea barely talking to me! Nanny B, she . . . she won't even look at me! And the worst fucking thing of all is," I heard his fist pound on something. "There's a possibility that my wife won't be able to conceive another child!"

I was trying to calm Jaylin down. It was obvious that some serious shit was about to happen.

"Man, you don't know that. And, I don't understand why Nokea got so upset when you told her what had happened that weekend, didn't you?"

"The CD tells a different side of the story! You've seen it! There's no fucking explaining that shit! I can explain shit all day long, but nothing compared to her seeing it for herself!"

"Jay, you need to calm down. It is not the end of the world. Sometimes things happen and nobody lives a life without troubles. You and Nokea live a wonderful life and many people would love to be in your shoes. Again, setbacks will happen, and as soon as Nokea gets well, things will work out."

"You got that shit right," he laughed. "You for damn sure got that shit right! I told you, if that CD made it to my house, what was gon' happen? What did I tell you Shane!"

Jaylin wasn't trying to hear me. A lifetime of happiness just wasn't no guarantee. "I wouldn't think you wouldn't risk all that you have—"

"You know what, Shane, you just don't fucking get it! You have allowed that bitch to get away with so much shit and that's why she continues to play the games she does. Well, game over! And you can tell that bitch it's on when you see her!"

The phone went dead.

Scorpio was wide awake, and she could hear Jaylin yelling through the phone.

"Who was that," she asked.

"It was Jaylin. But, I don't want to talk about it right now okay? Let's just go back to sleep."

Scorpio didn't say anything else. She laid her head back on my chest and I wrapped my arms around her.

Of course, I couldn't get back to sleep because there were so many "what if's" in my head. What if I'd never told Scorpio he was coming to St. Louis? What if I'd never asked him to stay for Trey's party? What if Felicia didn't have hidden cameras in Davenports, and most of all, what if Jaylin followed through with his threats about killing her?

He was known for being a man of his word, so I reached for the phone to call the airlines. I had to make plans to get to Florida and get there fast to stop him.

# Felicia

# 28

I sat in my office, thinking about how all these suckers thought they'd live happily ever after. First Jaylin and Nokea, and then, Shane and Scorpio. Yeah, right? I'd been through mega shit with both men, and to kick me to the curb like a piece of dirt wasn't cool.

Maybe, I would have left shit alone had Scorpio not brought her trampy butt back into Shane's life. He was hurt by what she'd done and I almost had him in the palms of my hands. We'd already been having small sexual talks over the phone, but when I'd go see him, all of a sudden, he'd have a change of heart. All I needed was one more week or two with him, and trust me, he would have been mine once again.

Since Scorpio was back, I hadn't heard from him. I figured she must have worked her charm on him, and again, all was forgiven. I was angry with Shane for allowing her to come back into his life. If anything, he knew darn well that he couldn't turn a ho into a housewife. He deserved so much better and I intended to make sure he got what he deserved.

I figured I wouldn't hear from him; so it was time to shake, rattle, and roll. So, that was why I overnighted my package to Nokea. I wasn't going to be played anymore by Shane or Jaylin. And, how dare Jaylin try to cut me out of that much money with the Mayor's Group? That was a dirty trick, especially after the work I put into that design.

See, men could continue to play all the games they wanted to, but they never ever know what kind of woman they're dealing with. Some women could walk away after being messed over, however, I was not one who could walk too far. Never will I sit back and allow anybody to get over on me without suffering the consequences and that goes for women, too.

As I stared out of the window, he cleared his throat. I snapped out of my thoughts and smiled at him. Over the last few months, we'd become quite a team. Not only had I been screwed over, but he'd been screwed over in the past as well. Of course, by Nokea, who was supposed to marry him. While at the altar, she decided that she was still in love with Jaylin, and left my friend standing there looking like a fool. Tell me, how many people were going to suffer for what Nokea and Jaylin had done? Yes, being on drugs had him tripping, but for Shane and Jaylin to turn their backs on him, at a time when he needed them the most, that was so sad, especially Jaylin. He was his cousin, and he thought blood was always thicker than water. So what, he'd screwed Scorpio when she came to him in her troubled time with Jaylin. If anything, he'd done Jaylin a favor. One that allowed him to open his eyes and see Scorpio for what she really was—a whore. Honestly, he was just as angry as I was, and we were determined to make their lives as miserable as they'd made ours.

Stephon placed his hands behind his bald-head. He glared over at me with his hazel eyes. The drugs he'd been on had messed up some of his good looks; however, since he'd been in recovery, he'd been looking a whole lot better.

"So, what's the plan," he said. "Since Scorpio's gotten her number changed, I ain't been able to call her."

I stood up and walked over to the window. I looked out, while folding my arms in front of me. "I'm sure Shane will somehow slip up and provide me with her new number. Until then, let's keep things on the down low. I want to wait and see what Nokea's response is to the CD."

Stephon nodded and stood up. He walked over and stood next to me. "Thank you again for helping a brotha out. If it wasn't for you, I don't know where I'd be."

"No problem. Just be there for me when I need you, okay?"

"No doubt," he said, leaning in for a kiss. Our tongues intertwined for a long time. I then brushed my fingers against his thick chocolate lips to wipe off my lipstick. "Hurry up and get finished," he said. "I hope to see you at my place in about an hour."

"I'll hurry," I said, as he walked to the door. He gave me a wink and left.

It was getting late, so I grabbed my briefcase to go. I turned down the lights in Davenports and headed toward the elevator. When it opened, I hit the L button to take me downstairs to the lobby. The elevator slowed, and as it was getting ready to make a stop, I looked down and searched for my keys in my purse. When the elevator stopped, the doors slowly separated. My eyes stared down at the expensive deep burgundy leather shoes, and then made contact with the navy blue pants that belonged to a Brooks Brothers suit. Next, I saw the diamond Rolex, and the lightly tanned sweaty hands were balled into fists. The bulge in his pants was there and the smell of Issey Miyake filled the air. I lifted my head and my eyes were locked with his cattish grey watery eyes that were red as fire. I tried to get away from him, but to no avail. All I witnessed was his fist go up and my entire face was numb. Suddenly, I saw nothing but darkness.